A CURE FOR
NIGHT

·A CURE FOR·
NIGHT

JUSTIN PEACOCK

DOUBLEDAY ■ NEW YORK LONDON TORONTO SYDNEY AUCKLAND

CD

DOUBLEDAY

Published in the United States by Doubleday,
an imprint of The Doubleday Publishing Group,
a division of Random House, Inc., New York.
www.doubleday.com

DOUBLEDAY is a registered trademark and the DD colophon
is a trademark of Random House, Inc.

This is a work of fiction. All characters are products of the author's
imagination and any resemblance to an actual person, living or dead, is unintentional.
While there are a number of real places mentioned in this novel, any situation in which
they are referenced is entirely fictional. Places and geography have been freely
altered to suit the demands of the story.

Book design by Ellen Cipriano

Library of Congress Cataloging-in-Publication Data
Peacock, Justin.
A cure for night / by Justin Peacock. — 1st ed.
p. cm.
1. Lawyers—Fiction. 2. College students—Crimes against—Fiction. I. Title.
PS3616.E225C87 2008
813'.6—dc22
2007050694

ISBN 978-0-385-52580-0

PRINTED IN THE UNITED STATES OF AMERICA

1 3 5 7 9 10 8 6 4 2

First Edition

To Melissa

A CURE FOR

NIGHT

PROLOGUE

THE DAY my life fell apart began like any other. Of course, it's almost impossible to pinpoint the exact instant a life changes—a million tiny events all conspire to bring us to every moment. But there can still be that day when things reach their boiling point and spill out into catastrophe.

I was a little late getting into work that morning. The truth was, I was often late those days; it wasn't particularly uncommon for it to be after ten by the time I came strolling in. I made up for it on the back end, often working deep into the night.

I was a midlevel associate at Walker Bentley Ferguson & Dunlop, one of New York's most prestigious law firms, and long hours came with the territory. In exchange for most of your waking hours the firm offered money, and lots of it. Still, it was easy for the associates to feel relatively poor in comparison to the corporate chieftains who made up our client base, or the partners who actually took home the firm's millions in profits.

It wasn't the sort of life I'd been born into, nor was it anything I'd ever particularly aspired toward, but it was where I'd ended up, and I'd gotten used to it. I hadn't been looking to blow it up, at least not on any conscious level. I hadn't gone looking for Beth, either; she'd simply shown up, a new paralegal at the firm assigned to one of my cases, a sprawling accounting fraud prosecution of a high-profile company and its senior executives.

I was spending almost all of my time on that case, plowing through the numerous tedious tasks that accompany a massive federal investigation: we were in the midst of turning over millions of pages of our client's documents to the government, every one of which first had to be reviewed. We were also conducting dozens of interviews with the company's employees, and drafting a sprawling white paper in an attempt to persuade the U.S. Attorney's office to drop the prosecution. It was the kind of case that racked up the billable hours, making the firm a lot of money, and making the lawyers who actually had to slog through it all thoroughly miserable.

I spent the dregs of the morning and into the early afternoon writing up my notes of a recent witness interview into a memo to files. I was still working on it while picking at the remains of a sandwich from the firm's cafeteria when Beth walked into my office and sat down.

I didn't like it when she did this. It made me nervous. Unfortunately, I'd made the mistake of letting her know, so she'd started popping in with some frequency, more to enjoy my discomfort than for anything else.

"Why you want people to gossip about us is beyond me," I whispered. Beth did not look playful, however; her mouth was drawn tight, her skin waxy and sallow.

"You got any candy in here?" Beth replied.

"Seriously," I said in a normal tone of voice.

"It's all your whispering that'll start gossip," Beth said, now speaking quietly herself. "There's nothing weird about my being in your office. People will just think you're telling me what to do."

"As if," I said.

"I really really need some sugar," Beth said.

"You know where the vending machines are."

"You don't understand," Beth said.

Looking at her, I did understand, but I didn't want to say the words out loud, not here in my office. Beth was craving sugar only to blunt her deeper need. "It's not that I don't understand so much as it is that I can't help you."

"I can take care of myself," Beth said. "How about you?"

"What about me?"

"You making it through your little day here?"

"My little day is going just fine, thanks."

Beth's voice again dropped to a whisper. "You coming over Friday?" she asked. I nodded.

"It's your turn to bring the supplies," she said in her normal voice.

"Why don't we just start wearing signs around our necks?" I said.

"Didn't you ever read *The Purloined Letter* or whatever it's called?" Beth asked. "Nobody ever sees the things that are hiding in plain sight."

Paul Frith, my closest friend at the firm and a colleague on the white-collar case, appeared in my doorway, hesitating when he saw Beth.

"Hey, Paul," Beth said, following the greeting with a pronounced sniffle. I saw how strung out she was because I knew what to be looking for, but nevertheless I had to think it was becoming obvious to anyone who cared to look.

Paul knew too—the only person besides me who did. He nodded at Beth in response to her greeting, glancing at her briefly, then looking away.

"You boys probably have important business to discuss," Beth said, standing, her clothes baggy on her thin frame. "I'll be down in the library if you need me."

I watched her go, idly remembering what it'd been like a few months ago, when she and I had first started up. It'd seemed like a bad idea at the start, but I'd had no idea how quickly it would get as bad as this. Paul closed my door, then sat down in the chair that Beth had just vacated.

"She's not looking so great," he said.

"I know."

"What are you doing about it?"

"Is there something I can do about it?"

"How long before that's what you look like?"

"I'm fine, Paul," I said, not asking myself whether I believed it. "Really."

"Isn't it time you just shut it down?"

"You don't have to worry about it," I said. "I mean, thanks, but you don't, okay?"

"Whatever you say, pal," Paul said, but he looked defeated. I tried and failed to think of something to say that would make him feel better, move us past this.

"So what's going on?" I said.

"Mary wants me to get everybody together for a team meeting at four today to talk about the status of the white paper," Paul said. "Since you and I are doing the heavy lifting on it, thought I'd check with you before I made it official."

"That's fine," I said. "That gives me a couple of hours to actually, you know, make some progress on it."

Paul stood, still looking deeply unhappy. I could tell there was more that he wanted to say. "See you then," I added, trying to cut him off.

Paul just looked at me for a moment, then nodded. "I'll see you, Joel."

I spent the next couple of hours glued to my desk, typing away at the white paper, which was already more than fifty pages long. Paul was writing the facts; I was writing the law. Essentially my task was to demonstrate that case law established that the actions taken by our client were not actually illegal. It was an uphill battle, but people didn't hire us to do the easy stuff.

IT WAS Paul who'd told me, appearing in my office doorway shortly before our scheduled meeting. I was so focused on my work I didn't immediately notice the ashen look on his face. "I take it you haven't heard?" Paul asked flatly.

"Heard what?"

"They found Beth in the ladies' room down in the library about an hour ago."

"What do you mean?" I asked, realizing as I said it that I already knew, my understanding racing ahead of my information.

"She was getting high," Paul said, a little anger entering his voice. "Who knows how long she'd been passed out in there before somebody found her?"

"They took her to the hospital?" I said.

Paul was unable to meet my eyes. "Apparently she vomited after losing consciousness. The old rock-star routine. I don't know the details, and don't really want to, but she was dead on the scene."

There was a high-pitched noise, a shrill metallic whine buzzing in my ears, loud enough to drown out everything else. I tried to imagine what my appropriate reaction to this news should be. Paul was telling me Beth was dead, which was impossible for me to understand. But Paul was also telling me that Beth had died in a way that would attract serious scrutiny, that questions would be asked, and that I myself faced enormous vulnerability.

"Joel," Paul said. "You really need to pay attention right now."

"I know," I said. "I am. I just don't know what to do."

"The police are here. This is going to be a thing."

"Do you think they'll come to me?"

"Don't you?"

I put my head in my hands. My emotions were so jumbled together that I couldn't tell what I felt. I was sad for Beth, of course, grief-filled and in shock, but those feelings jousted against my own raw fear. "I'm really in trouble, aren't I, Paul?" I said at last, looking up at my friend.

"I've been trying to tell you that for a long time," Paul said.

· P A R T ·
ONE

I SAT IN the tiny interview room, the back legs of my metal chair scraping against the brick wall behind me, waiting for my next client to walk in. A file—such as it was: a manila folder containing a badly typewritten complaint (I suspect that cops are virtually the only people left in the country who still routinely use typewriters, and they are apparently unaware of the existence of Wite-Out)—lay open on the metal table in front of me, but I hadn't bothered to do more than glance at it. I needed to have some idea of the police version of what'd happened, but there was no reason for me to have it nailed down in my head, confident from past experience that the words on the police forms would have little relation to the story I would hear when Chris Delaney walked into the room.

I spent my working days in the criminal courthouse on Schermerhorn Street, walking distance from the Brooklyn Defenders' office on Pierrepont. I'd been handling arraignments for about six months, five days a week of working out of the aging courthouse's dark and narrow rooms across from the holding cells, conducting five-minute interviews, then heading down the hall and up to the courtroom, where my clients would enter their initial pleas. Many minor misdemeanor cases ended then and there, a plea of guilty in exchange for time served, plus maybe a small fine or community service, perhaps a treatment program if it was a first-time drug bust. These pleas meant the defendant's main punishment was the twenty-four hours or so he'd just spent locked up waiting to be brought before a judge. Even after half a year this still bothered me: the system took somebody who'd just spent a more or less sleepless night on the floor of a giant holding cell, fifty other guys in the room, the court officers feeding him maybe some bologna with a drooping slice of American cheese pressed between a couple of wilted slices of white bread, and then along came a lawyer like me, telling the exhausted, scared, and hungry defendant that the whole thing could be over by copping a plea, the main punishment the experience just endured. That and a criminal record. What tired soul wouldn't accept that deal in exchange for getting to go home, sleep in his own bed?

There was a knock on the door. "Yeah," I called out after a second, a little thrown by the knock: many of my visitors, old hands at the game and naturally assertive to boot, didn't bother. The door opened and a young white man shuffled in. A user, no doubt about that, skin the color of dirty soap, bruise-colored puffs under both his eyes. His hair was curly and uncombed, spiraling down his face. Guy'd blow me for a fix, I thought, feeling an immediate sharp dislike for my newest client. This happened to me at least once a day, sometimes more. I had never mentioned it to another public defender, never asked if it was just part of the job, because I was afraid that it wasn't. I was afraid it was particular to me, especially with someone like Chris Delaney, a type I recognized in an instant, a type I'd narrowly escaped becoming myself, if I had indeed escaped it. He'd ended up where I'd been heading in the weeks before Beth's death. Of course, the cost had been high for me too, and a year later I was still paying.

"Have a seat," I said, picking up the file and making a show of looking at it. "Chris Delaney," I said. "That your name?"

The kid nodded. I put Chris's age at twenty. "I'm Joel Deveraux," I continued. "I'm with the Brooklyn Defenders'. I'll be representing you at your arraignment. Ever been busted before, Chris?" I asked.

The kid, this Chris, shook his head. "This will be more productive if you use words to communicate with me," I said, letting some irritation show. Despite all the talk in the trade about client empowerment, how you should make your clients feel that they were in the driver's seat, in my opinion that was just issuing an open invitation to a festival of bullshit. I didn't think letting clients try out an increasingly preposterous series of variations on reality was productive for anybody. It saved everybody some time and aggravation if the client understood from the beginning that I was in control.

"No," Chris said.

"But you've been using for a while," I said, not putting much question into it.

Chris looked at me, his eyes begging. He was clearly so spent, so sick, that it was hard not to feel a tug of sympathy. But pitying junkies was like crying over every death that took place on this earth: it would be a bottomless ocean of grief. Chris seemed genuinely humiliated, though, and didn't answer.

"I'm in this room every day, Chris," I said. "I can tell a junkie from a day-tripper a mile away. You may have been a dilettante once, a 'recreational user,' but that time has passed. It's all over your face."

Chris still just looking at me, resentment seeping in and mixing with the pleading in his eyes. "Why does it matter?" he said.

"It matters because I'm going to try and get you help," I said. "Are you ready to be helped?"

Chris appeared to really consider the question. "I don't know," he said softly, looking at the floor. "I hope so."

I glanced down again at the scant file in my hand. "Says here they snagged you up on the street. You know why?" Phrasing the question so that it didn't assume guilt.

Chris shrugged. "I think they must have been watching from a rooftop or something. They picked me up two blocks away, put me in a van with, like, six other people. After they caught a couple more they drove in—like, a whole bunch of them, cops, I mean—and rousted the dealers."

I wrote a summary of this down, not for any good reason, just to be doing something, make Chris feel like he was talking to a lawyer. "Cops say anything to you about testifying against the dealers?"

"No one said shit to me," Chris said. "Never even read me my rights. Isn't that illegal?"

"They don't really need to Mirandize you if they don't ask you any questions," I said. "So why don't you tell me what happened? From the start."

"Do you want me to tell the . . . you know, the bad stuff?"

"Anything you tell me is confidential, of course," I replied. "And even at this stage, the more I know about what the other side is going to know, the more effective I can be."

Chris nodded at this. He wanted to tell, I thought: often they wanted to tell. Sometimes to confess, sometimes to brag, sometimes a mixture of the two.

"I was down at the projects at Avenue H and Ocean Avenue, looking to score. There's some guys I'm pretty regular with. Everything seemed, you know, business as usual, until I got back up to Flatbush. Suddenly these two cops are right up behind me, digging in my pockets. They just came out of nowhere, far as I could tell."

"So when you bought, that was right on the street?"

"They deal out of the project, but they realize guys with my skin color don't want to go in there. That place is like a fortress or something. So they work it where you can order right on the street, even though they keep the shit in the Gardens. They take your order; then you go to this pay phone that doesn't work and pretend to make a call. Somebody else comes out with the shit."

I resisted the urge to nod. I knew the playbook, but that had nothing, I told myself, to do with this. "And when the cops grabbed you, you said they reached into your pockets?"

Chris nodded again, with some force now. "They were both yelling, saying how they knew I had it and where was it; all while they were grabbing at me. They didn't ask for permission to search or show a warrant or anything." The kid again looking to suggest he'd been the victim of some constitutional violation he knew about from TV.

"You in school, Chris?"

Chris nodded. "At Brooklyn College."

"You get federal loans?"

Chris nodded again.

"That can be a problem," I said. "For next year, anyway."

"What's going to happen to me?" Chris asked, his voice cracking slightly.

"You got any kind of criminal record at all?"

"You already asked me that."

"Yeah, well," I said. "Some questions are worth repeating."

Chris shook his head. "I'm not a troublemaker. I'm on a scholarship, taking five classes, working twenty hours a week sometimes to get by. I just need some help winding down sometimes, you know?"

I had never spoken to a client about the events that had led me from graduating from one of the country's top law schools and making over two hundred thousand dollars a year as a corporate litigator at a big firm to making under fifty thousand doing rookie PD work. There was a moment here when I was tempted, thinking that hearing it would benefit Chris, but it passed.

"I guess that help has paid off," I said instead, instantly regretting it, knowing I was overcompensating for my own vulnerability. Chris looked down sharply, like he'd been slapped.

"Okay," I said quickly, not wanting to let the unpleasant moment I'd created linger. "Here's what's going to happen now. We'll go before the arraignment judge, who'll ask you for a plea. From what I have here, their case against you isn't perfect, but it sounds like that's just laziness and that they can easily fill in the gaps if they have to. You plead not guilty, you get a trial, but you also face the risk of actual jail time. You plead this out, no prior record, a college student, jail's off the table. Depending on the judge's mood, we should be able to get you into a treatment program. This would mean you'd have to do NA meetings as an outpatient at a treatment center. There's a catch to this prize, though: assuming you plead to a B misdemeanor,

you'll also be on probation for a year. If you don't go to your meetings, or if you get busted within the next year, they can reopen the
charges, put you in jail. You follow that?"

Chris answered with his own question: "What about my student
loans?"

"You won't be eligible for federal loans based on a drug conviction," I said. "But your priority right now should be staying out of
jail."

"I can't afford to go to school without the loans. My dad's on dis-
ability; my mom works part-time. This is going to ruin my whole
life."

"Your life is going to be a lot more ruined if you actually go to
jail," I said. "There're other loan programs out there. You might have
to pay more interest, but that really can't be your focus right now.
This is an easy case for them to make. It's your call how to plead, but
you said you wanted to get help, and getting help is going to basically
be your main punishment if you plead out. So that's what I strongly
suggest you do."

Ten minutes later the two of us were standing before the judge,
the bailiff reading charges. Part of my job working arraignments was
to keep the easy cases from going forward. The system relied on dis-
posing of many cases at arraignment; it would break if most arrests
in New York City proceeded past that point. In the vast majority of
cases, a defense attorney's job was really just to convince his client to
take a plea. Actually going to trial was primarily reserved for those
rare cases where guilt was really called into question.

I had grabbed the prosecutor in the hallway outside the courtroom, made my thirty-second pitch about how this Delaney kid had
no record, was ready and willing for treatment, ripe for time served
and some sessions as an outpatient. The ADA, a smug little prick

named Diaz whom I had been dealing with at least once a week for the past half year, stared off into space as I spoke, and then said he'd see what seemed reasonable.

Another lawyer from my office, Shelly Kennedy, was doing an arraignment—an indecent exposure on a subway flasher—when I walked into the courtroom. There was a steady drone of voices from the back of the room, which was nondescript and worn, the only decorations being the words "In God We Trust" behind the judge and a half dozen of the ugliest chandeliers I'd ever seen in my life. The courthouse had been built in the 1930s and was coming apart at the seams.

Tired, I shut down a little during the lull as we waited, feeling a second of disorientation when Delaney's case was called. I picked up the file and walked toward the podium, nodding at Shelly as we passed, the familiar stage fright causing my heart to pound a little and my palms to sweat, as it always did, but it didn't bother me: I knew I'd be fine once I started talking. I looked down at the file as I walked, furrowing my brow as though sifting through conflicting evidence, when really I was just double-checking my client's name. I had a pathological fear of calling a client by the wrong name. I'd never actually done it myself, but I'd seen it happen more than once. To me, this was the bluntest possible reminder of the assembly-line nature of the work we did here, and I didn't think I'd be able to stand it if I ever made that mistake.

Two court officers brought Delaney over to stand beside me. One stood behind him, the other next to him. Delaney held his hands behind his back like he was handcuffed. ADA Diaz stated his name and office for the record, and I did the same. Then Diaz did his spiel, which I barely bothered to listen to, using the time to prepare what I was going to say.

"Your Honor," I began when my turn came, my voice going a half octave deeper, as it always did in court. "My client has never before been charged with any crime. He is willing to concede that he has a problem with substance abuse, and he would very much like to receive help for this. This is not a case where any term of imprisonment is warranted. If the state will agree to a B misdemeanor plea for probation and entry into an outpatient program, not only will justice have been amply done, but my client will have been genuinely helped."

Judge Davis looked over at Diaz, who was reading his own file on the case. "Counsel?" she said, wanting to see if the state would agree.

A long moment passed. At last the ADA looked up at the judge. "This does seem like a case where probation and outpatient could be warranted," he said.

Judge Davis nodded, turning her attention toward Chris. "Mr. Delaney, is it your intention to plead guilty to the charges against you in order to get the sentence just discussed?"

Chris looked at the judge, then back at me. Nobody was ever in a hurry to plead guilty. The defendants were usually a step behind at arraignment, except for the old pros, the lifetime-achievement-award winners who were in and out of the system all the time. I cupped a hand over Chris's ear and whispered: "You have to plead guilty to get the deal. Otherwise you have to plead not guilty, and then we go from there."

Chris considered this, then looked back at the judge and nodded.

"You have to say the words," Judge Davis said. "Is it your intention to plead guilty?"

"Yes," Chris said. "I plead guilty."

"And is that because you are, in fact, guilty?"

Chris nodded again, then caught himself. "Yes," he said, adding tentatively, "Your Honor."

And it was all over but the paperwork. Once the judge had accepted the plea and the bailiff was calling the next case, Chris turned to me. "What happens next?"

"What happens next is you leave this building, get yourself a nice meal, and go sleep in your own bed. You've got to pay a processing fine but it can wait, and they will contact you directly about the outpatient meetings. The most important thing for you to keep in mind is that this whole deal blows up if you get busted again—for anything—in the next year. The state will be able to just tear this up and charge you all over again. You understand?"

"Yeah," Chris said absently, but I couldn't tell if he was really listening. I had no idea how many of these deals did ultimately blow up—so far as I knew, nobody bothered to keep track. Everyone too busy just keeping the system running to bother tracking whether it was actually working or not.

I walked Chris out of the courtroom, shook his hand, uttered the usual spiel about staying out of trouble and going to the required meetings. Then we were done and my shift was over and I was free to take my paperwork back to the Brooklyn Defenders and call it a day.

·2·

I **DUMPED MY** new files onto the sprawling pile on my desk, feeling too tired to deal with them now. My officemate, Zach Roth, was at his desk when I came in, typing up a brief on his computer. Zach was short and wiry, high-strung, perpetually tousled. He was a couple of years younger than me, but had been with the office for a couple of years longer, worked felony cases. Zach was married to a big-firm corporate lawyer who apparently didn't mind subsidizing his idealism, so he seemed likely to stick around longer than most

PDs. The combination of high stress and low pay generally guaranteed a high burnout rate in our line of work.

"Hey, Joel," Zach said. "Our fearless leader was here looking for you."

"Isaac?" I asked. "Did he say what he wanted?"

"He said he was calling you up from the minors. He said it like you'd know what he meant."

"No idea, actually," I said. "What's up with you?"

"Just got back from wasting my whole afternoon at Rikers. Got an armed robbery of a liquor store, referred over to us from Legal Aid after the arraignment."

"This was your first time meeting the guy?"

"Yeah, it was my meet and greet," Zach said. "Turns out there was a little something they forgot to put in the arraignment report."

"What's that?"

"My guy's deaf."

"He's deaf?"

"As in he reads lips and talks with his hands," Zach said. "Or at least I assume he does those things. We didn't really get that far."

"I know what 'deaf' means," I said. "I was more just agreeing that it seems like something they should've put in their report."

"At least I didn't have to listen to any bullshit for once. There's something to be said for a client you don't have to listen to."

ISAAC WAS in his late forties, with curly brown hair just showing some gray and perpetually in need of cutting, a small diamond stud in his left ear. While I hadn't changed out of my suit after leaving court, Isaac was dressed in jeans and a sweater. My office clothes

were those I'd purchased during my four-plus years at Walker Bentley, and my wardrobe was considerably more formal and expensive
than what most of the office's attorneys wore when they were not
bound for court.

"Here's the thing," Isaac said without preamble when I walked
into his office. "It's not really that easy to evaluate someone who's doing what you're doing. Let's face it, you don't need that Columbia
law degree of yours to handle arraignments. You've been showing up
every day, you've gotten the job done, you've been just fine. But I
can't say you're some arraignments whiz. No knock on you, I just
think it's something I would never be able to say about anybody."

"I see your point," I said. "So it sounds like you need to give me
something where I can impress you."

Isaac smiled at this. "You weren't the only person that occurred
to," he said. "I'm gonna bump you up to concentrating on misdemeanors, maybe some minor felonies. You'll still have to cover arraignments from time to time, but the cases will be yours to keep."

"That's great," I said. "I won't let you down."

"I certainly hope not," Isaac said. "There's something else too.
We've got a big one I want to bring you in on. As you presumably
know, Myra's got a new murder, and it's a red-ball."

I nodded. The lawyers in our office were grouped into small
teams, the idea being to ensure as much brainstorming and collabo-
ration as possible. My team consisted of myself; our team leader,
Michael Downing; Myra Goldstein; my officemate, Zach; Julia San-
grava; Max Watkins; and Shelly Kennedy. We generally met for
lunch once a week, kept one another up to speed on our cases, shot
the shit, and debated strategy, and although Myra was a rare and re-
luctant participant in these meetings, I was well aware of her new

high-profile case. The death of a college senior, an honors student, who'd been gunned down in the projects was the rare Brooklyn murder that actually made its way into the newspapers.

"The white kid from Brooklyn College who got killed out in Midwood," I said.

"It's trouble. Black defendant from the projects, white victim from campus. Plus we've got a second victim who's still hanging on, though I gather he's touch-and-go. The press is sniffing around; the DA's office is putting their A-team on the case. I think Myra could use a second chair."

Isaac had taken me aback. This was far more of a break than I'd been expecting. "Happy to do it."

"I'm sure you are. I should warn you that Myra's used to doing things her own way—she's not in the habit of having another lawyer with her on a case. But I think she could use the help on this one."

"So you want me to provide effort."

"I figure you've been living on Eager Street for a while, you're going to have some effort to give," Isaac said. He paused, leaning back with his arms folded, making a point of studying me. "You want this, right?"

"I do," I said, and I very much did.

· 3 ·

SAAC'S FAVOR in assigning me to a high-profile murder case was nothing compared to the biggest favor he'd done me: giving me a job in the first place. After I'd served out the six-month suspension of my law license, none of the first-tier firms in the city—places that would normally hire someone with my résumé virtually as a matter of course—had even invited me in for an interview. I'd tried the second tier, then the third, undistinguished firms I never would have considered out of law school. I at least got a few interviews, but they'd proved skittish too. A lawyer with a documented drug problem and a spectacular flameout was just too big a risk, no matter how sterling my credentials. I understood that, but understanding didn't make it any easier. I'd kept working as a legal temp, doing cite checking and document review, floating around the big law firms that would no longer consider hiring me as a proper lawyer.

I had never denied that it was all my fault. Plenty of people dealt with the same mix of pressure, boredom, and long hours without turning to drugs. While it was easy for me to look back at Walker Bentley and see the aspects of my life there that had driven me to be so self-destructive, how did I then explain that I alone, out of all the firm's hundreds of attorneys, and the thousands more at similar places in Midtown and Wall Street, had wound up where I did? At the end of the day, there was no escaping the role my own character (or lack thereof) had played in what happened.

Like many law school graduates who went to a corporate law firm, I'd had only the vaguest idea of what I was getting into. It hadn't taken any time at all for me to realize I'd made a big mistake. Big New York City law firms were notoriously unpleasant and unhappy places to work, and it was no secret that the more prestigious the firm, the worse it treated its associates, expecting that in exchange for a six-figure salary and the prestige of having its name on our résumés, we'd be at the firm's disposal all day, every day.

Walker Bentley was an old-fashioned firm in many ways. It was almost a century old, named after WASP partners long dead. Unlike many such firms, it still maintained at least a pretense of the law being a profession rather than just another global business. This played out in somewhat schizophrenic ways: many of the older partners were patrician conservatives, while the younger associates tended to be liberals put off by the aggressively commercial stances of many of our rivals.

But like the rest of the profession, the firm's traditions were quickly falling victim to the bottom line. The steady drumbeat of rising profits required more hours billed, larger cases, an increased sense that the young lawyers were little more than fungible billing units serving to line the partners' coffers.

The firm was explicitly elitist, with the majority of its associates coming from a half dozen or so law schools, of which Columbia was one. Although it was more a meritocracy than an aristocracy, in my experience the line between the two is seldom very clear, and the assumptions of shared privilege played themselves out constantly, just as they had everywhere I'd gone since leaving my hometown.

The first year had been the worst, the weeks of working seventy or more hours, the constant shuffling between tedium and extreme pressure, the presumption of incompetence from the firm's partners. My friendship with Paul had been forged during those late nights at the office, the bullshit sessions over expensive delivered dinners eaten with plastic silverware in a conference room on the thirty-sixth floor of a Midtown office building. I'd figured I'd go the normal route—put in a handful of years at Walker Bentley, then head to a boutique or get an in-house job, but sometimes I wondered if I'd even make it through a year.

But I did make it, and in the process began to get used to the things I'd initially hated. During the course of my second year I felt that I'd gone a long way toward making my peace with the firm, and while I was still looking forward to leaving, the urgency of my dislike had faded.

It was toward the end of my third year that I'd met Beth. I'd been assigned to a new case—an interesting one, as such things went—a Fortune 500 company facing both a federal indictment and an SEC investigation involving accusations of accounting fraud and insider trading. The indictment had made the front page of the *Times*, accompanied by a photo of our client's CEO doing his perp walk, flanked by the firm's lead attorney handling the case. The firm had four partners on the case, plus nearly a dozen associates and a handful of paralegals.

There were two distinct kinds of paralegals at Walker Bentley. On the one hand were the lifers, people who'd been working as paralegals for years and were making it a career. On the other were recent college grads testing the waters for a year or two before either heading off to law school themselves or dropping the idea entirely and moving on to something else. Beth belonged to the second category: twenty-two years old, fresh out of Barnard College.

I was in thrall even before we'd formally met; just seeing her across a conference room, one of a couple dozen people at an initial team meeting. Not just because Beth was beautiful, though she was certainly that, a thin pale blonde. But there was something else that had drawn me: a sense of apartness. She struck me as someone who was doing a carefully observed impersonation of a normal human being.

I told myself that acting on my attraction was not an option. For one thing, I was essentially her boss. For another, she was twenty-two; I was twenty-eight—not a huge gap, but a noticeable one. I also quickly got the distinct feeling that Beth was trouble.

All these things served only to stoke my desire. I supposed boredom added fuel too—Beth as a possible way to trade the life I had for a more interesting one.

I'd compensated for my attraction by creating a distance between us, teasing Beth, flirting through aggression. I got the feeling that she understood what I was doing, and that she was comfortable playing it that way.

After getting off to an impressive start in her first couple of months on the case, Beth quickly became erratic. She seemed to grow even paler, her complexion turning waxy and sallow. She began turning up later and later, one day calling in sick at eleven a.m.

I hadn't had to deal with this sort of thing at the firm before, and didn't really know how to deal with it now. It made my life difficult if I couldn't rely on her: a couple of times I'd had to go digging through her office for documents, which wasn't a good use of my time. I considered simply passing the situation up the chain of command, but the fact was, I didn't want Beth to get in trouble. And it wasn't the sort of headache a partner would want to be bothered with; part of my job was to deal effectively with support staff.

A few months after she'd started Beth received her LSAT scores. I heard about it in passing from another paralegal: Beth had scored in the top two percent. I wasn't surprised; I'd known she was smart, and I imagined that Beth wasn't surprised herself. However, I wasn't sure how to reconcile this fact with her recent work habits. It was past time to address the situation, I decided, and this gave me the perfect cover.

I sent Beth an e-mail, subject line, *Congratulations*, and asked her to come by my office when she had a minute.

An hour later she arrived, eyes downcast, looking far more embarrassed than proud. "Hi," she said.

"You weren't even going to tell me?" I said.

"Why do you care?"

"What's that supposed to mean?" I asked. "Of course I want you to succeed. What schools are you looking at? Assuming your grades are strong, you should have a good shot anywhere."

Beth still hadn't looked at me. She shrugged. "I'm not really sure I want to go," she said softly.

"What are you talking about?"

"If you had it to do over again, would you?"

There wasn't an easy answer to this question, I realized, my hesitation no doubt giving this away. "You can go to law school and not end up where I'm at afterward," I responded. "Listen, we need to talk about some other stuff too—can I buy you a drink after work?"

I wondered if Beth could hear my thudding heart in the silence that followed. The idea had been to take her out to gently confront her about her declining work habits, but something had shifted; it wasn't clear even to me if instead I'd just asked her out on a date. "What else do we need to talk about?" she said at last, finally looking at me now that I could barely look at her.

"Well, frankly, I'm sorry to say this, but we need to talk about your recent job performance. You've been a little hit-or-miss as far as dependability, and it concerns me."

"It *concerns* you?" she repeated, mocking my words in a way I didn't quite understand.

"It does," I said. "I need to be able to rely on you. If you're going to go on to do this for a living, people are going to continue to need to rely on you."

Another silence. I wondered which of us was more uncomfortable. I suspected it was somehow still me. "Sure," Beth said at last. "You can buy me a drink; we can talk."

That night I learned that Beth's father was Leon Winthrop, one of those elite Washington lawyers who bounced effortlessly between prestigious positions in government and lucrative private practice, and that Beth had been groomed for a career in the law essentially since birth. I also learned that she was using heroin.

It'd made sense, in retrospect: her pallor, her waifish appearance, her ghostly, tardy manner. The only reason it hadn't occurred to me, I thought afterward, was because I'd never met a junkie before, and didn't expect to meet one at a place like Walker Bentley. She'd told me as a secret, making me promise I wouldn't tell anyone before I knew what she was going to say. Curiosity crowded against my disapproval.

We'd stayed in the bar for a couple of hours, Beth nursing a single drink. She said she didn't have a taste for alcohol, which I found somewhat amusing under the circumstances. "So," Beth said in parting, "we can hang out sometime. If, you know, you're up for an adventure."

It was only in retrospect that I came to understand her honesty that night for what it was: a sales pitch. Beth had been in search of a new partner in crime, someone to share her bad habit, and she, for reasons I would never know, had picked me as a target.

It wasn't like I was a virgin when it came to drugs: I'd smoked more than my share of pot in high school and college, done coke a few times, had also been known to crawl into the office with a wicked hangover on occasion. But it had all fallen into the category of recreational, nothing where I'd ever felt at risk of losing control. Not until this.

I'd known as soon as Paul had told me that Beth was dead that my own future was at risk. If anything, I'd underestimated my exposure. While the firm had managed to keep Beth's death from becoming a public scandal, Beth's father had flown to New York and started calling in favors. The next thing I knew, I was being cast as Beth's corruptor, facing utterly false accusations that I'd turned her on to heroin. An investigation was opened and I was interviewed by two detectives, but ultimately it didn't even go to a grand jury.

While the criminal investigation had been halfhearted and fleeting, Winthrop had also filed a formal complaint against me with the bar, alleging that I had procured the heroin that had killed his daughter. As best I could tell, Winthrop's only basis for this was his own need to believe it, but it wasn't an accusation I could easily disprove either. By then I had resigned from Walker Bentley to avoid being fired; I'd hired a lawyer with my own money to defend me before the bar investigation. Disbarment had been a real possibility, so much so that my six-month suspension for admitted drug use actually came as a relief.

I had been so swamped with my own troubles that I'd never properly mourned Beth. I hadn't attended her funeral, certain that I would not be welcome. Worst of all was the ugly fact that her death was, in part, a relief: there was a real sense in which I didn't miss her at all, that I felt myself lucky, an escapee. In my bitterest moments, I thought that Beth had died before she could finish totally ruining my life.

I pushed these thoughts from my mind. It was over, done with; I was where I was. I went to find Myra.

MYRA GOLDSTEIN had been a public defender ever since law school. Given our office's turnover rate, a half dozen years was enough to make you pretty senior, and Myra now worked exclusively on serious felonies. Even though we were on the same office team, I hadn't really gotten to know her. I'd always found her aloof and a little condescending.

The door to her office, which she now shared with our newest lawyer, Shelly Kennedy, was closed, which was unusual around here. I knocked, waited, knocked again. I thought I heard a voice on the other side of the door but couldn't make out what it was saying.

After a moment Myra yanked the door open. She was a brusque, angular woman in her early thirties, with dark, unruly hair that just barely snaked past her shoulders, and bulky hipster glasses. She was pale, with light green eyes that softened the slight harshness that the rest of her conveyed. While Myra was attractive, she appeared either not to know or not to care. She smelled of tobacco more than perfume. "I said 'Come in,' " she said.

"I couldn't hear you through the door."

"You're here on the Tate case," Myra said, moving back behind her desk, stepping lightly around the piles of paper that filled much of the floor of the office.

"Right," I said, standing awkwardly until I realized that Myra was not going to suggest that I sit, at which point I took Shelly's chair. The office felt especially cramped because of the disarray on Myra's half, which spilled well over into what should've been Shelly's territory.

"Isaac wants me to have a copilot on this one, I guess."

"He seems to think it's going to be a big one."

"Murder cases are all big ones," Myra said dismissively. "Isaac's just worried I don't have my head in the game."

"Do you?"

"Not at the moment. But I will."

"I'm sorry about the Gibbons verdict," I said, realizing I hadn't seen Myra since it'd come down.

"What do you know about the Gibbons verdict?"

"I know it didn't go our way."

"That's for sure."

"And I know you don't think he did it."

Myra shook her head. "It's not a question of thinking. I know he didn't do it."

"The jury thought so."

"Yeah well, the jury didn't know as much about crime as I do. The big thing was that Terrell had confessed."

"That's a problem."

"It was, yes."

"But you don't think it was legit?"

"I know it wasn't. They were in that room for about fourteen hours before Terrell confessed. He never stood a chance."

"You think they convicted just on the confession?"

"There wasn't any direct evidence. The only other thing the police had was the word of a supposed coconspirator, which they couldn't have brought in if Terrell hadn't confessed. The confession is what did him in."

"You have good grounds for appeal?"

"Nothing great, no. But you never know."

"Sorry. That must be tough."

"More for Terrell than for me. Anyway, we're here to work on Lorenzo Tate. So I made a copy of the file, what there is of it at this point, which is almost nothing. We've got the incident reports, a summary of the witness statements, some paperwork coming out of the actual arrest."

"What should I be doing?"

"First thing, of course, is we need to go talk to our client. I represented him at the lineup and arraignment a few days ago, but didn't get a chance to really talk to him then, other then to tell him to keep his mouth shut until he saw me again. We've got a meeting at Rikers set up for nine a.m. tomorrow. Where do you live?"

"Bergen Street, between Fifth and Flatbush."

"I'll come get you around eight fifteen," Myra said. She picked up a couple of large bound documents and handed them to me. "These are two pretrial omnibus motions from other cases. We'll steal as much as we can from these in assembling our motion papers, so you should read through them to get a feel for how we'll proceed."

"Anything that needs doing now?" I asked.

Myra shook her head. "It'll take you a while to read the file and look at these omnibus motions. You can do that between now and tomorrow morning."

. 4 .

OUR CLIENT, Lorenzo Tate, was twenty-six years old. He'd
been arrested on the basis of two witness statements. The sister of the surviving victim, Latrice Wallace, had told the police that
Lorenzo had come looking for her brother earlier on the night of the
shooting and had made threatening remarks. There was no statement from that victim himself, Devin Wallace. I figured this could
either mean that his condition was still too serious for him to talk, or
that he wasn't cooperating with the police. The eyewitness to the

shooting, Yolanda Miller, had said that while she didn't actually know the shooter, she'd seen him around the neighborhood, and had identified him by a street name, Strawberry.

It was after seven by the time I had finished going through the file. Suddenly finding myself working a murder had charged me up; I felt an excess of energy combined with being at loose ends, not a great combination for someone coming off a serious heroin flirtation. A cornerstone of the way I lived now was in how I structured my time, always knowing in advance what I was about to do, first breaking the day down into little pieces, then building it back up again with defined activity. I fought a vigorous campaign against dead air, and finding myself in an unplanned moment was enough to send me into a panic.

I needed to make a plan. Nothing better coming to mind, I called Paul at work.

My years at Walker Bentley had conditioned me to get straight to the point when talking to someone who billed out his time in six-minute intervals. "I just sort of got promoted," I said. "And I'm at loose ends tonight, thought I'd see if you wanted to get dinner."

I noticed the pause before Paul spoke. "Sure, pal, but it's going to have to be on the semi-late side. How's ten?"

"Fine," I said, trying not to think about the hours I'd have to kill in the meantime, trying instead just to focus on the fact that I had carved some order into my night. "Sure. Meet at Blue Ribbon, get the Black Angus for two?"

Paul laughed. "You can't afford Blue Ribbon anymore," he said.

"You're right," I said. "Steak's on you."

BLUE RIBBON Brooklyn was on Fifth Avenue in Park Slope, walking distance from my apartment on Bergen. I'd gone home first, changed out of my suit. I was still living in the apartment I'd rented back when I made a corporate lawyer's salary, a spacious one-bedroom with exposed brick walls and a marble fireplace that no longer worked. It was an irony of the New York real estate market that it was financially easier to stay in an apartment that I couldn't afford than it was to pay the broker's fee and moving costs to go somewhere cheaper. I'd had nearly a hundred grand invested and saved when I'd left the firm; much of that money was gone now, and more drained out with each passing month that I lived beyond my present means.

Even though I arrived at the restaurant a few minutes late, Paul wasn't there yet, which wasn't a surprise: he was usually late, just as I had been when I'd worked at Walker Bentley.

I ordered a martini, up with olives, and settled in at the bar to wait. The restaurant was crowded, loud; even the bar was full. Paul came bustling in ten minutes later, wearing a suit but no tie, making his way easily through the packed room. He was tall and thin, with carefully sculpted hair, the first faint signs of encroaching age starting to show on the outskirts of his face. He apologized for being late in the offhand manner of someone who always was.

"I do miss this," I said after we'd been seated and ordered our dinner.

"Miss what?" Paul said.

I gestured out at the restaurant, filled with well-dressed, attractive people eating expensive food. "The money," I said with a laugh.

"Don't worry about the bill—pay whatever you can afford; I'll cover the rest."

"I appreciate that," I said. "But I don't like it. I mean, in the sense that I don't like not being able to pull my end."

"We're friends and it's money," Paul said. "So who gives a fuck? At least you get to do something sexy. I've been practicing for over five years and I've spoken in court one time. That's when they sent me to a status conference to inform the court that we were not opposing the other side's motion for an extension of time. I can quote my entire speech: 'Your Honor, the defendant has no objection.'"

"Trust me," I said. "What I've been doing for the past six months has not been sexy."

"You get to hang out in court all day," Paul said. "Like the lawyers on TV."

"That's where the similarity ends," I assured him.

Paul raised his glass in a toast. "So, more important, congratulations on your new case. Skipping all the way to murder—you can't tell me that's not sexy."

"The murder isn't really my case—another lawyer's going to be the first chair. I'm just there to do research, that sort of thing—I assume, anyway. I'm going to be handling misdemeanors with most of my time—minor stuff, really."

"Fuck it, it's still sexy. All crime is sexy. I mean, you know the kind of shit I do all day. If I'm not careful, I'm going to officially become an antitrust lawyer. I can't even figure out my own taxes."

"You always seemed to like it okay," I said. "You always seemed to like it more than I did, anyway."

"More than you did isn't too hard to pull off, pal," Paul said. "But it does get empty. You know, the 'is that all there is' blues. Lately I've been seriously thinking of going back to church."

"*Back* to church?"

"When I was a kid I went to church," Paul said. "I wore a clip-on tie, went with my folks."

"And why are you thinking of going back?"

"I don't know," Paul said. "I want to be better."

"You're going to start going to church to get help being better?"

"That's what church is all about, right? How to be good?"

"You've got a whole lot of better to explore before you get to good," I said.

Paul gave me a look, narrowing his eyes while trying to suppress a smile. "I mean, no, I'm not in danger of pulling some variation of that prolonged cry for help you launched, but I know why I do it. I do it for the money, and because I failed to come up with anything more interesting to do. That's not really something I'm super proud of."

"Well," I said, "I guess you could say that I'm not super proud of how I've ended up where I am, either."

"You didn't get there the easy way," Paul agreed as the waiter brought us our steak. "But I do believe that in some way you got where you were supposed to go. And that's good enough for a fucking celebration."

WE ATE our steak and drank our wine, and after the meal we each had an Oban, straight up. I hadn't realized how tense I was until the alcohol relaxed me. I liked the camaraderie of eating steak and drinking scotch. Paul's company relaxed me too; I enjoyed his aggression, his thoughtless will, his attempt to bully the world.

Afterward, we stepped outside into the crisp spring air. The breeze was just enough to make me aware of the fact of weather. I heard Paul inhale a breath, taking in the night. When I glanced over at Paul he was smiling. "Let's go see if we can find some trouble," he said.

· 5 ·

Myra's car was already parked across the street when I went out to wait for her the next morning; she honked as soon as I stepped out of my building on Bergen Street. I'd overslept a little; Paul and I had ended up spilling whiskey at the Gate until a little after one a.m. I wasn't at my best; my stomach was clenched and sour, and I could still taste the scotch in the back of my throat.

"Morning," I muttered as I opened the door of her aging Volvo.

"Just throw that shit in the back," Myra said, pointing at the jumble of papers in the passenger seat. I scooped them up and tossed them onto the backseat. Myra was smoking a cigarette, had an old Sleater-Kinney song blasting on the car stereo, both of which were a little much for me first thing on a hungover morning.

"You've been out to Rikers before, right?" she asked as she pulled onto Flatbush.

"Actually, no," I said.

"Rikers isn't so bad," Myra said. "Compared to the real prisons upstate—Green Haven, Sing Sing—it's a weekend in the Hamptons. There're bad guys there who couldn't make bail on a hard-core felony, but they're heading to trial and they've got an incentive to behave. Everybody else who's there has been sentenced to under a year, meaning they're unlikely to be violent."

"I'm sure you get used to hanging out in jail," I said. "I just haven't had the opportunity to do so."

"It's bullshit that Lorenzo's being held on a case this thin," Myra said as she pulled onto I-278, which would take us out of Brooklyn, through Queens, and into the Bronx. "The judge wouldn't grant bail because of all the reporters in the courtroom, didn't want to see himself on the front page for letting loose the college-student killer. His only hook was that the police didn't find Lorenzo for a few days after they'd issued an arrest warrant, which he took to mean flight risk. How's that make him a fucking flight risk? He had four days to get out of town and they arrest him going into his apartment. If anything, he's proven he *won't* leave, even when given motive and opportunity."

"Did you argue that?"

"I thought about it," Myra said. "So, no offense, but I really don't get why Isaac decided to put you on a murder case. I'd been working as a PD for over three years before I had my first murder. I spent my first eighteen months doing nothing but juvie-court delinquent proceedings. Where'd you go to law school?"

"Why?"

"I bet you went to an Ivy League, didn't you?"

"What does it matter?"

"Harvard?"

"Columbia, actually. Why?"

"I knew it!" Myra exclaimed. "That explains why Isaac is putting you on this case. Even though he's a socialist, he's also such a total Ivy League snob. I mean, how fucked-up is that?"

"Every socialist I've ever met has also been an Ivy League snob," I replied.

"I'm just saying that guys like you don't necessarily pay your full dues. I went to Brooklyn Law School. People hear I'm a public defender, they assume it's because I couldn't get a real job. People hear you're a public defender and they assume you've got the world's greatest soul."

"I was a lawyer for four and a half years before I became a public defender," I protested, although my license had actually been suspended for those final six months. "Isaac told me when I started that I'd probably be able to move on to more serious cases after six months or so."

"So you go from arraignments to a murder case," Myra said. "Whatever. It's Isaac's call."

"Is there some reason you don't want me on this case?"

"I haven't had a second chair on any of my cases. Why is Isaac giving me one now?"

"So you can mentor me?" I said, which got me a quick sardonic look.

"It's because he thinks I'm rattled by the Gibbons case. He thinks my focus isn't there. Essentially you are a no-confidence vote in me."

"You don't really know that."

"Yes, I do."

"What Isaac told me is that it's a high-profile case, given the victim. I don't see why that's not a good enough reason to have me on board."

"I have my way of doing things. I'm not a supervisor, I'm not a trainer, I'm a trial lawyer. I run on instincts, and can't always explain why I do what I do, and don't have the time or inclination to try."

"Look, I'm just happy to be on the team, okay?"

"But that's the point," Myra said. "There is no team. This is *my* case."

WE DIDN'T talk much on the rest of the drive. As we finally approached the bridge that led to the jail we pulled into a parking lot and went to a wooden trailer, where we got our passes for entering Rikers. It looked to me like a border checkpoint between third-world countries. I felt a sort of joy at the sordidness of it all, that part of me that responded to being a criminal defense lawyer in a way I had no interest in analyzing.

We got back into the car and drove over the bridge, planes taking off from LaGuardia on our right side. Rikers wasn't what I had expected: the Los Angeles of jails, it was sprawling, disconnected, a bunch of buildings spread out haphazardly across a moody landscape.

We parked in a crowded lot and entered the squat control center. The room was crowded with people trying to get in to see prisoners. I followed Myra to the window for attorneys, where she handed over our passes and filled out a visitation card. The guard stamped our hands and gave us plastic tokens identifying us as lawyers.

Myra led the way out of the main building and back outside. There were seagulls everywhere, used to humans and ignoring our presence. We waited for a bus that took us to the facility where Lorenzo was being held.

Finally we ended up in an interview room, waiting for Lorenzo to be brought in. The room was small, drastically overheated, two chairs on one side of a metal desk, one chair on the other. One wall was a window, two court officers dimly visible on the other side—one had maybe just told the punch line to a joke; both were laughing.

Myra and I waited in near silence for ten minutes. I felt my nerves clutch; looking at Myra I could tell she felt it too, even with her experience. I supposed you never got completely used to sitting in the hostile space of a jail, waiting for a man accused of murder.

Myra filled the time reviewing the papers that made up our initial file; not knowing what else to do, I did the same. Finally the door behind us opened with a protracted metallic screech, and we turned to face our client.

I didn't know what exactly I'd been expecting, but Lorenzo Tate was not it. Perhaps more than anything I'd expected someone intimidating, and Lorenzo certainly wasn't that. He was relatively short, for one thing, under five-eight, and was smiling at us boyishly, looking more like a salesman than an accused murderer. He had fairly light skin, with a noticeable birthmark, a dark bruise-colored discoloration on the upper edge of his face, just above and to the side of his right eye.

Myra introduced me to Lorenzo and we all shook hands. She then launched into a brief overview of how having a public defender worked. The small, stuffy room was even more uncomfortable with Lorenzo in it; I felt myself starting to sweat. Myra asked Lorenzo if he could afford to retain a lawyer.

"How much would I be paying?" Lorenzo asked.

"Prices vary pretty widely. But for a murder case, if it actually goes to trial, I would think even the cheap side's going to be around fifty thousand," Myra said.

Lorenzo looked disappointed by this answer. He glanced down and shook his head. "No disrespect to you all, but do I need to be getting the money for a real lawyer?"

"To be honest, Mr. Tate, fifty thousand dollars wouldn't buy you a lawyer that's half as good as we are," Myra said, no hint of bragging in her voice. "Obviously this is a big decision, and you should do what you feel comfortable with. I'm not trying to sell you anything— I get paid the same whether you become my client or not. But don't hire a lawyer just because you've heard generally bad things about public defenders. Because we, in particular, are good."

Lorenzo was watching Myra carefully as she spoke. When she was done Lorenzo looked over to me, which made me aware that I was smiling slightly. I decided to let myself smile. I was enjoying this. After a long moment Lorenzo nodded.

"That's all right then," Lorenzo said. "I'm gonna be with you all."

"Then before we get started, I want to tell you two things," Myra said. "First, you should tell us everything you know, bad or good, that the DA's likely to know or find out. Anything they know that we don't is going to put us at a big disadvantage. We're here to help you, not to judge you, and we can't do that if we don't know what we need to know.

"Second, we're the only people you should talk to about this case. And I mean the only people, and I mean *anything* about this case. Someone here asks you what you're in for, you tell them traffic tickets. Anything you say to anybody who isn't in this room right now can come back to haunt us. You understand?"

"I feel you," Lorenzo said.

"Okay. I'd like to start just by getting a little background about who you are, before we get into the case itself," Myra said. "Were you born in New York?"

"I was raised up in the Gardens," Lorenzo said. "You know Glenwood Gardens? Off of Avenue I out in Midwood?"

"I don't," Myra said.

"We the old-school kinda project," Lorenzo said. "A big old compound of high-rises. Ain't no garden there neither."

Myra nodded. "And is that where you still live?"

"I'm up out of the project now," Lorenzo said. "Got me a place on the avenue."

"Did you finish high school, Mr. Tate?"

"No, ma'am," Lorenzo said. I couldn't believe my ears: an accused murderer from the projects had just called Myra "ma'am." I was taking notes while Myra asked the questions, and I wrote that down.

"Do you have a job?"

Lorenzo smiled a little, his head bobbing and weaving slightly. "Do you want to know what I do for green, even if I don't pay no taxes on it, you know what I'm saying?"

I did, and a quick glance told me that Myra did too. "You mean if you make money doing something that isn't legal, should you admit that to us?" she asked.

Lorenzo again with his boyish smile. I guessed that our client did all right with the ladies. "I know you can't turn me in or nothin'," Lorenzo said. "I just don't know if you want to know."

"Everything you tell us is privileged," Myra said. "Meaning exactly, we can't be forced to turn you in—unless you tell us about a crime you are planning to commit in the future. The other factor, though, is we pretty much can't let you say something on the witness stand that we know not to be true. So, for example, if you confess that you committed the murder in this case, we'd be limited in how we could let you testify in court that you didn't do it. Understand?"

"You don't have to worry about me confessing to no murder," Lorenzo said. "'Cause I sure enough didn't cap no mother's son. I ain't never shot me no gun in my life."

"Good," Myra said, although I could tell that our client's protestations of innocence didn't mean much to her. Defendants almost always insisted on their innocence to their lawyers, even when doing so was both laughable and unnecessary. The standard office theory was that clients assumed a PD wouldn't work as hard for someone we knew was guilty. What the clients failed to reckon with was that all PDs knew that the vast majority of our clients were, in fact, guilty. "In terms of how you made money, I think it's important enough that we know that you should tell us, even if it means admitting to something illegal."

"You can't come up through the Gardens and not be in the life. And when I was coming up the life meant slinging rock. Wasn't like you could come up through the Gardens and not sling some rock. But I got that shit behind me, and I ain't never looked back at it."

"Okay," Myra said. "You ever get busted?"

Lorenzo shook his head.

"*Never?*" Myra said, not trying to hide her skepticism.

"When I was out on the street, nobody cared about making no busts up in the Gardens. I got off the street soon as I was able, and I stayed off. I'm, like, all deep in the background now. Plus, these days I just be involved with the chronic. Ain't nowhere near the same green, but motherfuckers ain't getting capped over no Buddha."

"You're saying you're just involved with pot?" I asked.

Lorenzo nodded. "Got me this fine hydro shit, don't even have to bring it in from outside the city. It's like a bud grows in Brooklyn, know what I'm saying?"

"Well," Myra said, "it will certainly be helpful that you don't have a criminal record."

Lorenzo grinned his charmer's grin. "Knew there must be some reason I be keeping myself clean all this time," he said.

We all smiled at this. I found myself liking Lorenzo.

"Do you remember where you were on the night of April 6?" Myra asked.

Lorenzo nodded and leaned forward. "I been thinking on that. I was chillin' with my boy Marcus—I was at his crib until two in the morning or thereabouts."

"What were you two doing?"

There was a pause, and Lorenzo looked away. "Marcus and me, we're, like, on the same team, you know what I'm saying?"

Myra narrowed her eyes a little. "I'm not sure I do," she said after a moment. I didn't either: I wasn't sure if Lorenzo was revealing Marcus to be a fellow dealer or a boyfriend, but guessed the former was the more likely. "Do you mean you work together?"

Lorenzo smiled and nodded.

"That may mean he's not our ideal alibi witness," Myra deadpanned. "Do you know if Marcus has ever been busted?"

"Marcus just ain't as lucky as I am," Lorenzo said. "He's gone down a couple of times."

Myra didn't try to hide her disappointment. "A good alibi isn't necessary, although it certainly never hurts," she said.

"I was with Marcus till late that night," Lorenzo insisted.

"It's not that I don't believe you," Myra said. "But if we put Marcus on the stand and his record comes up, stuff about drug dealing, it doesn't make you look very good by association."

"I got you," Lorenzo said after a moment. "But it's still the truth."

"Okay," Myra said. "The police didn't arrest you until four days after the shooting. Did you know they were looking for you?"

"I'd heard about how the five-oh be looking to snatch me up on that," Lorenzo said. "So I kept myself on the low."

"How did they come to arrest you?"

"I finally go by my crib, see if I can get me some clothes, the po-po be watching my place; next thing is I'm in the system. Wouldn't never have happened that way if that white boy hadn't been capped."

"Do you know Devin Wallace?"

"Devin and I go back a ways, sure."

"And had you ever met the deceased?" Myra asked.

"The white boy?"

"His name was Seth Lipton," Myra said, a little coldly. She clearly thought Lorenzo should bother to remember the name of the person he was accused of killing.

"Never met the man," Lorenzo said. "He must've been copping."

"Why do you say that?" Myra said.

Lorenzo smiled. "He gonna have some other reason for being up in the Gardens?"

Myra responded with a noncommittal nod. "So you and Devin, you were friends?"

"We was all right."

"Not friends, but friendly?"

"Yeah," Lorenzo said. "Like that."

"Is that accurate?"

"We was all right," Lorenzo said again.

"How did you know Devin?"

Lorenzo fixed Myra with a careful look, then looked over at me. "How come you let her do all the talking?" he asked.

"I'm the second chair," I said. "It's Myra's case."

"That right," Lorenzo said, a slight skepticism creeping into his look now. I guessed that Lorenzo's opinion of my stature as a man had just plummeted.

"That's the way we work it," I said, feeling that I needed to cut this boys-against-girls crap off at the pass. "I'll be involved with every aspect of your case, but Myra's in charge. I think the question she asked you was how you knew Devin."

Lorenzo smiled at this. "We did some business together. I keep Devin hooked up with the chronic. I'm all out of the on-the-street shit, but I know people. I bring things together like. That's how come I'm still alive and never went to the joint: I ain't about declaring war and shit, getting all up in other people's business. I go along to get along."

"So you supplied Devin with drugs," Myra said evenly.

"Just with the chronic, though. I ain't touchin' that serious shit."

Myra leaned back in her seat and let a moment pass. There was only so much admitting to criminal activity we wanted from our client right off the bat. "Okay," Myra said. "How about this woman who said she saw you at the shooting? Do you know her?"

"Yo-Yo?" Lorenzo said. "I know who she is from around the Gardens and what-all, but I don't think we ever talked none."

"You don't think you've ever actually spoken with her?" Myra said, leaning forward slightly. "Not once?"

Lorenzo shook his head. "She and I never said word one."

"But it wouldn't surprise you that she knew who you were?"

"Course she'd know who I was if I know who she was. People *know* me up there."

Myra took a beat, clearly wondering if she wanted to follow up on that. It profited a defense lawyer nothing to hear the bad news from the prosecution, or worse still, in court, rather than from our client, where there might still be time to blunt the damage. On the other hand, knowing too much of the truth could limit our options. "When you say people know you up there, what do you mean?"

Perhaps realizing he'd gone further then he intended to, Lorenzo retreated back to his boyish charm. "I was around, is all," Lorenzo said. "The Gardens is where I come up."

"Do you think someone like Yolanda would know that you were in business with Devin?"

"Yo-Yo knew that, sure. Shorty was with Devin, at least from time to time."

Myra frowned at this, locking eye contact with Lorenzo. "Are you saying that Devin and Yolanda were a couple?"

"I don't know about no *couple*, but yeah, they was together."

Myra shut her eyes for a second, taking this in. "The eyewitness was dating the intended victim?" she said, trying to keep her voice neutral.

Lorenzo noticed her reaction. "That some kind of shit for you to work with?" he asked.

Myra nodded slowly. "It changes things. The bad side is, the jury might be likely to pay more attention to someone who was emotionally affected by the shootings. It probably also changes how aggressively we can cross her. The good news is, it potentially gives her a reason to lie, or at least to try and seem more certain than she otherwise would, that a complete stranger wouldn't have."

"Why does being Devin's shorty give Yo-Yo a reason to lie?" Lorenzo asked.

"It doesn't, necessarily," Myra said. "But it gives us something to investigate. Maybe she knows who really did the shooting and she's lying to protect him. Hell, maybe she did it. The thing is, with a complete stranger, there'd be no way to really claim that she was lying, because there's no reason why she would."

Lorenzo considered this. "So it helps us or it don't?" he asked.

"Too soon to say," Myra said. "But it certainly changes things. Tell me more about their relationship."

"What you wanna know?"

"How long had they been seeing each other?"

"They was . . . let's see . . . they first got together back in the fall, maybe October. That's the first I remember seeing her around."

"Was Devin seeing anyone else?"

Lorenzo smiled. "Devin and I weren't tight that way," he said. "But sure ain't gonna surprise me if he was."

"You think he might have continued seeing other people?"

Lorenzo, still smiling, shrugged.

"How about Yolanda?" Myra said. "Any idea if she was seeing anyone else?"

"Like I said, I ain't never spoke to Yo-Yo. I just knew her to see her around."

"Did you ever see her around with any other guy? It doesn't have to be someone you knew."

"I'm not recollecting nothing like that," Lorenzo said.

"Okay," Myra said, taking a second to consult her notes. "What about Devin's sister?" she asked. "What was your relationship with her like?"

"Latrice?" Lorenzo said. "She a fine-looking girl. A dime for sure."

"Did you ever have any kind of relationship with Latrice?"

Lorenzo laughed his easy laugh. "Devin ain't gonna like that. Latrice wasn't the kind to be with me anyway. Girl's got a *job*, that kinda shit."

"Are you saying she disapproved of you?" Myra asked.

"Latrice knew what Devin's business was," Lorenzo said. "She knew what my business was. She let it go, far as I know."

"She lived with Devin, right?"

Lorenzo nodded.

"Are they close?"

"They brother and sister," Lorenzo replied. "I'm gonna believe they tight."

"And you talked to her when you were over to visit Devin?"

"Sure."

"Did you talk to her on the night that Devin was shot?"

"That's right," Lorenzo said.

"Okay," she said. "Now according to the police reports we have, Latrice said you came by looking for Devin on the night of the shooting."

"I be looking for him, yeah, but that was before he got capped," Lorenzo said. "Lookin' to find a man ain't no crime."

"Do you remember what time you went by Devin's apartment?"

"Not for sure," Lorenzo said. "Maybe like seven?"

"Why were you looking for Devin?"

"About the green, you know," Lorenzo said. "Dude owed me some money, sure. But how he ever going to pay me if I shoot him?"

Based on what I knew from the police reports, Lorenzo's conversation with Latrice was a topic about which I'd at least half expected Lorenzo to lie. The hope was that, if he did, he would do it in a vaguely plausible way. It was always demoralizing when the client came out with some preposterous story that they expected you to sell.

Instead Lorenzo appeared to be telling the truth, but it wasn't a truth that helped us.

"This was for product?" Myra asked.

Lorenzo bobbed his head, confirming through body language what we already knew. "How much did he owe you?" Myra asked, keeping her voice neutral. We didn't care that our client dealt drugs. We did care that he'd been looking for one of the victims in order to settle a drug debt on the night of the shootings, because this made our job considerably more difficult.

"He owed me five G," Lorenzo said softly.

"Five thousand bucks?" Myra asked. Lorenzo nodded slightly, looking uncomfortable for the first time in the interview.

This wasn't good. Other than love, money was as bad as motive got. Because we were talking about marijuana, I hadn't expected that kind of number. I wondered how much pot five thousand dollars wholesale got you. We clearly weren't talking about dime bags of shwag weed. I willed myself to think past the buzz of worry that was trying to hijack my concentration.

"Okay," Myra said. "So you went over to Devin's apartment because he owed you money, and Latrice answered the door. Do you remember the conversation you two had?"

"I ask her if Devin there, she say no; I ask does she know where he is, she say no; I ask if he left the dead presidents for me, she say no. I'm like, 'That motherfucker thinks I'm playing with him.' Then I was out."

"Do you recall whether those were your exact words? 'Motherfucker thinks I'm playing with him'?"

"I wasn't carrying no tape recorder."

"I understand that," Myra said, making a show of patience. "But I still need to know if you think that's exactly what you said."

"Best I can remember, I say what I say I say," Lorenzo said. "What she say I say?"

"According to the police, she said that you threatened Devin," Myra said evenly.

"I threaten him to his own sister?" Lorenzo said incredulously. "What I do that for? Why am I going to threaten him to Latrice, then cap him a few hours later?"

"Is it possible that you said something that Latrice took as more threatening?"

"She can say 'motherfucker thinks I'm playing with him' be a threat if she want to. Ain't nothin' I can do about that."

"You don't think you might have said something more threatening?"

"I didn't say no kind of threat," Lorenzo said, for the first time looking angry. "Dude was my boy, and dude owed me money. Can't be my boy and can't pay me back neither if he's dead. So I got me two good reasons not to cap him."

OUTSIDE THE jail, I found myself squinting in the sudden daylight. We'd talked to Lorenzo for around two hours, circling back to his upbringing, his relationship with Devin, whether there was anything else he could tell us about Yolanda or Latrice, his alibi for that night. Even though I'd basically just sat and listened the whole time, taking notes, I felt exhausted, like my day should be done already.

It took one look at Myra to tell she felt the same. She'd lit a cigarette as soon as we walked outside, taking a deep drag. I'd expected her to have built up a shell by now, not to show fatigue or discouragement, but perhaps that had been unrealistic. "Is it just me, or was that a mixed blessing?" I said.

"It's never good when the client admits that the victim owed him money on a drug debt and that he'd gone looking for said victim the night he was shot. The alibi based on a dealer doesn't exactly help us."

"I guess the good news is, if he was going to lie to us he'd presumably have come up with something better than that."

Myra looked over at me, grinning. "You have a point," she said. "Not that it helps. We can't present a preposterous defense and then ask the jury to acquit based on how implausible our defense was."

"Are you sure?" I asked. "Have you ever tried it?"

"Why don't you test it out on a misdemeanor and get back to me?"

"Five grand sounds like a fuck of a lot of pot."

"You'd be surprised," Myra said. "Weed's become a high-end business in New York. First-rate hydro can retail out in the neighborhood of five hundred or more an ounce. Wouldn't shock me if five grand wholesale was just for a pound."

"I knew I was in the wrong line of work," I said. "What about that Devin was sleeping with the witness to his getting shot? That didn't turn up in any of the police reports."

"Like I said to our guy, I think it cuts both ways," Myra said. "It maybe gives her a reason to lie, which helps, but it might make her a lot more convincing on the stand. She's not some passerby who's not really paying attention; she's watching her boyfriend get shot."

We had crossed through the parking lot and reached Myra's car. "So what do you think?" I asked as I waited for Myra to unlock my door.

"What do I think about what?" Myra asked.

"You think he did it?"

Myra looked over at me from across the top of her car. "How the hell should I know?" she said.

· 6 ·

I HAD JUST arrived at the office the next morning and was still settling in when Myra came over to my desk. "You have anything important scheduled for right now?" Myra asked.

"I was just grabbing a chance to go over my new batch of files," I said. "There's a bunch of misdemeanors I haven't even looked at. What's up?"

"Come with me," Myra said. "We need to go on a mission."

"Where to?"

"The scene of the crime," Myra said.

We took the 2 train from Borough Hall out to its last stop in Brooklyn. "You ever been out here before?" I asked once we were seated. The train was pretty empty; the commuter rush was mostly over, and we were heading in the opposite direction of most commuters.

Myra shook her head. "That's the point of the mission," she said. "It's important that we have at least some kind of feel for the place where the shootings happened."

We got out at the Brooklyn College stop, onto Flatbush Avenue, a street that was to Brooklyn what Broadway was to Manhattan: it traveled through virtually the entire borough. But this stretch of Flatbush looked noticeably different from the stretch that passed a half block from my apartment. It felt as though we'd gone back in time a little, the store signs all looking like they'd been put up in the 1950s.

The commercial strip appeared lively enough, however, with fast-food stores, delis, clothing shops, everything open for business. Virtually everyone on the street but us was black. We walked aimlessly for a couple blocks, just getting our bearings, cutting over on Avenue I, then turning onto Bedford Avenue.

The neighborhood changed completely as we did so. Now it was Orthodox Jews who occupied the sidewalks, which were lined with detached houses with yards and garages.

Eventually we came across the campus of Brooklyn College. There were security guards at every entrance to the campus, which we made no attempt to enter. We hit Flatbush again, turned right, then left onto Avenue H. The fast-food restaurants and stores of Flatbush dropped away, the number of people dropped and scattered, and soon we were walking alongside Glenwood Gardens.

As Lorenzo had said, the Gardens was the kind of project New York didn't build anymore, a series of identical towers sprawling across several square blocks. Even in the late morning it possessed an aura of dilapidated menace.

I found myself hesitating when Myra turned from the street into the project. She turned back to me, offering a tight smile. "Anyone looking at us is going to think we're cops, lawyers, social workers, the IRS, something," she said. "They'll leave us alone."

Myra turned out to be right: the people we passed stared at us hard, but nobody said anything. We took a quick walk through, slicing across the middle of the project, between where the shooter had stood and where the victims had been. I had a hard time taking anything in, too worried about catching someone's eye in the wrong way. The courtyard was fairly empty; just a cluster of young men standing outside the doorway of one tower, a young woman watching a small child playing in the middle of the yard.

We crossed through the main courtyard of the project and turned right onto Avenue I, heading back to Flatbush. "So," Myra said, "I guess that's the Gardens. What'd you see?"

I glanced over at her, wanting to convey a little resentment that she was giving me a test, but also wanting to know if she'd seen something I hadn't. "The whole place is like a fortress," I said. "The courtyard is completely cut off from the street."

"That's true," Myra said. "But it isn't cut off at all from the project itself. There must be a couple of hundred windows that look out onto that courtyard."

"Sure," I said. "But our crime happened a little after midnight. Could be nobody was looking."

"Could be," Myra said. "They would've heard shots, but people in a project probably aren't all that likely to go stand in front of a window when they hear shots. But I still find it hard to believe no-body else saw anything. Even if they did, though, it doesn't necessar-ily mean we want to uncover what they saw."

"Because they might have seen our client?"

"You never know," Myra said.

"Okay," I said. "So that was educational. Now can we get out of here?"

"Not yet," Myra said. "We've still got to meet the neighbors."

·7·

YOLANDA MILLER was not happy to see us. Not that I'd
expected her to be, but the degree of her immediate hostility
took me by surprise.

She was talking to us from the doorway of her apartment, making no move to let us in. I felt exposed and vulnerable standing in a
hallway in the Gardens, but tried to put such thoughts out of my
mind.

"I don't got to be talkin' to you," Yolanda said once we'd introduced ourselves. "The DA told me I ain't got to say nothing to you if I don't want to."

"If necessary we can subpoena you," Myra said. "Did the DA tell you that?"

"What's that gonna do?"

"If we subpoena you it would mean you'd have to come down to court and talk to us under oath," Myra said matter-of-factly. "If you didn't show up the judge would issue a warrant for your arrest."

"You gonna arrest me now? For what?"

"I'm not saying we're going to arrest you, Yolanda," Myra said. "I'm simply telling you what would happen if we were forced to subpoena you and you didn't comply with the subpoena. I don't want to have to subpoena you at all. We only have a couple of questions."

"I ain't got nothing to say that's going to help you all. I saw Strawberry shoot Devin and that white dude."

"I'm not going to try to get you to say anything other than the truth," Myra said. "I'd just like to know exactly what you saw, step by step. Let's start with where you were."

"I'd just come out my building to go to the Arab mart down on Avenue J."

"What's the Arab mart?"

"It's just a deli," Yolanda said with a shrug. "Everybody be calling it that because it's run by these Arabs. They the only Arabs around here, what with all the Jews."

"What were you going to get from the deli?" Myra asked, apparently uninterested in exploring Yolanda's lack of political correctness.

"What you care about that for?"

"I don't, really. I just want to make sure I have a full picture, that's all."

"I got me a little boy. I needed to pick up some milk."

"You were going to get milk?"

"And I needed me some Newports," Yolanda said, drumming the fingers of one hand against the pocket of her jeans while the other hand held her front door.

"So you were going to get milk and cigarettes?"

"True that."

"Did you make it to the deli?"

"I didn't get out the Gardens."

"Okay. So what happened when you left your building?"

"I saw Devin across the way," Yolanda said.

"Did you know Devin?" Myra asked, playing it straight—we needed to know what story Yolanda was going to tell about her relationship with Devin.

"Me and him is together," Yolanda said, not making much out of it. While she was still hostile—her arms folded across her chest, her face tight and expressionless—she seemed to be reasonably forthcoming. But there was something jittery about her too, a nervous energy that seemed to go beyond the fact that we'd barged into her life and started asking questions.

"You're together?" Myra said, feigning surprise. "Meaning you're dating?"

"Like that, sure."

"I see. How long have you and Devin been together?"

"Few months now," Yolanda said dismissively.

"What was Devin doing when you saw him that night?"

"He was talking to the white dude that got hisself killed."

"You saw the two of them talking together?"

"They was just across the way."

"Could you see Devin's face when you spotted him?"

"Naw," Yolanda said. "I could see the white dude's face, enough to see he was white, anyway."

"What happened after you saw Devin and the white guy?"

"I was gonna go over there, talk to Devin. Just as I started walkin' was when Strawberry started shootin'."

"Did you see the shooter before the shots?"

Yolanda shook her head. "I wasn't looking 'round after I saw Devin. Then I heard a gat sparking, saw Devin and the white dude both go down. That's when I seen Strawberry. He come running by."

"That's when you first saw the person who'd been shooting? After the shots had been fired?"

Yolanda was getting a little more agitated, but not as much as I would've expected. While it was obvious that she didn't like talking about the shooting, she was able to do so without losing her composure, which was more than most people would've been capable of. I suspected she would make a decent witness for the prosecution. "He come running right by me."

"He ran past you?"

"That's right."

"How far away was the person who ran past you?"

"It was Strawberry," Yolanda said, raising her voice slightly. "I seen him. He wasn't no more than ten feet away."

"Did he still have the gun in his hand when he ran by you?"

"Yeah."

"He did?" Myra said, tilting her head slightly. "You saw the gun in his hand when he ran by?"

"Where else was it gonna be?" Yolanda said heatedly. "He wasn't gonna leave it there."

"What I'm asking, Yolanda, is whether you actually saw the gun in his hand," Myra said, keeping her own voice even and speaking slowly, clearly trying to defuse the conversation a little.

"Sure, I saw it when he run by."

"Which hand was it in?"

Yolanda glared at Myra with open hostility. "You trying to trick me."

"No, I'm not," Myra said. "I'm simply trying to understand what you saw. Now, if you saw the gun as he ran past, it had to either be on the side nearest to you or the side farthest from you. Do you remember which it was?"

"You ain't never been around when a gat went off," Yolanda said dismissively. "The whole thing happen in, like, one second, the shooting, seeing Devin go down, seeing Strawberry run past me. I wasn't looking for no kinda shit like what hand he got the gun in."

"So what did you see of the man you saw run by?"

"I seen his face."

"And you'd seen Strawberry before?"

"I'd seen him around here. He do business with Devin."

"What kind of business?"

Yolanda's glare grew even sharper. "You can ask Strawberry that your own self."

"And had you ever spoken to Strawberry?"

"I ain't got no cause to speak with him. But I seen him in the Gardens. I seen him enough to recognize him."

"Where specifically had you seen him?"

"I seen him over at Devin's crib."

"You were over at Devin's apartment when Strawberry was there?"

"Time to time."

"Were you in on their deals?"

"Hell, no," Yolanda said, and the way she said it I believed her. "I don't do that shit."

"Anyone you know ever have problems with Strawberry?"

"You mean, I got a reason to put this on him?" Yolanda asked, shaking her head. "It ain't like that."

"Did you talk to police the night of the shooting?"

"That's right."

"Did you tell them you'd seen the shooter?"

"I told them I seen Strawberry."

"Did you talk to the police between the night of the shooting and when you came to view the lineup five days later?"

"Only when that lady detective came by with those pictures she want me to look at."

This caught my attention: it was the first I'd heard of any photographs. I felt Myra tense beside me. She cocked her head slightly, gazing intently at Yolanda. "Detective Spanner came to show you pictures?"

Yolanda shrugged. "I don't know her name. The lady detective who been running the po-po's case."

"What kind of pictures did she show you?"

"She want me to tell her which picture be Strawberry. I tell her I know him if I see him in person."

"Did you look at the photos?"

"The lady detective show them to me."

"And did you pick out Strawberry?"

"I didn't pick out nobody. I told her I'd know if I see him in person."

"So you looked at the photos, but you didn't pick anybody out?"

"I pick him out at the lineup. You was there when I pick him out."

Myra smiled broadly. "That's right, Ms. Miller," she said. "I was there the first time you picked him out."

■ ■ ■

AS WE cut across the open space in the center of the Gardens, heading to the apartment that Latrice Wallace shared with her brother, I turned to Myra. "I'm not sure Yolanda liked us," I said.

"I'm not sure I liked her," Myra replied. "But that was huge just now. That was *Fantasy Island*."

"Because we've never been told anything about a photo array."

"We certainly have not. And we certainly should have. We've got a way to potentially throw out Yolanda's whole ID of our guy now."

"Really?"

"Absolutely," Myra said. "First of all we have the discovery violation—the DA had an obligation to tell us about the failed ID procedure. Second, the fact that Yolanda couldn't make an ID on the first try casts doubt on the accuracy of any subsequent ID she did make. We'll demand a *Wade* hearing, challenge Yolanda's lineup ID. We get that tossed, the DA's case is in serious trouble. Plus there's the fact that she admits that she was schtupping our vic."

"Did you just say 'schtupping'?" I asked.

"My mother taught me that good girls don't say 'fuck,'" Myra said. "It's too much of a coincidence, though, don't you think?"

"We're back to talking about the case now, right?"

"We're talking about the fact that the state's best witness was fucking the vic," Myra said. "Was that clear enough?"

"If we got rid of her ID, would that get rid of the whole case?"

"Maybe," Myra said. "Even if it still went forward, I don't see a way for them to win without Yolanda."

"Sounds like we should write a motion soon."

"I completely agree," Myra said. "Provided that by 'we' you meant you, and by 'soon' you meant right away."

· 8 ·

LATRICE WALLACE opened the door of the apartment she shared with her brother, Devin, with the chain on, peering out at us cautiously through the crack. We knew her brother wouldn't be there—he was still in the ICU. Myra introduced us, telling Latrice that we represented Lorenzo Tate and wanted to ask her about what she'd seen that night.

To my surprise, Latrice didn't show any resistance to answering our questions. On the contrary, she seemed resigned to it, as if she'd expected us. It didn't seem to occur to her that she could just refuse to cooperate, and it certainly wasn't in our interest to offer her that option.

Latrice was attractive, as Lorenzo had advertised: she was a thin, self-possessed young woman, with copper-tinted hair flowing halfway down her back. The three of us sat in the stylish living room Latrice shared with her brother, which was filled with better furniture than I had in my apartment. Given the condition of the Gardens generally, and of the building in particular, the apartment seemed completely incongruous. At least until I remembered what Devin Wallace did for a living.

"I just wanted to find out what you actually saw that night," Myra said. "It's my understanding that you spoke with Lorenzo Tate a few hours before the shooting; is that right?"

"I talk to him when he come by here."

"What did you two talk about?"

"He ask if Devin be home. I say no. He ask if Devin left money for him. I say I ain't seen nothing like that. Then he talked some shit."

"What do you mean?"

"He just said some shit 'bout my brother, something like, 'Motherfucker don't know who he's fucking with, but he's going to get his.' "

"What happened next?"

"Strawberry was out."

"And what time was this?"

"Must've been like seven, seven thirty or so, 'cause I'd just gotten back from work."

"And is that when you usually get home after work?"

" 'Round then, yeah."

"So after Lorenzo left, what did you do then?" Myra asked.

"I went back to what I was doing, cooking up something to eat."

"You didn't call up your brother, try to get ahold of him?"

"I don't get up in Devin's business," Latrice said again. "If my brother got something he want to say to Strawberry, he knows how to find him."

"Did you see either your brother or Strawberry at any point later that night?"

Latrice shook her head. "I didn't hear nothing about it till the police came, telling me 'bout how Devin got himself shot."

"Okay," Myra said. "We don't have to talk about that night anymore. Just one other thing: do you know Yolanda Miller?"

"Sure I know Yo-Yo. She live right here in the Gardens."

"What was her relationship with your brother?"

"He be with her from time to time, if that's what you asking 'bout."

"They're dating?" Myra asked.

"They hook up, sure."

"Are you friends with Yolanda?"

"Me and her is fine with one another."

"You know her pretty well."

Latrice shrugged. "We both come up here in the Gardens, but Yo-Yo's got a few years on me. We go back, I guess, but we ain't tight or nothing."

"Is she somebody you'd trust?"

Latrice jerked her head back like she'd been asked if she was willing to give Yolanda a kidney. "She never done wrong by me. She was doing awright back when she was with Malik. Things didn't get messed up for her until after she had his boy."

"Who's Malik?" Myra asked.

"Malik Taylor," Latrice said, as if that would explain something.

"Okay, so who's Malik Taylor?"

"He's from around the way. He and Yolanda were together for a couple of years, up until she had his boy. Not to say that Malik is like most of the men in the Gardens—he's awright—but he got up on out of there once that kid was born."

"Do you know where we can find Malik?"

"He run the sports store up on Flatbush."

"What store is that?"

"Midwood Sports."

"He owns it?"

Latrice laughed at this. "He don't *own* it. He just do the day-to-day. You know, like a manager."

"When did he and Yolanda have a son?"

"That was almost two years ago now."

"And has Yolanda not been doing so well since her son was born?"

"I don't know what all go on with her and Malik," Latrice said. The more she talked to us, the more she'd started to actually say things. "But I know she started getting high, shit like that."

"Yolanda started doing drugs after her son was born?"

Latrice looked away, pursing her lips, clearly regretting telling us. "Most folks around here get high," she said quickly. "Ain't like that's a big thing."

"But something changed in Yolanda, didn't it?" Myra asked, equally quick. "Otherwise you wouldn't have mentioned it."

"It wasn't just the Buddha no more; she was hitting the powder too. I know 'cause Devin didn't like that shit. He don't like to be 'round nobody who's into the serious product."

I thought back to Yolanda's jittery presence, the sharp edge that glinted out of her demeanor. A budding coke habit would certainly explain it.

"So you're saying that Yolanda had started doing coke?"

"That's what I just said, ain't it?" Latrice said, a new sharpness in her voice. "I shouldn't even be talking to you—it's my brother that got shot. You best just be getting up out of here."

MYRA MANAGED to keep a poker face until we were safely outside the building, at which point she turned to me and gave me a big grin. "That moved the ball up the field," she said.

"I didn't have you for a football fan."

"Is that what they do in football?" Myra replied. "I was referring to one of the DA's prime witnesses punking out the other as a druggie."

"How many yards does that give us?"

"It undermines her entire ID."

"Doing pot or coke wouldn't make you hallucinate."

Myra was clearly losing patience. "Maybe not. But drugs fuck up your perceptions, certainly, and they sure as hell make you seem pretty unreliable. Does any of it mean she didn't actually see what she claims to have seen? Not necessarily. Does it give us a lot of mud to throw on her, dirty up her clean little eyewitness testimony? Absolutely."

"And that's what matters."

"In law school I took a class with a famous criminal defense attorney. He had a saying: 'A criminal trial is a search for the truth, but the defense lawyer isn't a member of the search party.' "

· 9 ·

OUR LAST visit of the mission was to see Marcus Riley, our client's supposed alibi, who lived on Avenue J, a couple of blocks from Glenwood Gardens.

Marcus Riley was a large man, bulky and lumbering, and he certainly did not look thrilled to see a couple of white people in business clothes knocking on his door. Hip-hop rumbled out of the room behind him:

Kingpins put in bullpens, old connects get paro'
Break out of town when the Jakes take down the Pharaoh.

"We represent Lorenzo Tate," Myra said, when it was looking like Marcus was not planning on inviting us in.

"You represent him in what?"

"You know that Lorenzo has been charged with murder, right?"

"You mean you his lawyers?"

"That would be us."

"Well, you ain't his family, that's for damn sure," Marcus said, finally moving aside to let us in.

Lorenzo had told us that Marcus lived by himself. Even if he hadn't, I'd have been able to guess based on the condition of Marcus's apartment. The living room was cluttered, the furniture stained and ratty, although I noticed that the television was a large flat-screen. There were dirty clothes and empty beer bottles strewn across the floor, and it smelled like a locker room.

"Lorenzo said you were with him on the night of the murder," Myra said, her inflection halfway between a statement and a question.

"Yeah, uh-huh, true that," Marcus said, sprawling down on his couch, grabbing a tallboy from the floor, and helping himself to a hearty swig.

"You mind if I turn this down?" Myra said, pointing toward the stereo. She was still standing, so I was too.

Marcus shrugged, and Myra lowered the music until it was barely audible. "I'm going to ask too that you don't drink any more just now," Myra said. "You give us a statement, we write it up, your drinking a beer is the sort of detail that can complicate things."

"Ain't no thing," Marcus said, putting the can down on the floor. "Strawberry told me you all was gonna come by."

"What were you and Lorenzo doing that night?"

"We was just chilling."

"Where were you?"

"Where Strawberry say we were?"

"I want to hear it from you," Myra replied.

Marcus hesitated, his face going slack, his whole focus draining out. I realized that he was stoned. The smell of pot was still faintly wafting through the musty air. "We was here," he finally said.

"Just you and Lorenzo?"

"Ain't that what he say?"

"Listen, Marcus," Myra said, starting to lose her patience. "We can't just tell you what we want you to say. If you can't remember it on your own, you're not going to be any use to us."

"It was just him and me is how I'm remembering it."

"And what were you doing?"

"You know, just chilling. Wasn't getting in no kind of trouble."

"Were you here all night?"

"Strawberry ain't gonna want me to say we left, is he? Besides, I ain't looking to put myself in the mix."

"Nobody's suggesting you had anything to do with what happened in the Gardens that night, Mr. Riley."

"I know *you* ain't gonna be sayin' that, on account it don't help your boy. But how I know the law not gonna just come after me, I say I was with Strawberry? Then I don't help him none, and I'm facing time too."

"I really don't think that's likely to happen," Myra said. "All we're asking you to do is tell us the truth. Were you with Lorenzo Tate that night?"

"Lorenzo tell me that I was," Marcus said. "I know he'd been over to my crib sometime that week, but I didn't write down no date as to when it was."

"What'd the two of you do?"

"What's Lorenzo say we did?" Marcus asked.

"We need to know what you remember."

"Things are a little foggy in my mind just now," Marcus said. "Truth be told, I sparked up a Dutch before you all came knocking."

"Thanks for your time, Mr. Riley," Myra said, standing abruptly and heading toward the door.

"WHAT'S WITH the quick exit?" I asked once we were back on the street.

"There's no point in throwing good time after bad," Myra replied.

"Is that an answer to my question, or something you got off of a refrigerator magnet?"

"Do you think we can use him?"

"I can see some problems with using him."

"Yeah, like the fact that he's got a sheet, that he's drinking and high and it's barely noon, that he probably really doesn't even remember whether he was with Lorenzo that night. We put him on the stand, we virtually ensure a conviction."

"So we don't put on our guy's only alibi witness?"

"The burden is on them, not on us. We're allowed to just attack their version of what happened without presenting our own. But as soon as we offer our own version, the jury's going to be comparing the two, trying to decide which is more believable. We should only put a story forward if we either feel like we have to, or if we're confident our story is a lot more convincing than theirs is."

"So we don't put on Lorenzo's alibi witness, even if Lorenzo is telling the truth and he was hanging out with Marcus at the time of the shooting?"

"Whether or not something may be true isn't relevant for our purposes," Myra said. "The only thing that matters is whether or not it's convincing."

·10·

ICE OF you to join us for a change, Myra," Michael said, once we'd sat down with Zach, Max, Julia, and Shelly in a conference room for our weekly team lunch meeting. "Where are you on the Gibbons appeal?"

"The first thing was that Isaac had to review the trial transcripts for any potential ineffectiveness claim. He has and there isn't."

"No surprise there," Michael said. "So where does that leave us?"

"That generally leaves us with prosecutorial misconduct and judicial error, right?"

"The ADAs break any big rules?"

"Much as I love to bad-mouth prosecutors, I don't see anything there."

"Okay," Michael said. "That leaves judicial error. Or at least, I hope it does."

"It does indeed," Myra said. "The judge essentially cut our whole defense off at the knees. The first thing has to be that he wouldn't let our expert on false confessions testify."

"But the case law in New York supported that decision, right?"

"The case law in New York is wrong," Myra replied.

Michael raised his eyebrows. "That solves that," he deadpanned. "So we have point one. What else?"

"I'm working on it," Myra said.

Michael gave a mirthless laugh, shaking his head. "How's Terrell holding up?"

"I'm going up to see him on Saturday," Myra said. "I haven't had a chance to go up since he got sent to Sing Sing."

Michael looked at me. "You ever been to one of our real prisons?"

"Not unless Rikers counts," I said.

"It certainly doesn't," Michael said. "You should go up with Myra and see what high-stakes poker really looks like."

"Sure," I said, glancing over at Myra. She looked like she was trying to come up with a way of opposing the idea.

"I'm going to be leaving really early on Saturday morning," Myra said at last.

"That's fine," I said.

"It's actually a lovely little trip up alongside the Hudson," Julia said. "Until you get where you're going, that is."

"Ah, yes, the scenic prison drive," Zach said. "The public defender version of stopping to smell the roses."

"Speaking of prison visits, you ever find a sign language interpreter for your deaf guy?" I asked him.

Zach shook his head. "I took a sign interpreter, but it turned out he and my guy didn't speak the same sign language."

"People speak different kinds of sign language?" Max asked.

"Apparently Spanish sign language is totally different from American sign language," Zach said. "Or else the interpreter just wanted to fuck with me."

"What's your guy up on?" Julia asked Zach. Julia was the one member of our team who was fully fluent in Spanish, and therefore often ended up getting drafted into emergency translation duties, though this appeared to be beyond her skill set. She was first generation Cuban American, and entirely too fashionable to be working as a public defender.

"Armed robbery."

"How does someone who's deaf commit an armed robbery?"

"I've got a hard time picturing it myself," Zach admitted. "But maybe that's just the soft bigotry of low expectations."

"So how about you, Shelly?" Michael asked. "How's it been going so far?"

"Okay, I guess," Shelly said. "It's a lot to take in right away."

"Is it what you expected it would be?" Max asked.

"Sure," Shelly said. "It's really the number of cases more than anything else. It's hard to even keep track."

"So," Michael said to Shelly. "Now that you actually work here, as compared to an interview when everybody on both sides of the desk is lying about everything, what can we tell you about the job?"

"I don't know," Shelly said. "I guess I just wonder, with the pressure and everything, how people deal with it."

"Same as people deal with anything else," Zach said. "Sex and alcohol."

AFTER LUNCH I was to spend a half day covering arraignments, picking up additional cases. I walked over to the courthouse, took my familiar place in the glum meeting room across from the basement holding cells. My first client was a drug case, looked to be a street dealer rousted in a sweep of Grand Avenue in Clinton Hill. Even by the standards of the streets he was fairly young, just nineteen. But Shawne Flynt's face as he sat across from me belied his age; I didn't detect even a glimmer of fear in his eyes. I could tell without asking that this wasn't his first time in the system.

"So," I said to Shawne after doing my introductory spiel, "why don't you tell me what happened?"

"This ain't nothing but some shit, yo," Shawne said. He was tall and lanky, an athletic looseness about him. His face was narrow and angular, his eyes the stillest thing about him. "All they got on me was I was parked up on the street. Wasn't no product on me, wasn't even no cheddar. They just swoop me up when they clear the corner."

"They're charging you with possession with intent," I said.

"I just got done telling you I ain't possessed a goddamn thing when they took me. All they got on me is I was there."

"Did they sweep up a lot of people?"

"They took in everybody who be standing on Grand Avenue," Shawne said.

"Did they get anybody who was actually holding?"

"You arrest enough niggers on the corner, somebody's going to be holding, know what I'm saying? But that ain't got nothing to do with me."

"You know the guys who were caught?" I asked. The vibe I was getting that Shawne ran the corner, and that he'd been clean when picked up because he no longer had to take the direct risk.

"You ain't gotta worry about none of them," Shawne said dismissively. "They soldiers. None of that is gonna come back on me."

"Soldiers have been known to flip," I said.

"Not on Grand Avenue they ain't," Shawne said. "You got no call to worry about my crew."

"Your crew," I repeated.

Shawne smiled and offered a little shrug. If it'd been a slip it wasn't one that bothered him. "True that," he said. "They my crew. But they ain't gonna come back on me. You don't got to do nothing here, yo, else I'd get me a real lawyer to take care of it."

I ignored the offhand insult, which I'd gotten used to. "Why'd they pick you up at all then?" I asked.

"Politics as usual," Shawne said. "They trying to clear out the corner, fancy up the hood. They trying to do to the Hill what they done to Fort Greene, get shit all safe for the white folks to move in. The five-oh already shut the hotel where all the hos be trickin'; now they move on to the corners. They already snatched me up once before; didn't nothing come of it."

"When was this?"

"When this nonsense all started, two months back maybe."

"What happened to those charges?"

"The fuck you think happened? Ain't you been listening? They don't got shit on me."

"Have they actually been dropped?"

"Hell, yeah. Once they realized nobody was going to be snitchin' they backed up off of that shit."

"Okay," I said. "We're probably going to have to wait them out a little, but hopefully that same thing will happen here."

ONCE WE were out before the judge, Shawne slouched beside me, flanked by court officers, a vacant look on his face. It never ceased to amaze me how many defendants had to make a point of showing their indifference or hostility to the judge, despite the fact that a defendant's demeanor could be the single most important factor in the judge's snap judgment regarding bail: pissing him off was often the difference between going home and being carted off to Rikers.

"What do we got?" Judge Robinson asked ADA Narducci once Shawne's case was called, the bailiff reading a laundry list of charges—possession with intent, conspiracy to distribute, loitering, disorderly conduct. It sounded as though they'd rounded up a drug kingpin, rather than a teenager on a corner.

ADA Narducci went into a spiel about the numerous arrests that'd been made in the raid on Grand and Putnam, stressing that the police had discovered drugs with a street value of several hundred dollars along with several thousand dollars in cash. The numbers suggesting that the cops had only found the small street stash, not the major cache where the bulk of the drugs were kept. When Narducci was finished the judge turned to me.

"My client pleads not guilty to all charges, Your Honor. I didn't hear anything whatsoever linking my client to any drugs. No drugs were found on his person; he had roughly forty dollars in his pocket.

The fact that someone else somewhere on the block might have been holding drugs has nothing whatsoever to do with my client."

"The police made a sweep in which they picked up an entire drug crew," Narducci said.

"By 'drug crew,' you mean every black person who happened to be standing within fifty feet of the guy who actually had the drugs?" I replied.

"We're not trying the case now, gentlemen," Judge Robinson interrupted. "Bail's set at ten thousand dollars. Who's next?"

I huddled with Shawne for a moment before he was led away. "That bail number's ridiculous," I said apologetically. "It's just because of the number of charges they've thrown at you."

Shawne shrugged. "Not going to be no problem. I got a bondsman who know me. Me and mine be out of here later today."

I wasn't surprised; making bail was part of the price of doing business for the drug trade, just another form of overhead, like taxes for a regular business. "I'll make a discovery request of the DA, set up a meeting to see what they think they've got. I'll give you a call when I know where things stand."

"Just let me know when they're done with this nonsense," Shawne said, as the court officers led him away.

·II·

MYRA HAD assigned me the task of trying to speak with Seth Lipton's former roommate, Amin Saberi. We had Amin's name and address in Midwood from the police reports that had been turned over; they'd taken a statement from him. I noticed that Seth Lipton was still listed on the directory at the building's front door. I pressed the buzzer, waited, pressed again. I was getting ready to give up and walk away when a scratchy, unintelligible voice came blaring through the intercom.

"Mr. Saberi?" I said. "I'm a lawyer working on the Lipton case. Can I come up and speak with you, please?"

There was a silence that began to drag before Amin finally spoke. "I guess," he said.

I took the elevator up to the fifth floor, then walked the halls until I found Amin's apartment number. Amin opened the door in response to my knock, his brow furrowing slightly when he saw me. "I thought you were that guy Mr. O'Bannon again," he said. O'Bannon was the lead prosecutor on the case—Amin clearly thinking I was from the DA's office. I shook my head, following Amin into the living room of his apartment, deciding to hold off on admitting I was a defense attorney until I was inside.

The apartment was typical student-shabby, a futon instead of a couch, empty beer bottles lying on the floor. Amin was short, somewhat preppy in a polo shirt and khakis. His voice had the faintest wisp of an accent, but nothing I could place. I guessed he was of South Asian descent, but he seemed pretty thoroughly Americanized.

"No classes today?" I asked, not sure how to work my way into this.

Amin didn't look up at me. "I've got one at two," he said. "Why?"

I shrugged awkwardly. "No reason," I said. "I wanted to ask you some questions about Seth Lipton."

"Haven't I gone over this enough?" Amin said. "I've talked to the cops twice, plus that other guy from your office already—"

"I'm not from the DA's office," I interrupted, not wanting to let this misunderstanding go too far. "I represent Lorenzo Tate."

Amin took a step back, nearly stumbling over the futon that lined one wall across from the TV. "Are you allowed to come talk to me like this?" Amin asked.

"Of course I am," I said. "In fact, I'm allowed to subpoena you

and force you to testify. But I don't see any reason for that to be necessary. I'm just trying to get a sense of who Seth Lipton was, and how
he came to be in the wrong place that night."

"That part's easy," Amin said. "Seth was studying sociology, and
for his senior thesis he was doing this thing on the, like, structure of
drug dealers."

"The structure of drug dealers."

"In terms of as a business, basically, but not just that. As a sort of
corporate culture too."

I couldn't resist repeating again. "As a sort of corporate culture,"
I said. "I have to admit, I understand every word you're saying, but
I've got no idea what you're talking about."

"It's not that complicated," Amin said dismissively, at last flop-
ping down on the futon he'd just almost fallen onto. I followed suit,
sitting in the room's lone chair and taking out a yellow legal pad and
a pen. "The idea was just, like, to do a comparison, the culture of
drug dealers and the culture of, you know, like, a more conventional
business. But the other thing Seth was doing was, he wasn't just comparing the business models, like you would do in an econ thing, but
he was also looking at the culture, the sort of, you know, *code* by
which the business was run."

Amin looked at me expectantly, but my look in response was self-
consciously skeptical. I found the whole notion trite, fundamentally
collegiate.

"Whatever," Amin said dismissively, having picked up that I was
not a convert. "All of his professors thought Seth was brilliant."

"It never occurred to any of his professors that what he was doing might be dangerous?"

"Seth had the crew he was studying's *cooperation*," Amin said ve-
hemently. "He was supposed to be protected."

"Was Devin Wallace part of the crew he was studying?"

"The other guy who got shot?" Amin said. "I think so. I'd heard Seth talk about a dude named Devin down there. He was sort of the boss, far as I understood it."

"Did you ever hear Seth talk about Lorenzo Tate?"

Amin shook his head. "But Seth never gave me, like, the whole play-by-play," he said. "He told me more about the big picture. Truth is, I'm not sure I wanted to know the whole play-by-play."

"Why not?"

Amin looked away, the kid looking like he thought he'd said too much. "I don't know," Amin said finally. "I guess I'm just not as fearless as Seth was."

"So this thesis he was doing," I said. "Had he actually written it?"

"He was working on it, yeah," Amin said. "But he hadn't started putting together the final product."

"Did he have a rough draft or notes or anything?"

Amin looked back at me, clearly hesitating, trying to gauge the extent to which he could refuse to cooperate with me. I let the silence grow, knowing it would only increase Amin's uncertainty.

"Sure," Amin said. "I mean, he was working on it. Why?"

"I'd like to have a copy of whatever he'd done," I replied.

"Are you allowed to just do that?"

"What do you mean?" I said, smiling. "I'm a lawyer."

· 12 ·

"Y OU READY for your field trip?" Myra said when she picked me up outside my building on Saturday morning. A Common CD played on the car stereo—a good deal more mellow than the feminist punk rock that had greeted me the last time I'd been in her car. Myra was drinking take-out deli coffee and smoking a cigarette. I failed to understand how anyone could smoke so much first thing in the morning.

"Sorry if I'm cramping your style," I said. "When Michael suggested it I didn't really feel like I could say no. But I do realize this isn't a field trip."

"It sort of is, actually," Myra said. "I mean, there's no real point to this visit from a legal perspective. It's really just reminding Terrell that I'm still working for him, trying to make sure he doesn't check out on us."

"I don't imagine Sing Sing will let him check out."

"I mean punch his own ticket," Myra said. "Which Sing Sing certainly has let people do."

"Are you really worried that Terrell is suicidal?"

"Of course I am," Myra said sharply. "He's a borderline-retarded twenty-two-year-old who still lived with his mother on the day he was arrested and now finds himself in the big house for a murder he didn't commit. Being suicidal would be a pretty rational reaction to his circumstances."

"I hear you," I said.

Myra didn't reply, and we drove in silence for a full minute.

"You're really convinced he's innocent?" I asked, wanting to break the tension.

"Tell you what," Myra said. "After we meet with him, I'll ask you."

PEOPLE V. GIBBONS had been the biggest trial anyone on my team had handled in the time I'd been in the office, so I'd picked up a fair amount about it over the past few months. The case came out of a robbery of By Design, a jewelry store in the Fulton Street Mall, three masked men entering with guns drawn, leaving with money and jewelry, and leaving behind a dead store owner.

The store owner had gotten a shot off from his own gun before being killed, hitting one of the thieves. That turned out to be Kawame Jones, who'd been smart enough to travel to Newark before going to a hospital and claiming he'd just been shot in a drive-by. But it hadn't been far enough—the police had quickly connected him to the By Design robbery and placed him under arrest.

Once the police had linked the bullet in Kawame's shoulder to the gun in the store owner's lifeless hand, Kawame had sensibly decided to offer up information in exchange for a plea bargain on felony murder. Kawame had named one supposed accomplice, claiming that he'd never known the names of the other person who'd gone in or the getaway driver. He'd named Terrell Gibbons.

Based on Kawame's statement the police had picked Terrell up for questioning. After fourteen hours in police custody Terrell had confessed not just to being involved in the robbery, but also to being the shooter. The police had never been able to come up with any other direct evidence linking Terrell to the crime: their case had rested entirely on Kawame Jones's pointing the finger at Terrell and Terrell's having pointed the finger at himself.

Ever since his initial confession, Terrell had insisted he'd had no involvement with the murder at By Design, and that he'd confessed only after the detective lied about finding his fingerprints at the scene and told him that he would never go home or see his mother again unless he confessed. Terrell had an IQ located somewhere in the low seventies. This wasn't a characteristic you would look for in a prospective accomplice to an armed robbery. It was, however, exactly what you might look for in picking out a fall guy. And that was what Myra believed Kawame Jones had done.

Myra had tried to present at trial the testimony of a psychology professor at Cornell who had extensively studied false confessions. The judge hadn't allowed it, leaving Myra with no way to challenge the confession except by putting Terrell Gibbons himself on the stand. Terrell had done decently, but unsurprisingly he'd struggled on cross.

Despite Myra's passionate beliefs, it had always seemed obvious to me that she faced an extremely difficult task trying to persuade a jury to acquit. Convincing a jury that someone had confessed to a crime they weren't guilty of was virtually impossible. However hard a defense lawyer worked to put the jury in the shoes of the defendant, few people could imagine themselves admitting to a murder that they hadn't committed. Indeed, even while I understood that false confessions happened, my own understanding was at a certain level of abstraction. It certainly wasn't like I could imagine myself doing such a thing.

The jury had taken less than a day to convict Terrell of murder.

SING SING was on the edge of town in Ossining, near the Hudson River. It was New York's second-largest prison, one of its oldest, and certainly its most gothic. The prison held over two thousand inmates, more than half of them black. The overwhelming majority were in for violent felonies. About one out of every five was in for murder.

There was a residential street not far from the prison, although a turreted observation post occupied by armed guards made sure that the distance wouldn't be easily breached. The prison was dark brick, grim and foreboding, matching exactly my expectations of what a maximum-security prison should look like.

Myra and I arrived at the front desk in an open but stuffy room that was hardly an improvement over the sticky, humid weather outside, with a series of benches and a small scattering of people. The

CO at the desk told us they were conducting count inside, making sure all prisoners were accounted for; it meant that nobody could go into or out of the prison.

"This the real reason you agreed to bring me along?" I asked once we were seated on a bench. "Keep you company in the waiting room?"

"Actually I brought my cell phone and some case files for that," Myra said.

Because it was an attorney-client visit, we were given a private interview room within the open visiting area, with a glass door we could close for privacy. The main visiting room was expansive, a television set in the corner showing *Jerry Springer*, not exactly the fare I expected in a maximum-security prison. The air was thick and stale. We waited another ten minutes before Terrell was brought in, dressed in a loose prison jumpsuit that emphasized his frailty.

Myra gave Terrell a hug in greeting before introducing me. I was surprised by the gesture: she hadn't exactly struck me as the hugging type. Terrell was pudgy, with a round teddy-bear baby face that made him appear younger than his years. Even in a prison uniform he looked soft and unthreatening—a hard trick to pull off. "You holding up okay, Terrell?" she asked, keeping a hand on his shoulder while looking closely at him.

"I ain't supposed to be here," Terrell said plaintively. "I didn't do nothin' wrong."

"I know, Terrell," Myra said. "That's part of why I'm here: to make sure you know that I still believe in you, that I'm still fighting for you."

"Ain't nothing you can do for me in here, though, is there?"

"How do you mean?" Myra asked.

"Nothin' you can do to protect me in here," Terrell said. "I come up in Bed-Stuy; I seen some serious shit, known people who got capped, all that, but ain't nothin' out there like what it is in here."

"We're not going to be able to get you transferred to another prison," Myra said. "But we can see about getting you into some kind of protective custody, or get you away from a particular person who's giving you trouble."

"It ain't one person," Terrell said. "It be everybody. It be this place."

"The best thing we're going to be able to do for you in that regard is to try to win your appeal and get you out of here," Myra said.

"You think you can win?" Terrell asked. "You really think you can get me out?"

"It's never easy," Myra said. "But I think the trial judge made some mistakes; hopefully I can get the appellate court to agree, and we'll at least get you a new trial. I've got a couple of people from my office helping me out. Joel here used to work at one of the city's fanciest law firms. We've also got my boss working on your appeal, who's by far the best and most experienced appeals lawyer in our office."

"Even if we get a new trial, what's to stop them from getting me all over again?"

"That's a few steps down the road," Myra said. "If we get a new trial, we'll take it from there, but I think we'd have a good shot at getting an acquittal."

"I shouldn't be here," Terrell said again. "I ain't done nothing to be here for."

"I know," Myra said. "I'm going to do everything I can to fix that."

■　■　■

"SO TELL me, Counselor," I said as we were walking up the steep and crumbling stairway outside of the prison to the parking lot, "do you really think you can get Terrell's conviction overturned?"

"We've got some issues," Myra said. "But the appellate division isn't ever exactly eager to overturn murder convictions based on evidentiary decisions by the trial judge, which is really all we've got here. I can't pretend it's going to be easy."

"He's not going to make it if he stays here, is he?"

"Not for very long, no," Myra said.

I felt my body shudder slightly and tried to tell myself it was from the sudden breeze, which was, in truth, light and warm. "I can see why you want to get him out, then," I said.

"Does that mean you think Terrell's innocent?"

"There's no doubt in my mind," I said.

·13·

I CAN'T BELIEVE I'm eating this shit," Myra said, staring dubiously at the fast food in front of her. We'd made it about halfway back to the city when Myra had declared herself starving. We'd stopped at a food court just off the interstate. The seating area was large but nevertheless dense and chaotic, jammed with families, children everywhere, crying and running and horsing around. The fluorescent light was glaringly bright, highlighting the handful of tiny take-out restaurants, the store selling bags of chips and tacky souvenir knickknacks.

"You look incredibly out of place," I said. Myra was wearing black jeans and a dark purple tank top. She'd worn a suit jacket into Sing Sing but had taken it off once we got back to the car.

"What's that supposed to mean?"

"Just that, you know, when was the last time you actually left New York?"

"America frightens me," Myra said, deliberately glancing over her shoulder as she said it.

"Did you grow up in the city?"

Myra nodded, picking at her french fries. "Borough Park," she said. "All my grandparents came over during the course of World War Two. My parents were both born in Brooklyn as post-Holocaust kids."

I wasn't sure how to respond to that, so I just nodded. I'd known a good number of Jewish people, especially since moving to New York, but I'd never meaningfully spoken to any of them about the Holocaust, any more than I'd ever really spoken to an African American about slavery. The topics were always there, implicit on some level, hovering at the edges of the conversation, but I for one always froze at any indication that they were actually coming up.

"Where are you from?" Myra asked.

"I grew up in Holyoke, Massachusetts," I replied. I didn't have much of a connection left to my hometown; I hadn't been back there since the Christmas before last. I'd skipped it last year, having started a short time before at the Brooklyn Defenders, not feeling ready to present myself in my new humbled state.

"That's where that girls' school is, right? You get to bang a lot of failed lesbians?"

"You've really got the wrong idea about growing up in Holyoke," I said before taking a bite of my greasy, flavorless burger.

"Were your parents professors?"

"Everyone always thinks that Mount Holyoke must be in Holyoke," I said. "But actually the college is in another town entirely."

"So what's in Holyoke, then?"

"Nothing much. It used to be paper factories, but they've all gone out of business."

"Oh," Myra said. "So I'm guessing your parents weren't professors."

"Neither of my parents graduated from college," I said. My parents, who'd married young, had divorced when I was five. They still lived in Holyoke, both having remarried and started other families. I was the only kid from their marriage, although between them I'd ended up with five younger half brothers and sisters. Growing up I'd shuttled between their two households. I hadn't fit in with their new families even before I'd made the leap afforded by a privileged education. None of them had ever fully understood the life I was living in New York back when I'd had at least the appearance of success, so it wasn't clear to me that any of them really understood how far I'd fallen. It certainly wasn't something anybody ever talked about.

Myra looked embarrassed, even like she was blushing slightly. "Sorry," she said. "When you said you'd gone to Columbia Law School, it's possible I made some assumptions as to your background."

"You're not the first," I said, smiling, appreciating the fact that she was at least sheepish about it. "The whole time I was at Columbia, everybody always assumed I had the same sort of background as they did. I'd go over to people's apartments and they'd, like, be living in this two-bedroom on Riverside, rent must have been over three grand a month, while I was in a studio with a shared bathroom and kitchen. I'd just pretend not to notice the differences. I'm used to people assuming I'm much more privileged than I actually am."

"All right, Mr. Working Class Hero," Myra said, tossing a french fry at me. "So how'd you end up at a fancy-pants law school?"

It wasn't a story I'd told in a while, though it certainly wasn't anything I was ashamed of. I decided there wasn't any reason for me not to tell it to Myra. "I'd been a total B student in high school," I said. "After I graduated I went to Holyoke Community, along with most of my friends. A professor there took me under his wing. He read a paper I wrote, decided I was playing below my league, and got me into Amherst College as a transfer."

"Just like that?" Myra said skeptically.

"Back in the sixties Amherst had adopted a policy of taking its transfer students primarily from community colleges. It was a diversity thing."

"So you got to jump into the ruling class based on some kind of affirmative action?"

"Lucky me."

"That must've been weird," Myra said. "Changing worlds like that."

"It was totally weird," I said. I'd felt a little like a zoo animal my whole time at Amherst, although eventually I'd learned to make it work for me, playing up my outsider status in a way that people seemed to buy into. My lack of polish and connections became a sort of asset, which I accepted even while knowing how patronizing it was. "I never really did get used to it, if you want to know the truth."

"So what changed? In you, I mean. How'd you become an all-star all of a sudden?"

I shrugged, embarrassed by the question. "I'd always read a lot, taught myself things. It was just something separate from school for me. Growing up where I did, I guess I just didn't get the idea that doing well academically might be a ticket out."

"And I guess the rest took care of itself."

"It more or less did," I said. I'd done well academically after transferring, although I'd rarely spoken in class, had always felt like there were things that my classmates knew that I didn't. It'd been an adjustment not to feel like the smartest person in the room, but I'd welcomed it: I understood this was my gateway to a world I'd previously barely known existed. "Other than my feeling like a complete fraud all the time, it's really been a happily-ever-after sort of thing."

"Is that why you quit your big-firm job to become a PD?" Myra asked. "Because you missed keeping it real?"

I was relieved to hear that Myra didn't know the story of how I'd come to join the Brooklyn Defenders. I shrugged in reply to her question, taking another bite of my burger. "You're right," I said. "This food is disgusting."

"Well, I'm not exactly a Mount Holyoke girl myself," Myra said.

"So why did you become a public defender?"

Myra looked away, something like a smile on her face. "I usually only get asked that on dates," she said.

If she was trying to make me uncomfortable it worked. "Does that mean I'm not allowed to ask?"

"I never thought about being anything else in terms of becoming a lawyer," Myra said.

"Okay," I said. "So why'd you become a lawyer?"

"I went to college at Purchase thinking I was going to be an actress, realized after one semester that there was a whole other level of crazy that was required to really try to do that for a living, figured a courtroom was the next best thing to a stage and that I wouldn't have to audition to get the part."

"I guess I've heard worse reasons for becoming a lawyer," I said. "So why did it have to be working as a PD?"

"My stepdad had done a nickel at Green Haven," Myra said. "He'd had a thing with drugs, funded it by breaking into stores after dark. He was pretty good at it, I'm told, but a needle buddy flipped on a possession with intent and ratted him out."

"That's rough," I said. "He okay now?"

Myra nodded. "This was all before he became my stepdad," she said. "It's ancient history. Now he thinks prison's the best thing that ever happened to him. He cleaned himself up, got his life together. Six months after he got out he met my mom, and they've lived happily ever after, as far I can tell. But he kept where he came from with him. He goes to prisons now, does counseling stuff to try to help guys be ready for life on the outside."

"So you're following in his footsteps."

"He doesn't see it that way," Myra said. "He never wanted me to do this. I think he'd be happier if I was doing what you used to do and making a quarter million a year."

"That doesn't mean you're not following in his footsteps."

"I suppose it doesn't, no," Myra said. She picked up a french fry, looked at it for a moment, then put it down. "Well, I'm not exactly full, but I do feel like I'm about to throw up, so maybe we should call it a lunch."

WE WALKED out to Myra's Volvo. "So," Myra asked, lighting a cigarette as we settled into the hot car. "Any big plans for tonight?"

"I've got a party I've got to go to."

"You sound excited."

"I promised my friend I'd go," I said. "But I never pretended that I wanted to."

"Why not?"

"It's a friend from my old law firm. I guess that's just not my world anymore. To the extent that it ever was."

"I bet he'll have really expensive booze," Myra said as she pulled out of the parking lot.

"You want to come?" I asked impulsively.

"I don't go to parties where I don't know at least three people," Myra said.

I wasn't sure what had just happened. I didn't know if I'd just asked Myra out, and I didn't know if she'd just rejected me if I had. Perhaps neither. I'd been dreading going to Paul's party, and would've liked to bring reinforcements with me. I'd also been reacting to our conversation; it was the first time I'd felt Myra opening up to me, and it'd seemed to me like there was a connection, sparked by a mutual recognition in how we'd both gotten to the place that we were. Not that I'd told her my full story, of course, or even come particularly close. In truth, I hadn't really been tempted to; it wasn't something I wanted bleeding into my workplace, to the extent that I could prevent it.

Whatever I'd intended, it was hard not to be a little stung by how quickly Myra had said no. I understood not wanting to go to a party where you didn't know anybody, but her rejection had been so immediate and definitive that it was hard to sugarcoat it. Perhaps I'd overestimated what she'd actually revealed to me; she'd been very matter-of-fact in talking about her stepfather and the rest of it. Perhaps it was how she always presented herself, a way she could reveal herself without actually giving anything away. Maybe it was nothing more than her first-date patter. Not that a fast-food lunch in a highway food court on the way back from a maximum-security prison constituted a date. Unless, of course, it did.

PAUL HAD just bought a loft in Dumbo and was throwing himself a housewarming party. He'd made me promise to come, despite knowing I wouldn't want to. The party would be full of my former coworkers, rife with reminders of my fall from grace. But Paul had insisted; he'd argued that it would be good for me.

I waited until a little after eleven to leave for Paul's, wanting the party to be well under way when I arrived, hoping it would help me blend in. I was actively dreading going, not at all sure I could face meeting up with so many people who knew about my past. Since Beth had died I'd largely stopped going out, socializing only with those very few people who didn't seem to be either judging or pitying me.

Dumbo was Brooklyn's attempt at a downtown Manhattan neighborhood, with converted lofts and high-end stores, although it was too patchy and industrial to quite pull it off, feeling more like a movie-set version of SoHo than the thing itself. Paul's building was a converted factory redone in high style, a doorman in the lobby, contemporary art on the walls, moody, abstract daubs of dark colors. The door to Paul's apartment was open, and I let myself in. I'd brought a six-pack of beer and was putting it in Paul's fridge when I heard someone say my name.

I turned and found myself face-to-face with Ted Chandler. Ted and I had been classmates at Columbia and had both joined Walker Bentley after graduation. We'd been casual acquaintances for almost a decade without ever really getting to know each other. Next to Ted was an attractive woman whom I didn't recognize. She had long, curly red hair and a kittenish smile, and wore a tight V-necked shirt that emphasized her full breasts.

Ted and I went through the motions of acting happy to see each other, after which he introduced me to the woman. Her name was Melanie; she had just lateraled over to the firm from a job in San Francisco.

"So what are you doing now, Joel?" Ted asked, looking uncomfortable as he asked.

"I'm working as a public defender here in Brooklyn," I said.

"You left Walker to become a public defender?" Melanie asked.

"I suppose you could say that," I said, glancing over at Ted.

"That's awesome," Melanie exclaimed, smiling warmly at me. I'd inadvertently captured her attention: she had the wrong idea about my career change, but there wasn't exactly a way for me to correct it. "I mean, everybody says they're going to do the law-firm thing for a couple of years and then go do something cool, but nobody actually does."

"Well," Ted said dryly, looking from Melanie to me, then back to Melanie, "Joel always did have more of a sense of adventure than the typical Walker associate."

"It would be hard not to," I replied.

"Tell me about it," Melanie said.

"There you are," Paul said, coming up from behind me. "I was beginning to think you weren't going to show."

"Got here as soon as I could," I said. "What with all the fighting for justice I do."

"Were you working today?" Melanie asked.

I didn't know whether Melanie was oblivious to my sarcasm or deliberately ignoring it. I decided to assume the latter. "Actually, yeah," I said. "I just got back from Sing Sing a few hours ago."

"I was in the office all day reviewing documents," Paul said. "But you don't hear me bragging about it."

"What's your client in for?" Melanie asked.

"Felony murder," I said, keeping it deadpan, deciding to just go with the role that this conversation was assigning me.

"That sounds pretty intense."

"The prison is," I said. "The client wasn't."

"He's not scary?" Ted asked.

"Not in the least."

"You don't sit there thinking about how he's a murderer?" Ted pressed.

"He's not a murderer," I said.

"I thought you said he was in for murder."

"I did," I said. "But that doesn't mean he did it."

"Somebody must have thought so," Ted said.

"He was convicted, sure," I said. "And if your point is that our jury system is foolproof, well then I guess you got me there."

"You really believe he's innocent?" Melanie said.

"I'm pretty much sure of it."

"Why'd he get convicted then?" Ted asked.

"Because the police got him to confess."

"He confessed to a murder that he didn't commit?" Ted said skeptically.

"It happens more often than you'd think," I said. "Fourteen hours in the box with homicide cops isn't exactly a Socratic dialogue. Actually it sort of is a Socratic dialogue, only with threats taking the place of dialectic and prison taking the place of enlightenment."

"That's horrible," Melanie said. "Do you think you're going to be able to get him out?"

"You never know."

"So, Joel," Paul interjected, "aren't you just amazed by my apartment?"

"You want to give me the tour?"

"You can see pretty much all of it from where you're standing," Paul said. "But sure."

Paul walked me over to the far wall, which featured a large window looking out toward Manhattan. Much of the view was blocked by another building, but I could see a sliver of the East River and a random section of Lower Manhattan skyscrapers.

"I should've known that fighting for justice was a pussy magnet," Paul said.

"Owning a loft in Dumbo is a pussy magnet," I said. "Barely getting by pleading people out on misdemeanors, not so much."

"Melanie's totally into you," Paul said.

"Did she come here with Ted?" I asked.

Paul shook his head. "Ted's been skulking around her tonight, but I don't think he's much in your way. A librarian would find Ted boring. You, on the other hand, she thinks, have soul."

"I played along because I didn't see any other way to play it," I protested. "But it's not like I could actually fool anyone into thinking I'm an idealist. Maybe for an hour or so."

"How long do you need to seal the deal?" Paul asked.

"With Melanie?" I said. "Presumably more than an hour."

"She's not that kind of girl, sure, or at least she isn't going to admit she is by leaving a party filled with work people with some guy she just met. But ten will get you twenty that you can get her phone number before you leave here tonight."

"Ten will get me twenty, huh? Deal," I said as I looked around Paul's spacious apartment. "So this is what five-plus years of being a corporate whore buys you."

"I've never denied that I could be bought," Paul said. "The best you could ever say about me was that I don't come particularly cheap."

IT TOOK me about an hour to catch Melanie alone, by which time I'd had the opportunity to fortify myself with a couple of bracingly strong vodka tonics. I noticed her coming out of Paul's bathroom and walked over quickly to intercept her.

I told myself that I'd know in the first second Melanie saw me coming whether or not this was a good idea. To my relief, the smile she gave me seemed genuine. "So tell the truth," I said. "Are you actually surviving at Walker? I promise not to tell."

"It's been totally fine for what it is," Melanie said. "But I do hope one day to make the leap like you did. I mean, for me it wouldn't be a public defender gig, but something like that. You know, something that matters."

My guess was that I was only a year or two older than Melanie, but she was making me feel cynical and old. Her idealizing of the grubby, thankless work that I did seemed profoundly naive to me, although I remembered the way young lawyers at corporate law firms romanticized any other way of practicing law. "It's safe to say that it doesn't always feel like what I do matters," I replied.

"I probably shouldn't ask—" Melanie said, before cutting herself off.

I had no idea what she'd been about to say, but I figured whatever it was, I wanted her to ask it. "What?" I said, tilting my head, doing everything I could to appear welcoming.

"I was just thinking—I feel bad that this is even where my mind would go—but I was just wondering, what's it like to give the money up?"

I shrugged off a flash of disappointment; I'd expected something more personal. "It totally fucking sucks to give the money up," I said with a smile. "Actually, though, honestly, I find that I just get used to whatever amount of money I have and live accordingly."

"That's awesome," Melanie said. "You've just, like, gotten totally clear, haven't you?"

I wasn't entirely sure what she meant by this, but decided that asking her to explain might dampen the mood. Melanie touched my shoulder. "Listen," she said. "I think I could use another drink."

I made the slight mistake of glancing down at my own drink, which was conspicuously full. "Sure," I said, turning toward Paul's kitchen.

"Actually, I was thinking . . . it's just that if we stay here, I'm going to have to keep making bullshit talk with people from the office, you know. We might not get a chance to really talk about stuff."

I was out of practice at these things, but had enough game left to be able to hit the softballs. "We could get a drink somewhere else," I said.

"Sure," Melanie said, playing it like it was actually my idea. I told myself it was like riding a bicycle.

"Let me just tell Paul I'm heading out for a while," I said, phrasing it that way to get back at her a little, hopefully reclaim some of the power by suggesting I might be returning to the party. "I'll meet you over by the door."

"Why don't you meet me at the elevator?" Melanie said. I remembered what Paul had said earlier, about how Melanie wouldn't contemplate leaving a party full of her coworkers with me. It seemed he'd underestimated her, but she was savvy enough to camouflage it.

I dragged Paul out of a conversation with a couple of people I didn't recognize. "What's a cool bar around here?" I asked.

"My liquor's not good enough for you?"

"Just tell me."

"Why?"

"Because you totally owe me twenty bucks," I said.

·PART·
TWO

·14·

MYRA AND I had been waiting on the prosecutors in the Tate case, ADAs O'Bannon and Williams, for twenty minutes. It seemed a point of pride with ADAs to always keep defense lawyers waiting; perhaps it was taught as part of their orientation.

"What's making us wait like this get them?" I asked.

"They just want us to know how much they dislike us," Myra replied.

Finally ADA Williams arrived and gestured for us to follow her to a conference room. She was a tall black woman in her early thirties, willowy and aloof, her suit jacket buttoned up. Nobody bothered with small talk; Williams didn't even offer a token apology.

The conference room she led us to was cramped and viewless, merely functional and seldom cleaned. O'Bannon was not there. Myra hissed out a sigh, making a point of showing her annoyance. I guessed she was doing this deliberately, that she was perfectly capable of hiding her irritation if she thought it would benefit her case.

"Ted knows you're here," Williams said, a touch of apology in her voice. "I'm sure he'll be right along."

"He's known we were here for half an hour," Myra said.

"He's probably on his way," Williams said.

O'Bannon walked in on cue. A squat bulldog of a man, with a full head of gray hair and a face like drooping clay, he stood a couple of inches shorter than Williams. He wore a white dress shirt that was fraying slightly at the collar, and a striped tie. He was the only one of us not wearing a suit jacket. I took this as a deliberate gesture, an indication that he didn't deem us worthy of such formalities.

"Sorry to keep you waiting," O'Bannon said, not putting any effort into it, taking a seat at the head of the table, dropping down a Redweld folder onto the table in front of him.

"Next time I'll tie some bells around my ankles so you'll know I'm here," Myra said.

"I'd appreciate that," O'Bannon deadpanned. "Now, what can I do for you?"

"You can explain to me how come the photo array shown to Yolanda Miller wasn't part of the *Rosario* material turned over to us," Myra said, a tightness in her voice as she spoke.

I hadn't known what to expect in response, but what I saw on both ADAs' faces was confusion.

"What photo array?" O'Bannon said after a moment.

"Yolanda Miller told us that Detective Spanner showed her photos prior to the lineup, and that she didn't pick anybody out. I'd say that qualifies as *Rosario* material, wouldn't you?"

"I don't know anything about this," O'Bannon said. "The only ID I know about is the lineup." He turned to Williams. "Are you aware of any photo array?" he asked her. Williams shook her head.

O'Bannon turned back to Myra. "Are you sure you understood Ms. Miller correctly?"

"I'm absolutely positive," Myra said. "How could you not know about a failed ID procedure with your star witness?"

"I'll look into it and get back to you."

"I'd imagine so, and quickly too, I might add," Myra said. "We're moving for a *Wade* hearing to challenge Miller's ID, and we need a copy of the photo array as an exhibit."

"We'll certainly act quickly to verify whether or not a photo array was shown to Ms. Miller," O'Bannon said.

"If we get Yolanda's ID tossed your case goes right down the toilet with it," Myra said. "You want to put anything on the table before the hearing?"

"Here's the thing with that," O'Bannon said. "Even if there was an earlier ID procedure, you're not going to get the lineup ID tossed. And I haven't come across a notice of alibi floating across my desk. Which means this is something like a slam dunk, as far as we're concerned."

"This is more like a half-court shot," Myra said. "Other than the alleged eyewitness testimony, which is in jeopardy of getting thrown out, and which will at least take a big hit on cross now, you don't have any direct evidence at all. No physical evidence, no murder weapon, no confession. You can't tell me there's nothing on the table."

"What I'm willing to put on the table is he allocutes to murder two, we agree to twenty to life."

"Murder two is the top count he's facing," Myra protested. "And a conviction after trial gets twenty-five to life."

"Be that as it may," O'Bannon said. "That's the best on offer."

"The only reason for that would be—" Myra cut herself off, glancing quickly at Williams, who was looking nowhere.

"You were saying?" O'Bannon asked.

"You're really not going to make an offer here?" Myra asked.

"I don't believe that's quite what I said," O'Bannon said. "I believe I did make an offer, and it was twenty to life."

"This is the kind of case your office pleads out on man one all the time and you know it," Myra said. "What's the difference here? I mean, other than that you got a poor black defendant accused of killing a white college student?"

"I certainly didn't say that," O'Bannon said, standing, though he wouldn't look at us any more than Williams would. "Now, if you'll excuse me, I'm due in court."

IT WAS a short walk cutting across the bottom edge of Cadman Plaza from their office on Jay Street to ours on Pierrepont. Myra had stormed out of the DA's office, with me trailing in her wake. I caught up with her when she stopped to light a cigarette. "Those fuckers," she said once we were outside in the heat. "No way they don't put a decent offer on the table if it was Devin Wallace who'd been killed instead of Seth Lipton."

"Does that really surprise you?" I asked.

"Just because something doesn't surprise me doesn't mean it doesn't piss me off."

"Doesn't it?"

Myra gave me the look she had that I still couldn't read—I didn't know if she was pretending to be annoyed with me or actually was. "It means we're probably going to trial on this one," she said.

"That's good," I said. "For me, I mean."

"Not if you like sleeping, it's not," Myra replied. "We've got to start ramping up our investigation with an eye to whether we can actually win this."

"I'm ready when you are."

"You seem like you put some Kahlúa in your coffee this morning."

"I'm in a good mood is all," I said. "Don't worry, I'm sure it won't last."

"How was your party on Saturday?"

I hadn't expected Myra to bring it up; other than on the drive back from Sing Sing, we'd never talked about our lives outside of work. "It was good," I said. "You know, how the other half lives."

In truth, it'd been more than good. Melanie and I had ended up spending a couple of hours at a bar in Dumbo, then stumbled into a taxi together and gone back to my place. I hadn't been with a woman since Beth had died over a year ago, and I hadn't let myself acknowledge the extent to which I'd missed sex until the prospect of having it had suddenly reappeared in my life.

I thought I'd acquitted myself rather well. While my lack of recent practice probably hadn't done my technique any favors, it had again imbued me with the raw enthusiasm of my high school years, something that Melanie appeared to appreciate. We'd made a late night of it, not falling asleep until after four a.m., then made love again upon awakening before going for a leisurely brunch at Melt.

I knew strategically that I should probably wait a few days to call her, but I decided to call as soon as I got back from the meeting at the DA's office, establish my bona fides as not playing games. This was every bit as strategic a decision as not calling would be, but dating in New York was as much a matter of tactics as was practicing law.

As soon as Melanie came on the phone I knew that something was wrong. She sounded guarded, tense. I told myself she was probably just busy, distracted by some memo she was in the middle of writing. After a couple of minutes of desultory small talk I decided I should just bring the conversation to a close.

"Anyway," I said, "just wanted to say hi. I thought maybe we could get a drink or something later in the week."

The ensuing silence said it all. I closed my eyes, waiting for her to speak. I knew what was coming before it came.

"Listen, Joel," Melanie finally said, "I was talking to Ted this morning, and he told me."

"He told you what?" I couldn't resist saying.

"You know," Melanie said. "About the thing with the girl here, and how you got fired and all that."

"I didn't get fired," I protested weakly. This was literally true, although it wasn't true in any other way.

"Whatever," Melanie said. "You know what I'm talking about."

"I'm just saying I quit. I wrote a resignation letter and everything."

"I mean Jesus, Joel," Melanie said. "You're like some kind of junkie?"

"I'm not a junkie," I said. "I was never a junkie."

"You told me you left the firm to go be a public defender. I feel a little misled."

"I didn't say anything to you that wasn't true," I said.

"I don't think . . . I mean, I just started working here—it would obviously be incredibly awkward."

"I thought you didn't care about that sort of thing," I said miserably. I didn't really know why I was putting up a fight; it was just brute instinct and pride—I clearly wasn't going to win.

"When did I ever say that?" Melanie asked.

·15·

No sooner had I hung up with Melanie than Myra came knocking on my door, saying she'd just gotten off the phone with Midwood Sports after confirming that Malik Taylor was working that day. We left immediately, Myra driving us out. I didn't feel much like talking and spent the drive staring out the window, brooding about Melanie's rejection. We parked on Bedford, on the outskirts of Brooklyn College, then walked back onto Flatbush's commercial strip.

Myra led the way into the store, which was overly bright with fluorescent light, Jay-Z blaring. The teenage girl behind the register regarded us warily as we approached the counter.

"You need help finding something?" she asked.

"Someone, actually. We're looking for Malik Taylor."

"He's in the back," the girl said, picking up the phone and dialing a four-digit number. I was surprised that she didn't ask us who we were or what we wanted first. "Yo, Malik? Some folks out front be looking for you." The girl paused, listening, and then glanced back up at us. "They ain't say. They dressed all serious and shit, though. You forget to pay your taxes?"

After some more back-and-forth the girl hung up and told us that Malik would be out in a minute. I followed Myra to a spot away from the register, near a selection of running shoes, where nobody seemed to be around.

It was less than a minute later that a young black man came out from a rear door and headed over to the counter. The girl pointed in our direction and Malik turned, hesitating when he didn't recognize us. He was compact, stocky, his heavy face accentuated by a beard. Perhaps the beard was to make him look older; it didn't otherwise seem to fit. After a moment he headed over to us.

"What's up?" Malik asked.

"We need to have a conversation," Myra said.

"About what?" Malik asked nervously, looking away from her and toward me.

"We need to talk about Devin Wallace."

Just hearing Devin's name made Malik wince. "Yo, I'm *working* here."

"Fine," Myra said. "We can talk out on the street."

Now Malik wouldn't look at us. "What's this about anyway, yo? It don't got nothin' to do with me."

"So you want to talk here instead, do you?" Myra said, raising her voice loud enough that a couple of customers glanced over. "Fine with me."

"Awright, awright. I can't just walk on out. I'll meet y'all outside in five minutes' time."

"You're not going to go out some back door on us, are you, Malik?" Myra said.

"Yo, what I say? Five minutes."

"Go do what you gotta do," Myra said.

BACK ON the street, I asked Myra why she was so confident Malik would really come out to talk to us.

Myra shrugged, taking a deep drag on her freshly lit cigarette. "I'm not," she said, exhaling smoke as she spoke. "Tell you the truth, probably the best thing that could happen to us is he sneaks out the back, runs like hell, and is never seen again."

"So that we can make him out as a suspect?"

"Fuckin' A."

I nodded, turning it over in my mind. While she was never exactly a shrinking violet, I'd never seen Myra as aggressive as she'd just been with Malik. I'd thought for a second that she was actually a little out of control, but I realized that wasn't it at all, that she was deliberately trying to scare or provoke him. I was enjoying watching Myra work on the street.

"Who do you think he thinks we are?"

"I assume cops."

"We don't look much like cops."

"If he asks, I'll tell; if he doesn't, I won't."

It took almost ten minutes, but Malik did come out. After five minutes had passed I'd asked if we should go back in, but Myra had just shrugged without looking at me. It was hot to be outside in a suit, the sun glaring down at us. If either the heat or Malik's delay bothered Myra she didn't show it.

When Malik did arrive Myra gave him a big grin. "Here we are," she said, putting her hand on Malik's back and walking him down Flatbush to the next corner, turning onto the quieter side street. I trailed behind them, nobody talking.

"Awright boss, what's this about?" Malik said, shrugging out of Myra's grasp and turning toward her. "Why you comin' to where I work at and calling me out like this?"

"I was talking to a lady friend of yours not too long ago, Malik," Myra said. "Cute little kid she had too. Matter of fact, kid looked a lot like you."

"Aw, man—" Malik interjected feebly.

"'Man' is right, Malik," Myra interrupted. "'Man' is exactly what we're talking about here. 'Cause you know what a man does when he knocks a woman up, right? I'm not talking about, you know, what *you* did, but I mean what a man is *supposed* to do in that situation?"

"It's not like that, yo," Malik said. "I provide for them the best I can. Me and Yolanda see each other. This ain't none of your damn business nohow."

"What we hear is Yolanda found herself a new friend. Only now that new friend of hers is lying half dead in the hospital, they still don't know if he's ever going to take a breath that doesn't come out of a tube. He could still flat-out die, Malik. It's already one count of murder, could go to two."

This wasn't exactly true, but clearly Malik didn't know that. He tried to force out a laugh, but he was dry-mouthed and at least a little scared, because what came out was more like a hoarse cough. "No way you jamming me up on that," Malik protested. "I heard you all already put a charge on Strawberry for that."

"We know that you and Devin had your problems, Malik."

"More like he had problems with me than the other way around," Malik said. "I just be trying to see my son from time to time, trying to do something *good*, man, and Devin, he don't want to hear that. Started cussin' at me, telling me I can't come see my own boy." Malik stopped himself, perhaps realizing that everything he was saying sounded potentially incriminating.

Myra had picked up on it too. "He told you not to see your own son? When was this?"

"I don't know," Malik said. "Back in March maybe."

"What'd you say back to that?"

"I spoke back to him, sure," Malik said. "We got to shoving each other some. Yolanda told me to get gone, so I did. Wasn't like we even really went at each other."

"So why would you have a problem with Devin, right? He was only keeping you from seeing your own son."

"I ain't gonna be beefing with Devin," Malik protested. "Shit, yo, I manage a *store*. Me on my worst day look like a little girl next to that motherfucker. You know he sling rock, right? He got all that shit. He got the rock, the powder, the chronic, that D called Bin Laden all them junkies be craving. He *owns* that courtyard out there in the Gardens. I beef with him, win or lose, I lose. Devin's soldiers take me out for sure."

"Of course, that wouldn't happen if you killed him and got away with it," Myra countered.

"Come on, yo," Malik said. "Not like I even got no gun. And how am I supposed to think I'm gonna get away with that? First with you, then with Devin's crew 'round the way."

"Let me see if I have this, Malik," Myra said. "You're saying you would have liked to kill Devin, maybe even thought about it a little, but you were afraid you wouldn't get it away with it?"

"Motherfucker ain't even dead, is he?" Malik said. "If I capped him, he gonna get up out the hospital one day, tell his boys what's what, it's them walking into the store and taking me out 'stead of you coming in and just giving me shit. I capped that bitch, why am I still here? Besides, why am I going to give enough of a fuck to do that?"

"He's keeping you from your child," Myra said.

"That's no reason for me to get myself killed," Malik said.

"YOU OKAY?" Myra asked once we were in her car heading back to Cadman Plaza.

"What do you mean?"

"Nothing big and existential," Myra said. "Just that this morning you seemed like you were ready to burst into song or something."

"I'm fine," I said. "Just some personal stuff's been a little fucked-up." In truth, I wasn't okay. I'd taken Melanie's rejection out of all proportion to the impact it should've had; she'd exposed to me the fraud of my pretending that I'd actually gotten my life back together.

"Well, if you ever need to talk to someone," Myra said, "I hear Isaac's a pretty good listener."

· 16 ·

WE HADN'T been able to get in to see Devin Wallace as long as he was in intensive care, not being either law enforcement or family. We'd tried to see him after he'd been moved out of the ICU, but unsurprisingly Devin wasn't interested. I'd kept tabs on Devin's progress with periodic calls to the hospital, and I came to find Myra as soon as I learned that he'd been released.

Myra nodded and stood. "You realize we're wasting our time, right?"

"In what sense?"

"He's not going to talk to us," she said.

"Probably not," I agreed.

"But I do always like meeting a man who's worth shooting," Myra said.

MYRA LED the way to Devin's building. We passed corner boys, dead-eyed kids looking nowhere as we passed, their bodies tense with the possibility of hassle.

The elevator was broken, a piece of cardboard with NOT WORK-ING scrawled on it stuck to the door, so we took the stairs five flights. The walls of the stairwell were covered with graffiti, trash strewn around the stairs. I noticed a used condom on the third-floor landing.

Devin's door was opened by an attractive black woman, maybe twenty-five, dressed only in a bathrobe. She ignored Myra, stared at me with blank hostility. "What you want here?" she demanded.

"We need to speak to Devin," Myra said. "Since I don't think he's up for coming out, you'd better let us in."

"What you want with Devin?"

"What's your name?" Myra countered.

"Ain't no call for you getting up in my business," the woman answered.

"Then the least you can do is get out of mine and let me in to talk to Devin."

The woman hesitated, still standing in the doorway. "Who that?" a male voice demanded from inside the apartment, the timing keeping the woman from feeding us some line about Devin not being here. Myra smiled at her slightly with one side of her mouth and arched her eyebrows, letting her know that there was no percentage in her trying to give us a story.

"Why you always gotta be hassling us?" the woman muttered, moving out of the way, Myra instantly through the door and into the apartment, me in her wake. There was no sign of Devin's sister.

Devin Wallace certainly looked the worse for wear for having taken two bullets in the back. He glared up at us weakly from his bed, a glassy daze in his eyes, presumably from painkillers. Even in his present condition I could tell that he was a good-looking, powerfully built man. He was light-skinned, with cornrows and a gold hoop in his left ear. His bedroom, like the rest of the apartment, was expensively furnished, but with a level of adolescent garishness not found in the living room: there was an Xbox 360 hooked up to a flat-screen TV, a framed Beyoncé poster on the wall. No doubt many a white teenager's Upper East Side bedroom looked much the same.

"That your nurse you got out there, Devin?" Myra said as we moved into the room. "I like how you make her feel right at home. She bring the robe herself, or you supply that?"

"I already told you all, I ain't talkin' to no five-oh," Devin said. "You ain't got no right to come up in my crib like this."

"Yet here we are," Myra said. "That Yolanda Miller's robe your nurse is wearing?"

"Ain't like I'm fucking nobody just now," Devin said. "I can't even hardly breathe, dog."

"You see who shot you, Devin?"

"Shit, yo," Devin said. "I got shot in the goddamn back. I don't got no eyes in the back of my head."

"You didn't get any kind of look?"

"Ain't like I'd be telling you if I did," Devin said. "I solve my problems my own self."

"Who wanted you dead, Devin?"

"I knew the answer to that, I'd be takin' care of it," Devin said. "No need for me to be lettin' you into my business."

"Are you saying you wouldn't tell the police who shot you even if you knew?" I asked. Regret grabbed me the second I said it. I knew better by now than to get in the way when Myra was doing an interview. Devin fixed me with a look, his brows furrowing, his mouth opening, but not in a smile.

"You ain't five-oh," he said to us.

"You're refusing to cooperate?" Myra asked.

"Yo, who are you, man?" Devin said. "I wanna see a badge."

"Why would I show you a badge?" Myra said. "You already said you wouldn't cooperate."

"SORRY ABOUT that," I said. "Me and my big mouth."

We were walking through the Gardens again, on our way back to the subway. I was furious with myself for blowing our cover.

"Don't worry about it," Myra said, not even trying to sound like she meant it. "I think we'd got what we were going to get."

"Nothing."

"Not nothing," Myra said. "We got that Devin isn't cooperating with the police. Anything he knows about who might have shot him, he's keeping to himself and his crew."

"So what do we do with that?" I said.

"We don't do anything with it," Myra said. "It just means we know the police aren't getting anything from Devin either."

■   ■   ■

A PACKAGE from ADA Williams was waiting for me when I got back to the office. Inside was a brief, innocuous letter from her, saying that the enclosed represented additional *Rosario* material accumulated by the prosecution since their initial disclosure. I assumed they were doing this in order to provide cover for the photo array, make it appear to have been turned over as part of business as usual. Their ploy seemed too obvious to be effective, but I supposed they saw this as better than just turning it over by itself.

There were about fifty pages of documents that I flipped quickly through—I needed to review it all carefully at some point, but for now my focus was on finding the photo array, which was at the very bottom of the pile. I glanced at it, not expecting the array itself to have much interest, when something caught my eye. I picked up the page, which was a photocopy, fuzzy and in black and white, and brought it close to my face, squinting at the photos. Looking more closely, I realized what was strange: every one of the six men in the photo array had a birthmark on his face like Lorenzo's. In fact, the birthmarks all mimicked Lorenzo's: someone had clearly drawn them on. It looked like they'd done a decent job of tracking Lorenzo's actual birthmark, though it was hard to tell for sure on the poor-quality copy we had.

I decided this was something Myra would want to see right away.

"They added birthmarks to the photos?" she asked incredulously, as I handed it to her.

"Ever seen them do anything like this before?"

Myra shook her head, not looking up from the photo array. "There's not anything wrong with them doing it, I guess, except then they should have followed through at the lineup. This photo array highlighted Lorenzo's birthmark, which made it as easy as could be for Yolanda to pick him out at the lineup. And, of course, I didn't know about it at the time like I should have, which kept me from being able to raise it to challenge the lineup."

"Maybe that's why they didn't turn the photos over," I said. "They knew they'd made the birthmark a big deal, and they didn't want to play that up."

Myra was still staring at the photos. "Sounds plausible to me," she said. "Of course, I'm not who we're going to have to convince."

·17·

To MY surprise, I'd come to share Shawne Flynt's optimism regarding the case against him in the weeks since he'd first become my client. I'd assumed there'd be something—an informant, a flipped defendant, an undercover cop who'd made a buy—that would directly tie Flynt to the drug dealing on the corner of Grand and Putnam. But as I'd studied the so-called evidence that had been gathered by the police, all I saw was proof that *somebody* had been dealing drugs on that corner, with nothing linking my client to the dealing other than his physical proximity.

Perhaps the cops had hoped they could flip up the food chain the dealer they'd caught red-handed, or maybe they'd been content to make arrests they knew full well wouldn't ultimately stick, wanting to send a message that they were taking back the street and directing the business elsewhere. Or maybe they just hadn't made their arrest numbers for the month, were padding their stats by bringing in everybody they could find. Whatever the reason, this was a bullshit case, and I doubted any self-respecting DA would proceed with it.

None of which was to say that I thought Shawne Flynt was innocent. I had absolutely no doubt that he was a drug dealer, and that he was captain of the crew that had been swept up in Clinton Hill. But not being innocent didn't make him legally guilty.

I'd scheduled a four o'clock meeting with Shawne in my office, to which he arrived almost half an hour late. He didn't apologize, or even mention his tardiness. I told him that unless something changed I didn't see how the prosecution could go forward with the case against him.

"I done told you that back in the day," Shawne said. "This ain't no thing."

"I don't think the DA will even want to present this to the grand jury," I said. "If they toss it themselves it's on the police department for not making a good collar. If they present it and can't get an indictment then it counts as a loss, as far as the DA's office is concerned."

"Ain't even nothin' to drop," Shawne said. "They never caught me doing shit."

I was well past the point of expecting to be thanked on those rare

occasions when I delivered good news to a client, but I was nevertheless surprised by Shawne's complete lack of worry. Even a bullshit
charge was enough to make people nervous; if anything, this was
even more true in the case of actual criminals, who generally believed
the police wouldn't hesitate to manufacture evidence that would put
them away. But I'd never detected even a moment of concern from
Shawne.

"So how you getting along with Strawberry?" Shawne asked.

It took me a moment to understand the question. Grand Avenue
was a fairly long way from Glenwood Gardens, and Lorenzo struck
me as too small-time to have a reputation outside of his home turf.
Either I had underestimated him, or else I'd underestimated the extent to which Brooklyn's drug dealers from different neighborhoods
kept track of one another.

"You know Strawberry?" I said, stalling.

"He tell you he capped Devin Wallace?"

"You know I can't talk about what my clients tell me," I said, trying to keep my voice light.

"It was me that was where Strawberry's at, I'd be thinking how I
might be better off doing twenty-five upstate than going back out on
the street."

"What are you saying, Shawne?" I asked, my heart starting to
pound a little. The threat seemed clear enough; what I didn't understand was where it was coming from.

"I'm just saying, yo, way I hear it, Strawberry ain't even got hisself a crew. He want to take out Devin by ghosting up on the G's
back, that shit ain't gonna fly more than once. Strawberry ain't gonna
get no second try, you feel me?"

"Are you threatening Lorenzo Tate?" I asked.

"Naw, man," Shawne said, leaning back and barking out a laugh.

"What I be doing that for? That shit ain't got nothing to do with me."

"But you're saying it might not be safe for him out in the world if he gets acquitted?"

"The streets take care of their own," Shawne said. "That's all I'm saying. You ain't need me to tell you that."

While Shawne was stepping back from actually threatening Lorenzo, the implication was clear. I could think of only one person on whose behalf Shawne could be speaking. "Do you know Devin Wallace?" I asked.

"How 'bout you?" Shawne said, not even bothering to acknowledge my question. "Who's making you well?"

I wasn't keeping up with him, and there wasn't much sense in my pretending that I was. "Look, Shawne, the reason we're here is to talk about your case—"

"You told me you got that shit covered. I'm figuring you came correct on that."

"That's true, but we really don't have anything else—"

"You get yours on the street, or have you learned to move past that? Smart motherfucker like you, bet you got somebody who comes to you."

"I don't know what you're talking about," I said, although of course I did. It was hard to stay in my chair; everything in me wanted to bolt from the room. I could feel beads of sweat forming on my brow.

"It's all right," Shawne said softly, leaning forward now, the faintest smile on his lips. "You don't got to cover from me. Dope really fucked shit up for you, though, huh? You was a real lawyer back in the day."

"I don't know what it is you think you know about me—"

"Now, why you gotta disrespect me like that?" Shawne said, his demeanor shifting: all of a sudden I was face-to-face with the young man who ran a corner. "Don't you be stepping up to me and calling me a liar when we both know nothing I said been no kind of lie."

It was clear that Shawne really did know something about my past. I had no idea how he knew, or why he was raising it, what he was trying to get. What I needed was time to think, but I didn't see how that was going to happen.

"What does any of this have to do with you, Shawne?"

Shawne smiled, easing back again, putting aside the threat. "We just two motherfuckers in a room talkin' some shit. Ain't nothing else. You looking a little warm, homey. Want me to open you a window or something?"

"You did some homework," I conceded, brushing sweat off my forehead with my fingertips. "Or somebody did. So what is it you want?"

"I'm just trying to make sure you're well, yo," Shawne said. "You getting what you need?"

"I don't need anything."

"Some needs just don't play that way. Some needs, they get into you, they ain't never going away. I don't got to be telling you this shit."

I couldn't contain myself anymore. I stood up and opened my office door. "I think we're done here," I said.

Shawne stayed in his seat, looking up at me impassively. "That how you want it, that'll be how it is," he said finally, standing. "Thought you might be looking for a friend is all. You change how you feel, you know where I am."

■　　■　　■

AFTER SHAWNE left I went to the men's room, ran cold water in the sink, cupped it in my hands, and splashed it on my face. I did it again and again, trying to cool myself down. When I caught my reflection in the mirror I hated what I saw: I looked ashen, disheveled, strung out even. I didn't look like the person I thought I was.

Zach was waiting for me outside our office. I saw him do a slight double take at my appearance. "You okay?"

"Fine," I said. "What's up?"

"You're late," he said. "C'mon, Myra's ready for us."

Isaac, Zach, Shelly, and I were mooting Myra for the Gibbons appeal, which I'd completely forgotten about. Myra stood at the front of the table while we sat at the far end. Behind her evening had set in, Borough Hall illuminated faintly in the growing dark. "May it please the court," Myra began. "This is a case that hinged on the defendant's confession. Terrell Gibbons has an IQ that makes him borderline retarded. It is well documented that people at that intelligence level are generally more open to suggestion than the average person. They also tend to be more eager to please, to submit their will to someone else, than the average person. As a result, someone with the defendant's intelligence level is much more likely to falsely confess—"

"You're not denying that your client confessed?" Isaac interrupted.

"Not in the sense that he said the words, Your Honor—" Myra began.

"What other sense is there?" Isaac said.

"The sense of actually *meaning* the words," Myra answered. "Mr. Gibbons testified that he confessed because he was tired and scared and the detectives threatened him with violence if he didn't."

"And you made these arguments at trial, did you not?" Isaac asked.

"Yes, Your Honor," Myra said. "But our argument here is that the court below erred in denying our attempt to put on expert testimony in order to connect my client's limited intelligence with the likelihood that he could be manipulated into falsely confessing. The trial court incorrectly saw this case as on all fours with cases such as *Green* and *Lea*. It's not."

"The fact that your client is of limited intelligence is enough to distinguish this case from the earlier Appellate Division decisions?" Zach asked skeptically.

"The central holding of those earlier New York cases, Your Honor, was that a jury's own experience and common sense would allow them to understand the coercive aspects of a hostile police interrogation. Petitioner does believe those cases are wrongly decided and should not be followed. However—"

"So you are saying we should take issue with those decisions?" Zach pressed.

"Not necessarily, Your Honor," Myra said. "While it is our position that those cases should in fact be overruled, this court need not do so in order to grant my client relief. The distinction—"

"So you're arguing that we should say that anyone who wants to claim they falsely confessed should be able to bring on an expert, but that if we don't want to go that far we can carve out a space for people like your client who have documented intellectual or emotional problems that may make them uniquely susceptible to falsely confessing?" Shelly asked.

"Exactly, Your Honor," Myra said. "Given the decisions in other state and federal courts, and the developments in the scholarly community establishing that false confessions are an issue worthy of expert testimony, those earlier New York decisions have become outmoded. But regardless of that—"

"We're talking about decisions that are what?" Isaac interrupted. "Five years old?"

"I don't think that matters," Myra replied. "Not if a consensus has subsequently developed."

"And by a consensus, you mean the handful of cases from other jurisdictions discussed in your brief?" I asked.

"There's no doubt this is a developing area of law," Myra said. "I think the *Hall* decision from the Seventh Circuit is extremely persuasive in this regard. A national consensus is fast emerging that goes against the two previous opinions from New York appellate courts. And this sort of emerging national consensus is of particular relevance when the issue in question concerns the general acceptance of expert testimony."

We continued for another ten minutes or so, pressing Myra on the details of her argument. I thought Myra was good, but she seemed less comfortable in the role of scholarly appellate advocate than she did as a street-fighting trial lawyer.

Afterward we all went out for a drink at the Ale House. I was still distracted from my conversation with Shawne Flynt and hadn't been able to fully focus on anything else. I knew I should tell Myra about what Shawne had said. If he was reaching out on behalf of Devin Wallace, that was something she should know. But I didn't know how to tell her that part without including what Shawne had known about me. And that wasn't something I was ready to tell her.

"So?" Myra said once we were all seated. "How'd I do?"

"Your presentation is good," Isaac said. "But it felt a little academic to me. You let us set the discussion. You're not giving the judges any reason to feel they *have* to overturn this conviction. You're giving them an opportunity to make new law in New York, but you're not forcing them to do so."

"How am I supposed to *force* them to make new law?" Myra said, clearly not liking such blunt criticism, however constructively intended.

"It's a tough balance with an appeals court," Isaac conceded. "But I think you've got to interject more passion into it. You've got to convince them that Terrell is innocent, make them be looking for a way to reverse his conviction."

"Okay," Myra said. "How?"

"They're only going to be willing to do that if they think there's no other way to avoid a clear injustice."

"But, Isaac," Zach protested, "you know the Appellate Division assumes that anybody convicted at trial is guilty. I don't think you can backdoor an actual innocence claim on them. That kind of claim only flies when you've got new evidence, or prosecutorial misconduct, something like that."

"I'm not saying it'll be easy," Isaac said. "You want your work to be cut out for you, go join the district attorney's office."

ISAAC STAYED for only one drink, talking strategy the entire time. After he left the rest of us got another round.

"I can't imagine how much pressure you must be feeling," Shelly said to Myra.

"Why should Myra be feeling pressure?" Zach asked. "She's not the one who stays in jail."

"Well, no, obviously," Shelly said, looking unsure of whether or not Zach was joking. "But to have somebody else's life in your hands . . ."

"We always do," Myra said. "That's not the issue."

"What is, then?" I asked.

"Usually we're trying to help somebody get away with something," Myra replied. "Even for me, it's hard to lose too much sleep over the prospect that a guilty person will actually be punished for his crime. It's a bit different when it's somebody who didn't do anything who's looking at spending the rest of his life in jail."

"You actually think about whether your guy is guilty or innocent?" Zach asked Myra.

"You don't?" Shelly asked him.

"Not if I can help it," Zach said. "I mean, sometimes they're just so guilty that you can't really help noticing it. But to the extent that I can keep from thinking about it I certainly do."

"So you never lose sleep over a case?" I asked.

"I didn't say that," Zach said. "I can never sleep the night before a trial starts. But that's just nerves."

"Have you ever had a client you were sure was innocent?" Shelly asked Zach.

"I really don't think of it that way," Zach said. "I think of it more in terms of degrees of plausibility. It's about whether I think I can manage to sell the story they've given me."

"But you can't avoid wondering what really happened," Shelly protested. "It's human nature."

"You never know what really happened," Zach said. "So it's best to just let it go."

"Sure," Myra said. "Except it's not always that easy."

"It is if you make it," Zach replied. "Besides, you know as well as I do that what Isaac was peddling tonight doesn't play. The appellate courts are pretty much incapable of even thinking about innocence. It's not in their DNA. Their whole purpose is just to make sure the rules were followed. If they were, then they're going to affirm. If they weren't, but it's not egregious, they're going to affirm. If they weren't, and it seems sort of brutally unfair, they're going to reverse. That's why I hate doing appeals."

"I didn't know you hated appeals," I said.

"Plus the fact that they're all about the law. Meaning you actually have to do research, read cases, all that shit that almost made me drop out of law school. Bores me to tears. Give me a good old-fashioned blood-on-the-walls cross-examination any day."

"Me too," Myra said. "But I can't let this one go. That's never happened to you?"

"Honestly, no," Zach said. "And looking at you right now, I have to say I hope it never does."

·18·

MYRA AND I were overdue to pay another visit to Lorenzo Tate at Rikers, and we'd carved out time on a Friday afternoon to leave the office early and head out there. On the drive I updated Myra on the additional material we'd gotten from the DA along with the photo array. I still hadn't told her anything about Shawne Flynt, hadn't found a way to do so without bringing up my own past as well.

"There's only one thing that helps us," I said. "But it's pretty cool. Apparently Latrice was right about Yolanda Miller's budding drug habit. She quickly fell on black days after the shooting. She's had two quick busts, one for possession and one for assault. She's got both of those pending, could be facing some time in the system."

"No shit," Myra said loudly. We had the windows of her Volvo open because Myra was smoking a cigarette, and the wind was whipping around inside the car.

I nodded. "We still don't really have an angle in terms of her making Lorenzo the shooter," I said. "We can point out that her trial testimony is presumably in aid of her hoping to cut a deal, but it lacks some punch when she's only backing up her initial ID."

"So why would she fall hard into drugs right after she pins the shooting on Lorenzo?" Myra said.

"I can see two angles," I said. "One is she got all sad seeing her sweetheart shot in the back. Two, she couldn't carry the weight of fingering an innocent man."

"I know which one I like," Myra said, ashing out her window.

"What do we know about the state of Devin and Yolanda's relationship post shooting?" I asked.

"We know that Devin had his other caretaker when we just paid him a visit," Myra said. "But that doesn't necessarily mean anything. Every man in the life I've ever come across feels entitled to two or three women."

"Because theory three would be that Devin just dumped her," I said. "And she turned to drugs to knock her pain out of the park."

"One way or another, it's ammunition for cross," Myra said. "It's better than nothing, which is what you usually get."

I waited for a moment to see if she had anything else to say about Yolanda's fall into trouble. "We got some bad news too," I said.

"What's that?" Myra said, not taking her eyes off the road as she stubbed out the butt of her cigarette in the car's full ashtray.

"A new witness."

"A witness to the shooting?"

I shook my head. "A cellmate of Lorenzo's from Rikers. He's given a statement saying that Lorenzo confessed to him."

"Godfuckingdammit," Myra said. "I fuckin' hate jailhouse snitches."

I looked over at her as she drove, surprised by the depth of her sudden anger. I would've thought a half dozen years of working as a PD might have inured her to developments like the abrupt appearance of new witnesses, but that didn't seem to be the case. "We told Lorenzo not to talk to anyone about what he was accused of," I said.

"This doesn't mean he did talk to anyone. Most of the snitches I've dealt with are straight-up lying."

"So what do we do about it?"

"The first thing is to find out what Lorenzo knows about the guy," Myra said. "Best-case scenario is they've never even met."

ONCE CLEARED through Rikers, we sat in a small interview room, glass running the length of one wall. I couldn't tell if it was the same room I'd been in the first time we'd come to see Lorenzo, or a different room with the same characteristics. I supposed that was part of the idea of jail.

We waited for Lorenzo for nearly twenty minutes. When he was finally shown in I was surprised by the genuineness of his smile: Lorenzo looked truly happy to see us. On second thought, why wouldn't he be? We represented the outside world; we were working for free to help him; we were the closest approximation of hope currently in his life.

We shook hands all around; then Lorenzo sat down across from us.

"Let's start with the bad news," Myra said. "The DA has a statement from a new witness."

"Can't be no witness," Lorenzo protested. "Because ain't nobody gonna see me do something I didn't do."

"It's actually someone from Rikers," I said. "Do you know Lester Bailey?"

Lorenzo's brow furrowed. "There's a dude named Lester here, sure. We was in the same cell for a couple of weeks, but I ain't seen him lately."

"That's probably because the DA moved him away from you once they'd gotten a statement from him," Myra said.

"How can he be saying anything about me?" Lorenzo demanded. "He don't know shit."

"He claims you confessed to him," I said.

Lorenzo's whole body jerked back, his chair skidding away from the table. He held his arms open wide, his face contorting with disbelief. "What he trippin' on?"

"You ever say anything to him about the shooting?" Myra asked.

"Why I gonna cop to something I ain't even do?" Lorenzo protested.

"But you did speak to him?"

"Motherfucker was up in my cell, sure, we talk. But I ain't ever admit to no killing."

"Did you tell him what you were accused of?" Myra asked.

"He'd heard from around the way."

"From who?"

"I don't got clue one. Ain't no secrets in Rikers for nobody."

"Did he ever ask you about it?"

Lorenzo was focused now on figuring out how Lester Bailey had played him. "He did ask me. I didn't think nothing about it, but now as I'm thinking on it, he was trying to get me to tell him shit."

"So what did you actually tell him?" Myra asked.

"I didn't tell him nothing, 'cause I ain't got nothing to tell him," Lorenzo said. "He sayin' I flat-out copped to the shooting?"

"He is," I said.

"I never said nothing like that."

"Be that as it may, this could cause us problems," Myra said. "If Lester Bailey wants to get on the stand and lie, there's not a lot we can do to stop him."

"This is some bullshit, yo." Lorenzo was still agitated. "They gonna be puttin' me away 'cause some snitch is gonna lie?"

"We'll see what we can do," Myra said. "We'll try to speak to Bailey, see if we can rattle his cage a little. Maybe we can get him to back down."

"What about my boy Marcus?" Lorenzo said. "I got me an alibi on this shit."

"We've talked to Marcus," Myra said. "And we don't feel we should put him on."

"Not put him on?" Lorenzo said, smiling like he thought Myra was kidding. "But he was with me that night."

"Marcus was pretty out of it when we talked to him. I think he'd make an extremely bad witness. Plus, if he takes the stand, the DA's going to be able to cross him on his criminal record. That'll just ensure that the jury associates you with drugs."

"But I ain't got Marcus, I ain't got no alibi," Lorenzo protested. He was already thrown off by the news of Lester Bailey, and it was clear that our lack of interest in his alibi witness was making things considerably worse for him.

"We don't think Marcus would be seen as a reliable alibi witness by the jury," Myra said. "He's going to hurt a lot more than he's going to help."

"What kind of defense we gonna have without Marcus?"

"We don't win on establishing our case," Myra said. "We win on tearing down theirs."

Lorenzo looked at her, a little challenge in it; then he rubbed his hands over his face, taking a deep breath as he did so. "So what's your good news?" he asked after collecting himself.

"What do you mean?" Myra asked.

"You said you were startin' with the bad news. So what's the good news?"

"I didn't actually mean to imply that there was good news," Myra said. "But we have made some progress. Do you know someone from the neighborhood named Malik Taylor?"

"Malik? I know him from around, sure, how come?"

"Apparently Devin Wallace told Malik to stay away from his girl, meaning Yo-Yo, despite the fact that Malik was the father of her child," Myra said. "Malik isn't ready, willing, or able to pretend that he was down with that. You ever hear anything on the street about Malik and Devin? Any beefs?"

"Now you say, I do remember hearing something," Lorenzo said after a moment. "Word 'round the way was that Malik was all up in Yo-Yo's crib on nights when Devin ain't around. People be talkin' some shit 'bout how them two were back together."

I glanced over at Myra, who was staring at Lorenzo with as much surprise on her face as I'd ever seen her show. "Who told you this?" she asked.

Lorenzo shrugged. "Don't remember who I heard that from. It was just what people be sayin'."

"Did Devin know about this?"

"I sure wasn't gonna tell him. Ain't none of my business. I got no need to get mixed up in some shit like that."

"Devin ever say anything about it, anything at all?"

"Now you got me thinking, I remember he say something about how Malik was disrespecting him, how he was gonna have to educate the motherfucker on how to behave."

"How did this come up?"

Lorenzo looked away from us as he tried to remember. "He was just talking about shit that needed to get took care of. He said something about how Malik had gotten up in his business where he didn't belong."

"Do you think Devin was saying he knew about Malik and Yolanda?"

"I didn't pay it no mind back then. You put them two things next to each other now, it do seem that way, sure."

"Assuming Devin did know about Malik and Yolanda," Myra said, "what would he have done to take care of it?"

"Way Devin sees it, the Gardens is *his*, you know what I'm saying? The whole damn place belongs to him. You the number one dealer in a project, you gotta make sure anybody who steps up to you gonna get took down real quick."

"So maybe Malik decided he needed to strike first," I said. "Maybe he shot Devin Wallace over this, and Yolanda's lying to protect him."

Myra's dismissive glance told me that in her view I was stating the obvious. "Lorenzo," she said, leaning forward in her chair, "why didn't you tell us this before?"

"I didn't think how it could mean Malik capped Devin," Lorenzo said. "A civilian like Malik don't take out a gangster like Devin. That's just not the way the game is played."

"And you're sure you can't remember who told you about this?" Myra said. "This helps us a lot more if we have a witness who can testify about the relationship between Malik and Yolanda."

"I'll think on that," Lorenzo said.

"Please do. And we'll do our own investigating, see what we can find out about it on our end."

"You think we can put this shit on Malik?" Lorenzo said.

"He's got a motive, and it gives their only eyewitness a reason to lie," Myra said. "This could change everything."

"I guess I should have thought to tell you all sooner, you put it like that."

"You should err on the side of telling us too much, Lorenzo," Myra said. "You never know what's going to make the difference."

"I feel you."

"So I guess the other thing we have to talk about is the pretrial hearing," Myra said, turning to me.

I explained the issue with the photo array, and how we would try to use it to suppress Yolanda's identification. "I hear you," Lorenzo said when I was finished. "That gonna be enough?"

"Not necessarily," I said. "But there's also the fact that the DA didn't turn over the photo array to us—we're going to argue that the ID should be suppressed due to their discovery violation."

"Generally speaking, there's two ways we can go at Yolanda's ID of you," Myra said. "Either she's mistaken or she's lying. For purposes of the *Wade* hearing, we're arguing that the ID procedures may have caused her to make a mistake. But is there any reason you can think of why she'd lie about seeing you?"

"If Malik tried to take out Devin, she might lie about that," Lorenzo said.

"But in that case she could just lie and say she didn't see anything, or that she didn't recognize anybody," I said. "Any idea why she'd pick out you?"

Lorenzo looked me in the eye. "Ain't no kind of reason for that," Lorenzo said.

MYRA WAS playing Notorious B.I.G.'s *Life After Death* as we drove back from Rikers, the thumping bass filling the car.

"I didn't have you pegged for a gangster-rap fan," I said.

"I can't stand most of it," Myra said. "All that 'I'm gonna smack my bitch' shit. But you can't work the streets of Brooklyn and not give it up for Biggie."

I unbuttoned the top button of my shirt and loosened my tie. "Long week," I said.

" 'Cause of this?"

"I admit I lost a little sleep over fucking up your interview with Devin Wallace," I said.

"It was a rookie mistake," Myra said. "But, you know, you're basically a rookie, so there it is."

"I'm not a rookie, though," I protested. "I've been practicing law roughly as long as you have."

"You want me to be your rabbi, maybe while I'm navigating rush hour is not the best time."

"I'm pretty sure I don't want you to be my rabbi," I said.

"I wasn't trying to be rude," Myra said.

"I don't think trying is really the issue for you."

"What I meant was, you want to really talk about the job, we can do that. But not while I'm already on the cusp of road rage."

"You want to go get a drink?" I said. I hadn't been planning on asking, hadn't known I was going to an instant before I did.

"As a matter of fact," Myra said, "I think I could use a drink."

WE WENT to Great Lakes, a bar on Fifth Avenue in Park Slope. Myra ordered a cosmo; I got a Maker's Mark on the rocks. "I can't believe you drink cosmos," I said. "They're so *Sex and the City*."

"It just so happens that I liked *Sex and the City*," Myra said. "And even if I didn't, cosmos are yummy. What do you think I should drink, chardonnay?"

"I had you down for more like a whiskey sour or a gimlet," I said. "You know, something film noir that would put hair on your chest."

"What's that supposed to mean?"

"I wasn't being literal."

"Because my chest is hairless."

"Glad to hear it."

"Entirely hairless."

"Perhaps if you drank whiskey sours."

"Is that what you want for me?" Myra asked.

"A cosmo is just on the girlie side, is all," I said. "Not an adjective I associate with you."

"Just because I'm a criminal defense lawyer doesn't make me Barbara Stanwyck," Myra said. "I'm allowed to be girlie when I want to be."

"I don't think I've quite figured you out, have I?"

"I didn't know you were trying to."

We got another round as the evening settled in around us. Myra went over to the jukebox, spent five minutes picking out songs. I watched her do it, but she didn't seem to notice, never looking away from her task. It occurred to me that it'd been a long time since I'd picked out songs on a jukebox. Watching Myra, it seemed like a fine thing to do.

"Are you going to tell me when your songs come on?" I asked when she came back to the bar.

"I never tell," Myra replied.

"So how bad do you think this Lester Bailey is going to be for us?" I asked.

"Hard to say until we set eyes on him," Myra said. "With any luck he comes across as a stone-cold liar who can't keep his story straight."

"You think there's any chance he's telling the truth?"

"You never know," Myra said. "But I really don't think so. Lorenzo strikes me as too savvy to give it up to somebody at Rikers like that."

Bob Dylan came on the jukebox, "Visions of Johanna." I looked at Myra, who grinned. "You really know how to lift the spirit of a bar," I said.

"I love this song," Myra said. "It's such a great New York song. It couldn't be written about anywhere else."

"I think of it as less about a place than about a time of day," I said. "It's a four-in-the-morning song."

"That's true. Fitting for us, I guess, seeing as we have a four-in-the-morning job."

"A four-a.m. job?" I said. "You mean because if our clients just went to bed at a reasonable hour, a lot of them wouldn't be in trouble?"

"That's what criminal law is: it's how the day tries to correct the night's mistakes. Most of my cases, people have done something they never would've dreamed of doing in broad daylight."

"What does that make us?" I said. "The night's janitors?"

"We're absolutely that," Myra said, sipping her cosmo. "What else do we do but clean up after it? That's why we'll never run out of work. Not unless someone invents a cure for night."

· 19 ·

PRETRIAL PROCEEDINGS on the Tate case were scheduled for nine thirty in Judge Ferano's courtroom. There were
two issues before the court: The first was the *Wade* hearing, which was
our attempt to suppress Yolanda's identification of Lorenzo as the
shooter. Second, the prosecution had filed a *Molineux* motion—
meaning that they wanted to introduce evidence relating to Lorenzo's
other criminal conduct. In this case, it wasn't criminal acts for which
Lorenzo had ever been charged or convicted—his record was clean—

but rather they wanted to be allowed to present evidence seeking to establish that Devin Wallace owed our client money arising out of a drug deal. This would be admissible only if the prosecution could establish a sufficient connection between the uncharged crime and the crime Lorenzo was charged with, and if the court found that the evidence of the uncharged crimes was more probative of guilt than prejudicial to the defendant's right to a fair trial. The DA was arguing that the evidence had to come in because the drug debt was the motive for the murder.

I'd researched and written our motion papers a few weeks back and would be conducting today's proceedings. Myra had been busy with the Gibbons appeal, as well as the rest of her felony docket. She'd looked over our papers before we'd filed, made a handful of revisions, but essentially the pretrial motions were mine to handle.

We were in a different courthouse from the one I was used to, as felony cases in Brooklyn were tried in a separate court from lesser crimes. The felony court on Jay Street was large and new; from the outside it looked more like a corporate office building than a traditional courthouse, and it was a good deal nicer than the rather dilapidated conditions I was used to. Our courtroom was on the twenty-first floor, the windows at the end of the hallway offering a view of Manhattan across the river.

This would also be our first appearance before the judge who would be trying the case, Al Ferano. The judge's rep was that he wasn't on the bright side, but that he didn't try to be, that he relied instead on his instincts and sense of rough justice. He was considered a pretty good draw for the defense, but nobody you wanted to get fancy with. Because the Democratic Party so thoroughly controlled the selection of judges in Brooklyn, you could pretty much count on getting a liberal on the bench every time, but many of them were nevertheless aggressively law and order. This wasn't because of politics, but rather the tabloids.

Judge Ferano kept us all waiting for about twenty minutes before taking the bench. He was in his late fifties, visibly portly even in a judicial robe, with a full head of graying hair he wore slightly long.

Lorenzo had the right to appear at any proceedings in his case, so he'd been brought down from Rikers for the argument. We'd done our best to explain the legal points we'd be addressing, and Lorenzo had at least made an effort to appear interested, but I got the distinct feeling he viewed this more as a break from the monotony of prison than he did an opportunity to get key evidence in his case thrown out.

Per Myra's instruction for all courtroom proceedings, Lorenzo sat in the middle seat while we flanked him. As a practical matter this could be slightly inconvenient, as it was far more likely that Myra and I would need to communicate with each other in court than that we'd need to communicate with Lorenzo, but Myra was convinced that the symbolism was important: she didn't want the two of us to appear to exclude our client.

The prosecution called as its witness on the ID issue Detective Kate Spanner, the detective who'd been the primary investigator of the Lipton murder. Detective Spanner was a stocky woman in her late thirties, with short hair and a military bearing. ADA Williams ran the detective through her background: the number of years she'd been a cop, then a detective, then a homicide detective. I barely paid attention: it was routine stuff, simply establishing that Spanner was competent and experienced, generally givens when dealing with homicide detectives.

Finally Williams shifted ground. "Turning your attention to the night of April 6 of this year, were you the responding detective to a shooting at Glenwood Gardens?"

"Me and my partner were, yes. I was the primary investigating officer."

"Were you the first police officers on the scene?"

"No," Spanner said. "When we arrived there was already two sets of uniforms, EMS, a crime scene unit. That's typical."

"What did you do upon arriving?"

"What we do is we talk to everybody who is already there," Detective Spanner said. "Get the overview from the uniforms, find out victim status from EMS, see if CSU thinks they got anything we can work with."

"When you talked to the officers who were already there, what if anything did they tell you?"

"They told me that two people had been shot, one dead at the scene, the other critical," Spanner said. "They also told me they had an eyewitness who could identify the shooter."

"Was the eyewitness still there when you arrived?"

"Yes. The witness, Yolanda Miller, was in the back of a patrol car."

"Did you ask her if she could identify the shooter?"

"I didn't even get the chance to," Spanner said. "Ms. Miller immediately volunteered that she had recognized the shooter, and she gave us a street name."

"What name did she say?"

"Strawberry."

"Did you ask her to describe this Strawberry after she identified him as the shooter?" Williams asked.

"Yes," Spanner said. "Ms. Miller described the man she called

Strawberry as a black male between five-foot-seven and five-nine, thin build, dressed in black jeans and a black shirt, white doo-rag, birthmark just above his left eye."

"Did you consider this sufficient evidence to arrest this man, as-suming you could identify him?"

"We did," Spanner said.

"Were you able to identify who Strawberry was?"

"We were able to that night, yes."

"How were you able to do that?"

"Uniforms knocked on a bunch of doors in the project," Spanner said. "Several people said Strawberry was the street name of Lorenzo Tate."

"Did you then feel you were in a position to arrest Lorenzo Tate?"

"Absolutely," Spanner said. "We were already prepared to arrest Mr. Tate based on what Ms. Miller had told us, but before doing so we thought we'd do the photos to allow Ms. Miller to make an iden-tification of Mr. Tate. But since she'd given us his street name, it was really just a sort of formality."

"When was the photo array conducted, Detective?"

Spanner requested and received permission to review her notes. "The day after the shooting."

"And where was it conducted?"

"I brought it to Ms. Miller's residence."

"Is that your usual practice?"

"Normally we'd bring someone in to look at photos on our com-puters, see if they could pick someone out," Spanner said. "This was different, though, because Ms. Miller had already made an ID of the defendant. This was really just a belts-and-suspenders approach."

"Did Ms. Miller say anything to you regarding the photo array before you showed it to her?"

"Yes," Spanner said. "I recall that Ms. Miller indicated that she didn't like the idea of viewing a photo array, that she would prefer to see the defendant in person."

"Was there a reason you nevertheless conducted a photo array rather than a lineup?"

"I'd already put the photo array together and brought it over to her," Spanner said. "Plus the fact that we did not have Mr. Tate in custody at that time."

"Did you have a warrant for Mr. Tate's arrest?"

"We did, yes," Spanner said. "But Mr. Tate didn't have the courtesy to turn himself in."

"So you proceeded with a photo array despite Ms. Miller's having voiced some discomfort with the idea?"

Spanner was starting to look uncomfortable herself, pausing a little before answering. "I suppose so, yes."

"How did Ms. Miller react to the photo array?"

"She barely looked at it," Spanner said quickly, regaining some confidence.

"How long would you say she looked at it?" Williams asked.

Spanner shrugged. "Maybe five seconds, tops."

"What happened after that?"

"I asked her if she recognized anyone."

"What did Ms. Miller say?"

"Ms. Miller again said she'd prefer to do it in person," Spanner said. "I was a little frustrated, to be honest, because she hadn't really looked at the pictures. So I asked her again if she recognized anyone, and again Ms. Miller said she'd know Strawberry if she saw him in person."

"What happened after that?"

"I thanked Ms. Miller for her time and told her that we'd have her back when we had Mr. Tate in custody."

"In your view, Detective, do you think that Ms. Miller failed to make an ID when shown the photo array?"

"In my view, she didn't try to make an ID on the photos. I didn't consider it relevant to the question of whether or not she could identify Mr. Tate, because she made it clear that she didn't want to pick him out from photographs."

"One last thing about the photo array you prepared, Detective," ADA Williams said. "In putting it together, was there anything you did to alter the photos themselves?"

"There was, yeah. In her initial ID, Ms. Miller had described the defendant as having a noticeable birthmark. That birthmark was visible in the photo I had of him. I'd looked for other photos where people had similar birthmarks but couldn't find any. I didn't want some defense lawyer claiming that Ms. Miller had just picked out the only picture of somebody with a birthmark on his face. So what I did was, I just drew the birthmarks on the other photos, then photocopied them so the birthmarks would blend in better."

"Had you done something like that before?"

"Once or twice I have, yeah," Spanner said.

"Is doing so normal police department procedure?"

Detective Spanner looked a little uncomfortable with the question. "Far as I know," she said.

ADA Williams then proceeded to walk Spanner through the in-person lineup they'd done once Lorenzo was in custody. Myra had been present at that lineup, although at the time she'd known nothing about the photo array, or even Yolanda's description of Lorenzo on the night of the shooting. Myra had objected to a couple of other lineup participants as in no way resembling Lorenzo, but she hadn't known to raise the birthmark issue.

"What happened when Ms. Miller was brought in to view the lineup?" ADA Williams asked.

"She looked for a couple of seconds; then she identified the defendant."

"How did she seem when she made that identification?"

"Confident," Spanner said. "She didn't hesitate."

"Thank you, Detective," Williams said, nodding once at Spanner before heading back to her seat.

I felt my heart start pounding as I stood to cross-examine the detective. I'd slept terribly the night before, unable to shake my nerves at the prospect of this hearing. This was my first proper cross-examination, and even though I was as ready as I could be, that didn't calm me down.

"Detective Spanner," I began, "you selected the pictures that appeared in the photo array and the individuals who appeared in the lineup, correct?"

"Yes."

"In doing so, you wanted to have people who had a general resemblance to Mr. Tate?"

"That's the idea."

"So, for example, everyone in both the photo array and the lineup was African American, correct?"

Detective Spanner shifted uncomfortably. "Well, yes, of course they were. The witness had described an African American, so it would have been silly to include someone of a different race."

"Because skin color was a core part of Ms. Miller's initial description of Mr. Tate?"

"I don't know what you mean by a core part," Detective Spanner said. "But yeah, she told us the shooter was black."

"The description given by Ms. Miller formed the basis for your assembling the photo array and the lineup?"

"I suppose so, yes," Spanner said. "I also had an old picture of Mr. Tate from the Housing Authority, back from when he lived at Glenwood Gardens, which is what we used in the photo array."

"Now, Detective Spanner, I would like to ask you specifically about the photo array. You testified that you added a birthmark on the other photographs, right?"

"I did, yes. Like I said, I couldn't easily find pictures of other people who had this sort of birthmark, so I added them on."

"How did you add them on?"

"I just used a pen and drew them on."

"I wasn't clear from your earlier testimony: are you authorized to modify photographs in that way?"

"Why wouldn't I be?" Spanner said. "I was just making sure that the photo array was as fair as I could make it."

"Because the birthmark was part of the witness's description, right?"

"She mentioned it, yeah."

"So just like everyone in the photo array was African American, so too everyone had a birthmark, because both of those were fundamental parts of the witness's description?"

"I don't know about fundamental," Spanner said.

"Did you ever receive any training on modifying photos in this way?"

"Training by who?"

"By the police department."

"No."

"Do you have any special experience in drawing?"

"Experience in drawing?" Spanner said quizzically. "I mean, I can draw."

"But nobody taught you how to draw identifying characteristics onto lineup photos?"

"I'm not aware of anyone who's been taught how to do that," the detective responded.

"Your department employs sketch artists, does it not?"

"Sure. For getting witness descriptions."

"Wouldn't they be trained to draw identifying characteristics such as birthmarks?"

"I suppose so."

"But you didn't think to have a professional sketch artist assist you here."

"I can't say it occurred to me to do so."

"And after Ms. Miller failed to identify anyone in the photo array, when it came time to put together the lineup, you didn't have birthmarks added then, did you?"

"It's obviously harder to do on real people," Spanner said. "Besides, your colleague was there, and she didn't say anything about it."

"Were all the people in the lineup African American?"

Spanner paused, clearly fearing a trap every time I brought up race. "I believe so," she said.

"Same as the photo array, right?"

"Far as I know."

"Because the witness had identified an African American?"

"Like I said before, yeah."

"So the race of the people stayed consistent between the photo array and the lineup," I said. "But in the former everybody had a birthmark too, and in the latter only my client had a birthmark."

"I have no reason to believe that played any role in Ms. Miller's being able to pick out the defendant. She knew what he looked like."

"Had the photo array been turned over to the defense at that time?"

"I don't believe so."

"Had the defense even been informed that a photo array had been presented to Ms. Miller?"

"I don't believe so."

"That's because you hadn't included it in your case files, correct?"

"It wasn't evidence of anything," Spanner said. "As I've explained, it wasn't that the witness failed to make an ID; it's that she didn't try to make an ID."

"She looked at the photos, right?"

"Briefly."

"And Lorenzo Tate was included in that photo array, right?"

"He was."

"And Ms. Miller didn't pick him out when shown the photos, right?"

"She said she wanted to see him in person."

"Meaning she didn't pick the defendant out when shown the photos, correct?"

"She didn't pick anyone out from the photo array."

"Thank you, Detective," I said, figuring this was as much of a concession as I was likely to get. "And was it your decision not to include the photo array in your investigation file of this case?"

"Yes. As I said—"

"How about the witness statement in which the birthmark was

highlighted as part of Ms. Miller's identification? Was that given to the defense prior to the lineup?"

"I don't know."

"Would it surprise you to learn that it hadn't been?"

"I guess it wouldn't surprise me, no," Spanner said. "We were still in the early investigation stage of the case."

"So if neither Ms. Miller's previous description nor the existence of the photo array had been disclosed to the defense, there wouldn't have been any reason for defense counsel to realize that the birthmark had any significance, would there?"

"Maybe not."

"Isn't it true that in the photo array, all the photos featured prominent birthmarks, while in the lineup only Mr. Tate had such a distinguishing characteristic?"

"I suppose so."

"And that Ms. Miller was unable to identify Mr. Tate in the photo array but did so in the lineup?"

"Like I said before, I don't think it's that she was *unable* to identify him in the photo array," Spanner said. "I don't think she really tried."

"When you interviewed Ms. Miller the night of the shooting, did she tell you what she was doing outside at that time of night?"

"She said she was on her way out to a bodega on Flatbush."

"What was the relationship between Yolanda Miller and Devin Wallace as of April 6?"

"It's my understanding that they were dating at the time of the shooting."

"And she just happened to be out in the project at the same time as the shooting of Mr. Wallace?"

"I believe Mr. Wallace spent a lot of time outside in the project,"

Spanner said. "He and Ms. Miller lived in the same complex. I don't think it's that huge a coincidence."

"Isn't it possible that Ms. Miller was actually out looking for Mr. Wallace that night?" I asked.

"That's not what she told me."

"Did you investigate the possibility?"

"No."

"But it's possible?"

"Anything's possible."

"Did Ms. Miller describe to you what she saw after she left her apartment?"

"Ms. Miller told me that she came out of her building and saw a man who she recognized as Mr. Wallace standing on the far side of the projects," Detective Spanner answered. "There's a large open courtyard in the middle of the Gardens project. I guess maybe it's where the garden was supposed to be. According to Ms. Miller, Mr. Wallace had his back to her and was talking with another man, who turned out to be the deceased victim, Mr. Lipton. Ms. Miller was considering heading across the square to speak to Mr. Wallace when the shooting started. Ms. Miller pressed herself against a wall as she realized the shooter was to the side of her, firing at Mr. Wallace's back. About a half dozen shots were fired in quick succession; then the shooter ran past her. That was when she had a chance to see him and to recognize him as Lorenzo Tate."

"Were there any other eyewitnesses to the shooting?"

"None that have come forward so far, no."

"Now, Detective Spanner, the nature of your job means you are pretty familiar with the Glenwood Gardens project, correct?"

"It's part of my precinct, so I suppose I'm familiar with it, yes."

"You've had occasion to investigate other crimes there?"

"Sure."

"The Gardens are known as a sort of open-air drug bazaar, aren't they?"

"Objection, relevance."

"Objection sustained," Judge Ferano said after a moment. "Move on, Counsel."

I looked over my shoulder at Myra, raising my eyebrows. She shook her head slightly.

"No further questions," I announced, returning to counsel's table.

"Does the state wish to call any further witnesses for the purpose of this hearing?" Judge Ferano asked.

Williams declined, and the state rested.

"I'll hear whatever arguments anyone wants to make," Judge Ferano said.

I had barely sat down, but quickly returned to my feet. I began by arguing that Yolanda's ID should be suppressed on the grounds that the police hadn't disclosed the photo array. I then argued that the identification procedures used by the police were both unfairly suggestive and not independently reliable. When I was finished ADA Williams took her turn, arguing that Lorenzo's birthmark hadn't played an important role in the identification, especially in light of the fact that Yolanda had seen Lorenzo on several previous occasions.

"Thank you, Counsel," Judge Ferano said when we were through. "I'll reserve my decision. Next up is the *Molineux* issue. The People seek the admission of evidence relating to the allegation that the defendant had sold one of the victims illegal drugs."

Williams again took the argument, claiming that testimony that the money Devin owed Lorenzo arose from a drug debt should come in to establish Lorenzo's supposed motive. The judge seemed skeptical, particularly when Williams revealed that the testimony they were proposing was that of Latrice Wallace, who had no firsthand knowledge regarding the nature of the debt, rather than Devin Wallace. This was good news for us in that it confirmed that Devin was still not cooperating with the police. When it was my turn I kept my argument short, wanting to stress my confidence that this proposed evidence did not fit the *Molineux* exceptions. After I finished, the judge again indicated that he would reserve his decision.

On our way out of the courtroom Myra and I were approached by a small, middle-aged man, his hair and goatee going gray, wearing a paisley tie whose fashion date had expired some years back and a worn sports jacket. "Got a second, Myra?" he asked.

"For you, Adam," Myra replied, "no."

The man turned to me, smiling. "Myra's charming," he said. "Isn't she charming? When people ask me about Myra, first thing I always mention is the charm."

"Joel, this is Adam Berman from the *New York Journal*. He's here because a white kid got killed."

"That's not entirely true," the reporter said, following us out into the hallway. "The college student angle plays a part too."

I recognized Adam's name from the newspaper. I'd been keeping track of the press coverage on the case, regularly checking the Web sites of all the New York papers for any articles. I read everything I came across, but in many ways it just felt like I was reading the same article over and over. From the shrillest populist tabloid to the most restrained establishment national paper, they all expressed the same perspective, the only difference being one of linguistic restraint, some papers blaring in headlines what others would only imply between the lines. However loudly they did it, they all demonized Lorenzo while practically deifying Seth Lipton.

There was absolutely no sign anywhere of the presumption of innocence. In its place the press appeared to have settled on a collective story, one in which an innocent young white person made the mistake of showing curiosity about the nonwhite people around him and paid for his youthful enthusiasm with his life. This was the story that sold, apparently, or else it was just the story the papers thought sold.

"What do you want, Adam?" Myra asked as we walked toward the elevators.

"You really think you can suppress the ID here?"

"I don't comment about stuff like that," Myra replied.

"What about the rumors I'm hearing that the DA's looking to add a hate-crime charge here?"

This stopped Myra in her tracks. "That's total bullshit. The DA feeding you that crap?"

"You know I can't tell you where I'm hearing it. But if I'm hearing it, that means other reporters are too, and maybe somebody who isn't as . . . *scrupulous* as myself decides to print it."

"Somebody's really feeding you a line about this being a race thing?"

"Black defendant, Jewish victim, deep in the heart of Brooklyn. You're old enough to remember the Crown Heights riot."

"Give me a fucking break," Myra said. "This is not that."

"Listen," Adam said. "I don't need to point out to you that your guy's getting bad press. I'm just giving you a chance to even the scales a little bit."

"How?" Myra asked.

Adam shrugged. "You can give me a little preview of what you've got. What's your defense going to be?"

"That'd be premature."

"You got anything you want to give me?"

"Slip me a card," Myra said, "and I'll let you know when I know."

·20·

I **WASN'T REALLY** hoping to ever see you again," I said to begin my meeting with Chris Delaney. Chris looked significantly
worse than he had the first time we'd met, a remarkable achievement
considering how bad he'd looked then.

I'd been given a heads-up by Shelly the day before, after she'd
represented Chris at arraignment. This new bust meant that Chris
was in violation of his probation from his earlier plea, and that he'd
almost certainly be facing prison.

Isaac had given me the case because of my having previously represented Chris. I hadn't argued with him, but the fact was I didn't want it, didn't want Chris as a client. I hadn't liked being around him; he'd gotten under my skin.

"I know, I fucked—I messed up, I'm sorry," Chris said.

"You did fuck up," I said. I didn't quite know why I was being so hard on Chris, but even just the initial sight of him had brought it out of me. The truth was, I really hadn't wanted to see him again, or even think about him. If anything, I wanted to assume he'd gotten himself together and lived happily ever after, scared straight by his brush with the law. I had no interest in being confronted by the depth of his trouble, in being reminded of just how far a downward spiral had to go for some people before it reached anything like the bottom. My own state was still far too precarious for me to welcome such reminders.

It was wrong of me to feel this way; I knew that: my job was to worry about his problems, to fix them the best I could with the crude tools the law provided, and I would do my job, but that didn't mean I welcomed his presence back in my life. "You remember what I told you after you were arrested the first time? Your staying out of jail was conditioned on your not getting in any more trouble for a year. Your initial deal is gone now."

Chris nodded slowly, not looking at me.

"That means you're going up with two pending drug charges," I said. "That means you're facing time."

"Look at me," Chris implored. "I can't do time."

"Yeah well," I said, "that's not really how this works."

"What should I do?" Chris said. "How do I get out of this?"

"I can try to get a deal," I said. "But I certainly can't promise it's not going to involve actual time. I think it probably will."

"I can't go to jail," Chris said, sticking with his motif.

"I've read the charges, Chris," I said. "They found the drugs on you, they watched you buy them, they've pretty much got this sewed up."

"Aren't you supposed to be my lawyer?" Chris demanded plaintively, clearly losing it a little. "Whose side are you on?"

"Deceiving you about your situation isn't being on your side," I said. "But I'll talk to the DA's office and see what they'll offer."

"I need help, man," Chris pleaded. "I'm sick. I need to get treatment, not go to jail."

"I can see if they want your testimony to go after the dealers," I said. "That might get you a deal that would keep you out of jail, but it would mean potentially testifying at trial against your dealer. There're obviously downsides to that."

"Would they kill me?" Chris asked with a skittish, failed laugh.

"That's an example of a downside," I replied. "I can't promise you that they wouldn't consider it. Though I certainly think it's unlikely."

"Maybe I could tell the cops something about Seth Lipton," Chris said hesitantly. "He's the guy from my school who got killed."

I'd never thought to ask Chris about Seth, or even mentioned to Chris that I was working on the case. "You knew Seth Lipton?" I asked after a moment, trying to keep my voice neutral.

"Sure, I knew Seth," Chris said. "It's kind of a small world, us BC druggies."

"You're saying that Seth Lipton did drugs?" I asked.

"That's not the point, though, right?" Chris said.

"What is the point?"

"Maybe I could tell the cops something about his little scheme," Chris said. "Maybe it would be like a motive or something for his getting shot."

"His scheme?"

"At school. Seth bought from the dealers in the Gardens, like in bulk, and dealt it on campus. He was the college's number one dealer."

"I beg your pardon?" I said.

·21·

I'D GONE looking for Myra as soon as Delaney had left, but she was over at the Appellate Division, arguing the Gibbons appeal. I finally tracked her down in her office first thing on Friday morning and related what Chris Delaney had told me about Seth Lipton. I'd expected some show of enthusiasm, congratulations, something, but Myra just looked at me.

"You should've been in touch with me the second this kid said Lipton's name," she said at last. "I'm the first chair on this case. No offense, Joel, but you're still a rookie at this. There're some potential conflict issues that need to be addressed."

"Meaning?"

"You're proposing that this Delaney testify about his knowledge of criminal activity, right?"

"Not his criminal activity, but yeah."

"And you found out about his knowledge of this activity while representing him, right?"

"Yes."

"Do you think you are in any position to objectively counsel Delaney about whether he should testify on matters where he may incriminate himself on behalf of another defendant who you represent?"

"He brought it up," I said. "I just wanted to find out what he knew."

"I get that," Myra said. "Which is why you should've found me right away."

"You weren't here," I said testily. "So I did the best I could in your absence. I'm sorry for not being you."

"Okay, so that wasn't fair on my part," Myra said after a moment. "Now can we move on?"

"Did you just apologize to me?"

"Don't get used to it."

"So what do we do?" I asked.

"First off is, we need to figure out whether we'd even really want to use his testimony. Assuming it's all true, what does the fact that Seth Lipton dealt drugs actually get us?"

"It makes the jury hate him, one," I said, leaning forward slightly in my chair. "And it makes him a more plausible target as the intended victim, two."

"Okay. So you'd want to put Delaney on?"

"I think so," I said, hesitant after her rebuke. "Wouldn't you?"

"Probably."

"So what do we do?"

"We'd better get Delaney a new lawyer. We'll have to 18-B him, to be on the safe side. I can walk you through that. Then it'll be up to his new lawyer whether Chris takes the Fifth on some things. He does too much of that, all his testimony is likely to be tossed, but you can't really unring the bell with the jury, so I think it's probably a chance worth taking."

"So," I said, still wanting some acknowledgment for this new evidence, even if it had just fallen into my lap, "how significant do you think this is?"

Myra shrugged. She was clearly still thinking it through, but I didn't get the sense of excitement from her that I'd been expecting. I wondered if it was because I was the source of the information. I didn't like the disconnect between how we talked away from the office and times like this, when she acted like my boss, but I decided not to say anything about it now. "It doesn't do anything to rebut Yo-Yo's testimony. But we do need to ask our client again what he knows about Lipton, given this new info. Let's see if we can come up with a credible theory whereby Lipton was somebody's intended target."

"I'm on it," I said.

"What's your, you know, actual plan?"

"I was thinking this new angle meant I should go back and have another talk with Lipton's roommate," I said. "Amin would be a better witness to use to get this stuff in than Delaney, assuming he knows anything and will talk."

Myra nodded. "There's no more important skill in what we do

than in taking advantage of your occasional lucky breaks," she said. "Maybe we can play this one out into something."

"I've got another idea with that. I think I should at least bring it up."

"What're you thinking?" Myra asked.

"That we should leak it to that reporter guy, Berman," I said. I hadn't been sure whether to raise this or not, worried that Myra would be offended by it, like I was suggesting that we cheat. "Change the focus of the story out there a little bit."

"How does that actually change the focus?" Myra asked. "The fact that Lipton was involved with drugs doesn't change that he was murdered."

"Not literally it doesn't, of course," I replied. I'd expected her to say something like this, and I felt sure it wasn't a sufficient objection. After all, she'd been the one to tell me that our job here wasn't to help find the truth. "But I think people's sympathy for Seth Lipton, drug dealer, will be different than it is for Seth Lipton, college student."

"I try cases in the courtroom, not in the tabloids," Myra said.

"Our jury pool reads the *Journal*. It gives us a leg up to have this out there."

"It's just not my style," Myra said. "But if you think it really might change the balance, I guess I'll let you take your shot." She reached into her purse, took out her wallet, and handed me the reporter's card.

"Why me?" I said.

"Why not you?" Myra said. "It was your grubby little idea."

"Fair enough," I said. "So how did the Gibbons argument go?"

Myra's face scrunched up like she was sucking on a lemon. "They asked me one fucking question."

"Just one question the whole time?"

Myra nodded.

"You never know," I said. "That might not mean anything."

"It might not," Myra said. "But as signs go, I wouldn't exactly call it good."

·22·

I **HADN'T BEEN** able to reach Seth Lipton's former roommate on Friday. So on Saturday morning, figuring that no self-respecting male college student got out of bed before noon on a weekend, I just showed up at his apartment.

A groggy Amin opened his door, dressed in sweatpants and a school T-shirt. I hadn't buzzed his apartment; instead I'd walked into the building when a young woman on her way out for a morning jog had left. I was wearing a suit despite the summer heat, largely in hopes of intimidating Amin; it also didn't hurt when it came to getting into apartment buildings.

I began introducing myself again when Amin interrupted, saying he remembered who I was. Amin stood in the doorway, not making any move to let me in. "Some new information has come to light regarding Seth Lipton," I said. "I need to ask you about it."

"What does anything to do with Seth have to do with anything else?" Amin asked. "He was hit by a stray bullet."

"You can't think of anything that would suggest Mr. Lipton might have been the intended target?"

"Look, you woke me up—"

"When I subpoena you to testify in this trial, are you really going to deny knowing that your roommate was dealing?" I interrupted. "Because you'll be under oath, and I assume a college student like you needs no introduction to the concept of perjury."

"What're you talking about?" Amin said, taking a step back, allowing me to step into the apartment as he did so.

"Which came first," I said, ignoring his question. My adrenaline was flowing, so strong and sudden that it caught me off guard. I'd prepared myself for a confrontation, and now I was acting out my part in one before Amin even understood why I was there. "Seth's sociological interest in drug dealers, or his professional interest in dealing drugs?"

"It wasn't like that."

"I already have a witness," I said. "Someone with firsthand knowledge that Seth was dealing right out of this apartment." This last part wasn't true—Chris Delaney hadn't said anything about dealing inside the apartment, but I wanted to make Amin feel that he too might be implicated. It wasn't entirely ethical, but I considered it necessary. I was here to break Amin, and I intended to do so. He knew something that might help my client, and I couldn't concern myself with the fact that it would also hurt Amin's dead friend.

"That's a lie, man. There was never any dealing here—"

"So you don't deny the dealing, just where it took place?"

"I wasn't involved." Amin was pleading now, maybe forgetting that I was only a defense attorney, not law enforcement. "And I told Seth, never out of our place."

"So you knew Seth was dealing to other students?"

Amin nodded miserably, then turned and collapsed onto the futon that served as their couch. I followed him in, propping myself on the armrest of the room's sole chair. "And you never told this to anyone after he was murdered?"

"They were trying to kill the other guy," Amin said. "What does it matter why Seth was up there?"

"It might matter quite a bit if the reason he was standing there was to buy a large quantity of drugs."

"Whatever he was doing there, he didn't deserve to get shot," Amin said. "I've met Seth's family. This comes out, it's going to be all anybody ever remembers about Seth. It's not fair."

"That's not your call," I said, lowering my voice, trying to take the confrontation down a notch. "I don't want to drag Seth's name through the mud. But I don't understand. This is an honors student we're talking about—how'd he ever end up in this?"

"You gotta understand, Seth was a guy who totally didn't think the rules applied to him. He didn't set out to do this. It was originally just the sociology project. I mean, sure, he got off on it, I guess— hanging with the homeys on the corner. I think the reason he got involved with the other thing, really, was to show them that he didn't think he was better than they were just because he was white."

"So you're saying Seth started dealing drugs so that the drug dealers would think he was down," I said.

"I know that whatever I say is going to sound like a lame-ass excuse," Amin said. "There's no good reason for someone like Seth to risk throwing his whole life away like that. I'm just explaining it to you as best as I understand it."

"Okay, sorry," I said. "I know this guy was your friend; I don't mean to disrespect his memory. I'm just trying to understand. So what you're saying is, it really all started as a legitimate sociology project?"

"He *cared* about those people, man," Amin said. "Whatever you think of that, he did care. He was trying to do something *real.*"

"So with all that, how did he end up dealing?"

"I don't know all the details," Amin said. "Seth was doing his own thing mostly. What I do know is, he got pretty tight with this one dude in particular. It was that other dude who got shot."

"Devin Wallace."

"Right," Amin said. "Devin let his crew talk to Seth; that was how Seth was getting a lot of his material. And he and Devin were spending a lot of time together. They hit it off in some weird way. Seth's from this pretty conservative Jewish community out on Staten Island—most of his family is Orthodox; they're pretty uptight about stuff. I think the only reason they let him leave home for school was because this area's so Jewish too. You should have seen the look on his mother's face the first time she met me. But, you know, coming here was his chance to become his own person. Same as it was for me, I guess." Amin shook his head, shifting uncomfortably in his seat. "So anyway, from what Seth told me, it was Devin who came up with the idea of having a white college kid pitching to the other white college kids. The idea was that there was this untapped market at the school, you know, white boys who'd be happy to score if you offered them a comfortable way, but who weren't ever going to head down to the projects on their own and cop from some brothers."

"So Devin proposed that Seth sell for him on the campus?" I asked. "Be the go-between?" The fact was that I understood Seth Lipton a lot better than I was letting on. I knew what it was to be self-invented. I knew the thrill of seeing the line you weren't supposed to cross in your rearview mirror. I also knew about the lure of drugs, not just their high but also how they set you apart, allowed you to view yourself as outside of the normal life that surrounded you. Perhaps I was being a hypocrite; there was certainly something a little perverse in my pretending to be shocked by what he'd done. But I wasn't there to express my own views or to show my understanding; I was there to try to get as much information out of Amin about his roommate as I could.

"I didn't know anything about this shit when Seth was first getting involved," Amin said. "It's not like he ran it by me, asked if I thought it was a good idea."

"So how did you learn about it, then?"

"When I found, like, a whole mess of fucking coke chillin' out in our freezer," Amin said. "I like freaked the fuck out, you know?"

"I would think so," I said. "So you confronted Seth?"

"Fuckin' A," Amin said. "He made it sound like it was some perfectly natural arrangement he'd reached with Devin—like, 'You help me with my senior thesis, I'll help you move drugs on campus.' The thing was, Seth was the kind of guy who *could* make that sound normal—like that was how the world worked, a deal like that, and if you thought otherwise, it was just you being naive."

"So he was running drugs for Devin?"

"Well, I mean, you know, Seth wasn't exactly your typical corner boy. I don't really know the details of what they worked out."

"Okay, sure, but essentially Seth was working for Devin, right?"

"They were doing this together, sure," Amin said. "But I don't think Seth was, like, Devin's *employee*."

"Fair enough," I said. "So what else should I know?"

"What else should you know?" Amin asked incredulously. "Man, you shouldn't even know what you already do."

· 23 ·

IT'S REALLY pretty simple," I said to ADA Narducci. "In order to convict Shawne Flynt of a crime, you need to have some evidence that he actually committed one."

Narducci had been blowing me off for a couple of weeks, clearly stalling, hoping something would turn up that would allow him to proceed with his case. I'd finally resorted to threats to get him to meet, telling him that I would be recommending that my client file a civil suit for malicious prosecution if the DA's office took it to the grand jury.

"Your client runs that corner," Narducci insisted. We were in a conference room at the DA's office, glare from the window behind Narducci causing me to squint. "This is the second time he's been picked up on the block in the last couple of months. What do you think he was doing there?"

"Standing on a corner isn't a crime," I replied. "Not even on Grand Avenue."

"We made a buy and bust from a guy who was standing five feet away from your client."

"Has the dealer on the buy and bust identified my client?"

"Just because he hasn't flipped yet doesn't mean shit."

"Actually, what it means is you don't have any evidence. You've got a possession-with-intent charge on a guy who didn't possess anything; you've got a conspiracy charge without any conspirators. Look, I understand the police sometimes feel the need to clear a corner, send a message by pulling everybody in. You stip to dismissal, then this is on them. You try to go forward here, the grand jury's no-bill goes down as a loss on your stat sheet. Why should you take the heat for the fact that they didn't make a case?"

"You really think my decision making about whether to go forward with a case is that cynical?" Narducci asked.

I smiled at this. "I don't think of it as cynical," I replied, meaning it. "I know your boss keeps track of your win-loss record, and I know you'd better be winning a fuck of a lot more than you lose if you want to be considered a player. And a no-true-bill isn't just a loss; it's an embarrassment. Especially if it's followed by a civil suit. So you tell me how you think you can make a case here."

"Your guy's just going to go right back out on the corner," Narducci said. "Shoveling poison to his own community."

After my last conversation with Shawne, I wasn't overly anxious to have him free and clear myself. I still had no idea why he'd been toying with me, or what, if anything, he actually wanted, but I had the feeling I hadn't heard the last of it. I didn't need Narducci to tell me that Shawne Flynt was bad news. But I couldn't let that get in the way of doing my job.

"What do you want me to do, let you put him in jail because he's a corner kid?" I said, hearing the frustration in my voice. "I'm not saying he's some kind of humanitarian; I'm just saying you don't have anything on him."

"He'll be back in the system next month, the month after that. It'll just keep happening until we do have enough to put him away."

"I know that," I said. "Hell, he knows that. But that doesn't change anything about the present. You gonna drop this one?"

Narducci sighed heavily, not looking at me. "Congratulations, Counselor," he finally said. "You've put another drug dealer back out on the street."

"SO, JOEL," Adam Berman said, "what can I do for you?"

We'd met at O'Connor's, a dive bar a block away from my apartment. O'Connor's was a relic of an earlier, dingier era in the life of the neighborhood, but its dark and gloomy interior had been adopted by the local hipsters, without displacing the seedy old barflies who made up the bulk of the clientele in the early evening of a weekday. I'd chosen it because I wanted to meet a good distance from the courthouse. There wasn't a gag order in place in the Tate case, so there was nothing preventing me from talking to Berman or any other reporter. Nevertheless, I didn't want what I was about to tell him ever being directly traced back to us. I wasn't here to tell him my client had an airtight alibi, or that we had proof a witness was lying. I was here to throw mud at the dead.

"Actually, Adam," I replied, "I'm here to do something for you."

"I'd imagine both of those things are true," Berman replied. "They usually are. What do you want to tell me that will do something for the both of us?"

"First of all, this whole thing has to be off the record," I said. "You can use it, but can't attribute it to me personally or Tate's defense generally."

"Done," Adam said immediately.

"We've come across some interesting information about Seth Lipton," I said. "It might make a good story."

"You're giving me dirt on Lipton?" Berman asked.

"I guess that's one way to put it," I answered. "I'm going to get a beer. You want anything?"

"I don't drink while I'm on the job," Berman said. "But I'll be happy to buy you a beer."

"This is on the job?" I said, gesturing at our surroundings.

"Of course it is. But I got no problem with my sources drinking while they talk to me. On the contrary. You want I'll buy you a shot. I can expense it."

Adam went to fetch me a beer. I found myself enjoying him without actually liking him. And although I supposed he was right that what we were doing here now constituted work, the fact was, I could use a beer. I'd never been a source for a reporter before, and while I was relatively at ease with Berman, I nevertheless felt exquisitely uncomfortable with what I was about to do.

"So," Adam said, placing a bottle of Sam Adams before me. "What is it you want me to know?"

I found myself hesitating, feeling for a moment as though I were about to commit some sort of betrayal. "The police have always said that Lipton was at the Gardens that night because he was doing his senior thesis about the projects."

"Wasn't he?"

"He was."

"Can I assume there's a 'but'?"

"But that wasn't the only thing he was doing at the Gardens."

"He scored drugs?"

"Yes," I replied. "But he took it up a level from there. He bought drugs in the Gardens and dealt them at the college."

"Lipton was dealing?"

"He was in business with Devin Wallace."

"What's your sourcing on this?"

"One that I can't tell you; the other is Lipton's former roommate."

"Why can't you tell me who your other source is?"

"I can't tell you that either."

"A client?" Berman asked. "I'll take anything other than an outright denial as a confirmation it's a client."

"It's like I said."

"You think the roommate will talk to me?"

"He doesn't want this to come out," I said. "So I doubt he's going to be eager to talk to a reporter."

"I can't run with this unless somebody who actually knows it firsthand will talk to me," Berman said. "But I'll look into it."

"It'd be worth printing, wouldn't it?"

"If I can flesh it out, sure. It'd be a big enough story, especially given that Lipton's been played up in the press like he has. But that's going to depend on whether I can get anyone to talk. You sure you can't give me anything on your secret source? I can keep him off the record."

"I'll ask," I said. "But that's all I can do."

·24·

PRETRIAL PROCEEDINGS in *People v. Lorenzo Tate* were the first thing scheduled on Judge Ferano's morning calendar. It was a regularly scheduled status conference, but with the twist that we expected the judge to rule on the two motions that we'd argued before him a few weeks earlier. Lorenzo had again been brought down from Rikers for the hearing; Myra and I huddled on either side of him.

"What he gonna say?" Lorenzo asked.

Myra shrugged. "There's no way to predict," she said. "We'll find out soon enough."

It wasn't that soon: Judge Ferano kept us waiting once again, coming out a half hour after our scheduled nine thirty start time.

"This is my decision and order relating to the defendant's motion to suppress the identification procedure used by the police in this case," Judge Ferano began, before reciting a brief boilerplate description of the issue before him. Although this took only a couple of minutes, it seemed to me to stretch out into eternity. My stomach churned—I wanted to win, to have my first big triumph as a public defender. It was purely selfish, I realized, having little to do with Lorenzo Tate and much more to do with myself.

After summarizing all of our arguments, the judge proceeded to systematically reject them all. At one point Lorenzo muttered something under his breath as I felt him tense beside me. I put a hand on his arm. Judge Ferano looked up briefly, expressionless, then looked back at his papers. The judge continued talking, but I stopped listening carefully. I tried to maintain a poker face, although I felt brutally disappointed. I glanced over at Lorenzo, who was still making no attempt to hide his own anger. I looked over at Myra, but she kept her eyes on the judge, her face neutral, not giving anything away. The judge took his time with the legalese before formally concluding that our motion to suppress Yolanda's identification was denied.

"All right," Judge Ferano continued. "Let's turn to the *Molineux* question. Evidence that Mr. Wallace owed Mr. Tate money is itself clearly admissible, and goes toward motive. The court notes that Mr. Tate has no prior convictions for drug activity, and that the People's belief that this debt was drug related is fundamentally speculative, resting primarily on the criminal history of the victim, Devin Wallace. Telling the jury that this debt arose from illegal activity would add little in terms of motive, while being highly prejudicial to Mr. Tate, and would create a grave risk that the jury would consider him more likely to have committed the crimes at issue because of his other, uncharged and unproven, crimes. The People will therefore be able to elicit testimony that Mr. Wallace owed the defendant money, but will be precluded from attempting to establish that this debt had any connection to illegal drugs."

AFTER WE were done in court we met with Lorenzo in a holding cell in the court's basement. Lorenzo still hadn't calmed down; he was unable to sit still. "It don't matter Yo-Yo say she pick me out," he said. "She just be lying about seeing me that night. 'Cause I wasn't there."

"That she's lying is harder to prove," Myra said patiently—we'd been over this before. "We don't have an eyewitness that goes against her, and we can't prove that she wasn't where she says she was. Have you come up with any reason why she would lie about this?"

"I don't even know her," Lorenzo said. "I got no idea why she be saying this shit."

"Well, unfortunately, she is going to be able to testify," Myra said. "There's nothing we can do now to keep her testimony out; but we can still try to find a way to minimize it or, ideally, to expose it as untrue."

Lorenzo nodded without seeming to agree.

"There's something else we wanted to talk to you about," I said. "We found out some new information about Seth Lipton."

"The white kid? What's anything with him got to do with anything with this?"

"He was in business with Devin," I said. "Seth went to Brooklyn College, not far from the Gardens, and apparently he was dealing on campus—selling to the white kids who were scared to cop on the street."

"You saying he was in the game?"

I nodded. "You ever hear about anything like this?"

"Matter of fact, Devin say something about it," Lorenzo said.

"What do you mean?" I asked.

"He say how he got this white boy could unload the product at that school, make deliveries, like. Devin told me about it 'cause of how he owed me that money, so this was something he had for making some more green."

"Did you know who Devin had running the drugs?"

"You tell me now it was that boy who got capped, but I don't recollect ever hearing his name."

"Lorenzo," Myra said softly, "you have to tell us these things."

"I didn't never put Devin's thing at the school together with his getting a bullet," Lorenzo said. "I figure the white boy who got put out that night was just some kid looking to cop. Ain't like it would be the first time. What's it got to do with anything?"

"We don't know," I said. "But for one thing, it means that there's at least some possibility that Seth Lipton was the intended target, rather than a missed shot."

Lorenzo sat for a long moment, thinking it through. "You saying somebody might have been looking to cap the white dude to begin with?"

"He'd opened up a new territory in neighborhood drug dealing," I said. "Couldn't that have pissed some people off?"

"Ain't like nobody else would be selling direct at the school,"

Lorenzo said. "Those boys want a taste, they got to come to us. Besides, I thought you was looking at Malik Taylor. He's who got a reason to be taking out Devin."

"So what you're saying is, no other dealer would want to take out Lipton because he was working the college?" I asked.

"I'll tell you one thing, though," Lorenzo said.

"What's that?" I asked.

"I got no reason to kill the white boy who was selling Devin's product. My boy owed me money; I ain't going to cap nobody who was bringing him green."

AFTER MEETING with Lorenzo, Myra and I walked back to our office. I knew I shouldn't be particularly disappointed, that no judge was going to be eager to throw out the cornerstone of a murder case. But losing gracefully had never been one of my strengths.

Finally Myra spoke. "Well, there's good news out of this."

"The *Molineux* ruling?"

"No," Myra said. "That we've got our first grounds for appeal."

"Well," I said, "that's something."

"I am a glass-half-full sort of gal," Myra said as she stopped walking to light a cigarette. "What else do we got? You ever track down the roommate?"

"I found him over the weekend," I said. "He shuffled and danced for a while, but eventually he admitted that he knew all about Lipton's dealing. But I don't think he was involved at all."

"So how does he come across compared to your other guy, Delaney?"

"I think Amin is clearly the keeper. His eyes aren't yellow, he doesn't look like bugs are crawling inside of his skin, he doesn't have the liability Delaney does in terms of a record, and his knowledge is more firsthand."

"Did you already 18-B Delaney?"

"I hadn't yet, no."

"I guess you can keep him then," Myra said.

·25·

WHY ARE you yawning?" Chris Delaney asked.

It was a fair enough question from his perspective. Unsurprisingly, Delaney himself was wide-awake, probably as awake as he'd ever been in his life.

I'd yawned because I hadn't been sleeping well lately, had been dragging in the mornings until the caffeine carried me up. I hadn't intended it to be disrespectful, and it wasn't because I was bored, but I understood how Chris Delaney could take it that way.

It was a little before nine in the morning. Chris and I were in my office, talking about the fact that in just over a half hour he was scheduled to plead guilty to misdemeanor drug charges.

"How are you holding up?" I said, instead of responding to his question.

Chris looked at me incredulously, as if I'd just asked him if I could go on a date with his mother. "How am I holding up?" he said. "I'm about to go to fucking jail. My parents have basically disowned me, and I've had to drop out of school. That's how I'm holding up."

"I got you the best deal I could," I said, meaning it. The ADA had agreed to a sentencing recommendation of three months, after which Chris would do six months at a halfway house. It offered at least the possibility of helping him, and since his sentence was relatively short he'd do his time at Rikers—no picnic, but an order of magnitude better and safer than a proper prison like Sing Sing. It was a good deal for someone with back-to-back drug arrests, but "good deal" was always relative when talking about jail time.

"What about what I told you about Seth Lipton?" Chris asked. "You said you might want me to testify."

"We're not going to need you to, actually," I said.

"I probably couldn't anyway, right?" Chris said. "Being in jail."

"It's not that," I said. "We've got Lipton's roommate, who's admitted that Lipton was dealing out of the apartment. But there's a reporter who's interested in talking to you about Seth."

"A reporter? Why's he want to talk to me?"

"He knows about Lipton's dealing."

Chris raised his eyebrows. "What's in it for me?"

"Nothing whatsoever," I said.

"What's in it for you?"

"Nothing direct. It's just that right now, the story's about how

Seth Lipton was this honors college student, and our client was this dangerous black drug dealer from the projects. We'd just like to have the full story out there."

"So you want me to tell the world that Seth was a drug dealer? I mean, the dude's dead. Shouldn't we just let him rest in peace?"

"Unfortunately, I don't have that option. But you do. If you don't want to talk to the reporter, don't. It's your decision. I'm not going to try to pressure you."

"You really think it'll help your case?"

"I don't know. But I'm pretty sure it won't hurt it."

"Will he have to use my name in his article?"

"That'll be up to you. You can tell him you'll talk to him only if he agrees not to identify you."

"Okay," Chris said. "If you think it'll help your guy, I guess you can have the reporter call me."

"Great," I said. "I appreciate it, Chris."

"Is that why he killed Lipton?" Chris asked. "Because of drugs?"

"What makes you think Lorenzo's guilty?"

"People who are arrested usually did it, right? I mean, I admit that I'm guilty. I guess most people probably don't tell you, though. I bet they come up with some story that you know isn't true, you sit there trying to pretend you believe it, probably have to keep yourself from laughing half the time."

I smiled in acknowledgment. "You pretty much nailed it," I said. "But my client in the Lipton case isn't one of those. Obviously I can't really talk about it, but off the record and between you and me, I honestly have no idea whether he did it or not."

"That must drive you crazy."

"To tell you the truth," I said, "I don't really think about it."

"Really?"

"It's not my job to figure out whether someone's guilty or inno-cent. It's just my job to defend them as best as I can."

"What if you thought I was innocent?" Chris asked. "Would you still let me go to jail?"

It wasn't a question I'd yet had to face, and it certainly wasn't something I'd ever thought about in regard to Chris. "Accepting a plea is never my decision. My recommendation isn't based on whether or not I think the client is innocent; it's solely based on how strong the DA's case looks and how good the offer is compared to what could happen at trial."

"You really think it doesn't make any difference to you whether the person you're representing is actually guilty?"

I shrugged. "Maybe on some subconscious level, sure," I said. "But not in any way I'm aware of."

"Do you ever see people after they've gone in?"

I was a little surprised by the question, not sure what Chris was getting at. "Not usually, no," I said.

"So you don't know what happens to them in prison?"

"What do you mean?"

"I just don't want—from the movies and whatever—you know, the drop-the-soap-in-the-shower shit."

I'd never had a client bring this up before, and had no idea how to respond. "Rikers is the safest place you can be in terms of a New York prison," I said, repeating what Myra had told me. "Most of the people there are awaiting trial, so they're not looking for more trouble, and nobody who's doing their time there is in for anything violent."

"So you think I'll be safe there?"

"I mean, you know, it is a jail. Keep your eyes open, and be as careful as you can be."

"Is there anything you can do to protect me?"

There wasn't, of course, not really, but I recognized that this wasn't what Chris wanted to hear. "If you start having trouble in there you can call me and I'll do what I can. But until there's an actual problem, there isn't going to be much I can do."

"So you're saying you can help me once somebody decides to make me his bitch, but not until then?"

"What I'm saying is, I think there's a good chance that won't ever happen, but if it does I can try to help you," I said. I checked my watch—we were due before the judge in less than ten minutes. I looked over at Chris, but he wouldn't meet my gaze. "We've got to go to court. Are you ready?"

Chris still wouldn't look at me.

"Listen," I said. "You don't have to plead. But if we go to trial on this you're going to be looking at doing real time, and they've got a good case. I don't recommend lightly that anyone accept a guilty plea. I understand that you don't want to go to jail—nobody does. But this is as good as you are going to get."

Chris put his face in his hands. It took me a moment to realize he was crying.

For the first time I saw Chris clearly for what he was: somebody no different from me, except that his luck had turned even worse than mine. He was what I'd just barely escaped being. My knee-jerk dislike for him had always been rooted in our similarities, of course, but only now did I realize that my disdain had been a form of self-hatred, a way to judge myself for similar faults. I truly wanted to protect Chris, to keep him safe, but there was nothing more that I could do. "You'll get through this," I said.

Chris lifted up his head and looked at me, letting me see his tear-streaked, terrified face. "How do you know that?" he asked.

"Because people do," I said.

·26·

So, BUDDY," Paul said. "Long time no see."

It had been. In fact, it'd been some time since I'd seen any of my friends from what I'd increasingly come to view as my past life. A gulf had opened up between what I'd done and what I was doing, and as someone who was, for better or worse, defined by my work, this separation had made it hard for me to talk about my present with people from my past.

I hoped this wouldn't be true of Paul, who'd been my closest friend since I'd graduated from law school. He'd supported me during the worst crisis of my life, even at some risk to his own career at the firm. I owed him for that, but I also knew that it was going to be hard for us not to be divided by our work.

"It has been," I said. "Too long." It was Friday night, and we were drinking martinis at Loki, a neighborhood bar that had a sprawl of mismatched couches spread through an open loftlike space. Paul and I were settled side by side on a plush purple couch that could easily pass muster as either hipster accoutrement or grandmotherly tackiness. The place was full, an old Pretenders song playing on the jukebox, a crowd that looked like they'd all wandered over together from a grad school seminar—typical for Park Slope's bar scene.

"I've barely seen you since you got on that murder case," Paul said. "Not since my party."

"It's been keeping me busy," I said. "We're just about to start picking the jury."

"You think you're going to win?"

"I honestly don't have the faintest idea," I said with a smile. "And don't ask me if I think he did it."

"I saw the article in the paper yesterday. The thing about your victim."

"About Lipton being a drug dealer?" I said. "Yeah, how about that?"

Adam Berman's article had just run in the *Journal*, and other than the fact that it'd made me feel disgusted with myself, I'd liked it very much. Berman was a diligent reporter; he'd ferreted out a number of students who'd confirmed that Seth Lipton was dealing on campus. The story had run just before we'd started picking a jury, which meant that our jury pool had a chance to see it before coming in and being warned by Judge Ferano to ignore any press accounts of the case.

"Did you know about his dealing before the article ran?"

"There's a limit to what I can say here."

"I'm going to take that as a yes," Paul said, looking closely at me. "Shit," he said suddenly with a laugh. "You fed it to them, didn't you?"

"Neither confirm nor deny."

"You diabolical motherfucker," Paul said. "I love it. A little poisoning of the jury pool before trial."

"I don't play to lose," I said.

"Apparently not," Paul said, shaking his head. "Speaking of playing, I know about what happened with Melanie. I'm sorry about that."

"It's not your fault," I said, a little thrown by Paul's abrupt transition. I hadn't planned on bringing Melanie up.

"I kinda feel like it is. I mean, I insisted that you come to my party, even though I knew it was going to be full of people from the firm. I thought it would be good for you to show your face, but I realize that was dumb. You can't go home again, right? I mean, you're better off just moving on."

"I'm not complaining," I said. "It was a fun little frolic, anyway, even if that's all it was."

"Was she the only person you've been with since Beth?"

"It hasn't been my priority," I said. "I mean, I've just gotten back to the starting gate, you know? It took me over a year to get my life even close to back in order."

"Welcome back," Paul said.

I lifted my martini glass in a toast to that and took a long drink. "Besides, I've been so busy at work that I don't really meet anyone outside of that."

"They've got this thing called the Internet now," Paul said. "It's like a dating smorgasbord. There's, like, a quarter million New York girls for you to choose from."

"What am I going to talk about on a first date with someone I met on the Internet? My job? You know what the highlight of my week was? Pleading out a junkie college student on drug charges—before we go to court to do the plea, he asks me whether I think he's going to get raped in prison. I mean, it's pretty hard to turn that into a cocktail-party anecdote."

"I'm sure there are girls out there who dig that sort of thing," Paul said. "They've probably got a closetful of handcuffs and leather masks, but nobody's perfect."

"Besides, how many serious relationships have you gotten into with girls you met online?"

"That's asking the wrong question. Why don't you ask me how many girls I've fucked who I met on the Internet? I'm not saying you should get married; I'm just saying you need to get back in the game."

"You're right," I said.

"I know I'm right," Paul said.

"I guess too it's that I've gotten used to being alone. It feels safer, you know?"

"What's so great about feeling safe?"

"You've got to remember just how thin the ice got for me there. Beth's father was trying to get me criminally prosecuted for her death. I could have ended up with manslaughter charges against me. Even when I got through that, I didn't know if I'd ever work as a lawyer again. Safe feels pretty fucking good."

"Fine, be safe. But for Christ's sake, get yourself laid, at least."

"I'll see what I can do," I said.

"What about the girl you're working with on the murder case?" Paul asked. "How's she?"

I hadn't really talked to anyone about Myra, hadn't acknowledged our intermittent flirtation, which often felt more rooted in anger than it did in potential affection. I still wasn't sure if it really meant anything, or if it was just something the two of us were doing in the absence of the will to do anything that might carry actual risk.

"She's cool," I said. "It's weird, a little—sometimes we get to really talking about things; other times she's all business. She lets me in and then she kicks me out, if you know what I mean."

"That's all fascinating," Paul said. "But I meant how does she look?"

"She's cute," I said. "Actually, she would totally beat me up if she knew I described her as cute, so maybe that's not the word. But she's a little too threatening to actually be called hot, so I guess somewhere between the two."

"You made any moves?"

"I don't exactly have the best track record when it comes to office romances."

"If anyone has nowhere to go but up in that department, it's probably you," Paul said.

"I won't argue with that," I said. "But also, she and I are in the middle of a murder case that's going to trial. The last thing we need is for me to throw some kind of a pass at her. However she responded, it would be a bad idea."

"What about after the trial?"

"I'm thinking about it."

"Ten will get you twenty if she says yes."

"Why are you always trying to bribe me to have sex with women?"

"I don't know," Paul said. "It's probably one of those things we shouldn't talk about."

· 27 ·

JURY SELECTION in the Tate case began on Wednesday morning. Jury selection was always a drawn-out chess match, especially in a murder trial, and never more so than when race came into play.

The judge had called for a jury pool of eighty, out of which we would pick twelve jurors and two alternates. We wanted as many blacks on the jury as possible, while knowing the prosecution would want as many whites as they could get. Neither side was allowed to strike jurors explicitly based on their race, but everyone in the system knew that in a case like this, both sides were doing exactly that.

After two days, we'd ended up with a fairly mixed jury, mainly because we'd struck as many whites as we could get away with while the ADAs did the same thing to blacks. The fourteen spots had gone to three black women, two black men, one Asian woman, two Hispanic men, four white women, and two white men. Their ages ranged from twenty to seventy, their education ranged from a high school dropout to a PhD. It was a jury that more or less looked like Brooklyn.

When we'd finished late on Thursday afternoon the judge had announced that we would start the trial at nine thirty on Monday morning. "All right," Myra said as we left court. "So we've got three days before this trial starts. Maybe we should talk about what the fuck we're going to do."

"Sure," I said.

"I could use a drink," Myra said. "Let's have our meeting at the Ale House."

We got a booth in the back. I took out a legal pad and a pen. Myra looked at it, smiling. "You really can't take notes in a bar," she said.

"Why not?" I said. "People will think you're someone famous."

"I mostly just wanted to talk about strategy. Which isn't anything we'd really want to write down, even if there was a reason to."

"Got it," I said. "No notes. What is it you want to strategize about?"

"I'm thinking we don't have enough here to just be playing defense," Myra said. "I think we need a counter story after all."

"I thought you told me we don't win by building our case but by tearing down theirs."

"It's generally true. But I'm worried their whole is going to be more than the sum of their parts. The fact is, nothing we say about Yolanda Miller is going to erase the fact that she claims she saw the shooting with her own eyes, and that she recognized our guy as the shooter and told the police his street name. Throw in credible motive by way of the sister, and then the supposed confession through the snitch, and they've got a case."

"So what do you want to do?"

"I wish we could put what's-his-name on—Lorenzo's friend."

"Marcus?"

"Yeah, Marcus," Myra said. "An alibi wouldn't hurt."

"Don't you think it's possible that Lorenzo's telling the truth and he was with Marcus at his apartment that night?" I asked.

"Sure, I think it's possible. But there're only two people who can tell that story to the jury. The first is Lorenzo, and he can't tell it without opening himself up to a full-scale cross-examination, which I don't think he'd survive. The second is Marcus, and he couldn't tell it so that it sounded like he believed it."

"But if it's the truth—"

"It doesn't matter if he's telling the truth if it doesn't sound like he is," Myra said. "Plus, bringing him into it would allow the DA to backdoor drug stuff into the case."

"Giving up our client's alibi seems like a high price to pay."

"You'd call Marcus to the stand? First of all, you really feel confident he'd say he was with Lorenzo? Marcus seemed like the last thing he wanted was to put himself even in the outside corner of a murder investigation. My guess is he's got a thing or two to hide."

"So what's our plan of attack then?"

"Way I see it, our most important target is Yolanda Miller. We get her credibility out of the way, the links between the rest of their case don't look so strong."

"As we've always said, the two possibilities are she's lying or she's wrong," I said. "She's wrong seems difficult, given that she'd seen him before."

"Okay," Myra said. "So why's she lying?"

"Because she's covering for Malik Taylor."

"And why did Malik Taylor shoot Seth Lipton?"

"He intended to shoot Devin Wallace."

"Why'd he want to do that?"

"Love triangle," I said. "And over the kid. Plus, he's got to shoot Devin before Devin shoots him, given what Lorenzo told us about the word on the street."

"Why would Yolanda lie about it?"

"Telling the truth puts her in the middle of a murder. Plus, it guarantees she loses both the men who are helping to take care of her son."

"Why does she pick Lorenzo as her fall guy?"

"Haven't got the slightest fucking idea."

"Okay," Myra said, leaning back in her seat and finishing off her drink. "We've got the start of a story there, but it still needs a lot of work. You got anywhere you need to be? Because I'd like to brainstorm around this for a few hours."

"You know me," I said. "I've almost never got anywhere I need to be. You want another drink?"

"Absolutely," Myra said. "There's a reason we aren't having this meeting in a conference room."

MYRA AND I spent a couple of hours throwing ideas around about what our counterstory should be and how we'd present it. We agreed that Malik Taylor was our only real option as an alternative suspect, although there were obvious problems with trying to pin it on him: he appeared to be a solid citizen, and while we had at least some kind of motive for him, we didn't have anything in the way of evidence that he'd actually done it.

"I guess the other thing we need to talk about is who's going to do what," Myra said. "Isaac came by to talk to me the other day. He said that he wanted to make sure that I wasn't just treating you as my bitch."

"Did you confess?"

"You have no idea how I treat my bitches," Myra replied.

"So what did Isaac tell you to do?"

"Just to make sure you actually got to do some stuff at the trial. My thought was to have you do a lot of the defense case. I think that's a good time to bring in a new face—it'll get the jury's attention. Hell, they'll think you're our closer."

"We have a defense case?"

"We've got Lipton's roommate; we've got Malik Taylor. Who knows, maybe we'll find an alibi witness over the weekend."

"That's great," I said. "I'll do whatever you'll let me do."

"I'm sure you will," Myra said. "Listen, I'm starting to get drunk, and I'm absolutely starving. I think that's my strategizing for the day."

"Sure," I said. "You want to order some food here?"

"Why not?" Myra said. "We can just segue right into the evening."

We ordered some bar food and another round of drinks from the waitress. "So what else is going on?" Myra asked me.

"I pled out Chris Delaney last week."

"Who's Chris Delaney?"

"He was the addict who told me about Lipton being a dealer."

"Right," Myra said. "The names all blur. I can barely keep my own clients straight, let alone anyone else's."

"He was really scared," I said. "I mean, I've had other ones who were scared, but he was all the way up there. I didn't know what to tell him."

"It's not like you can tell him it's not scary," Myra said. "It is scary. I certainly wouldn't want to go to jail."

"You ever get in any trouble with the law?" I couldn't resist asking.

"Me? Never. Not even close. My stepfather would've killed me. Why, did you?"

Isaac was the only person in the office who officially knew the full story about my past, but I'd wondered if the truth had gradually leaked out to my coworkers. If Myra knew anything she was being a good actress. "Nothing where I actually thought I was going to jail," I replied.

"What does that mean? You got bench warrants riding on you I should know about?"

"I'm in the clear," I said. "Honest."

I could tell Myra wanted to ask me more questions, so I decided I needed to quickly change the subject. "You ever gotten someone off who you were absolutely sure was guilty?" I asked.

Myra took a second to think about it, leaning back in her seat. "I had a repeat felon on a gun charge; the cops' search was blatantly illegal and I got the whole thing tossed. There was no doubt he'd had the gun on him. So I guess, yeah, I mean, everybody knew that guy was guilty, but he walked."

"Were you okay with it?"

"Sure," Myra said immediately. "Cops can't do warrantless, suspicionless searches just because somebody's black and is walking down the street in East New York. It didn't have much to do with me, anyway. Any lawyer would've been able to get him off—the DA shouldn't have gone forward on it after the cops fucked it up."

"You never worried that he'd go out and shoot someone?"

"If he did, it's on the cops, not on me. My job is just to make sure that everybody else does their job correctly. If they do, then there's usually not a whole lot I can do to change the outcome of the case."

"You honestly think it wouldn't bother you?"

"I honestly don't think about it. Why are you?"

"I don't know," I said, regretting having brought it up. What was bothering me was Shawne Flynt, but I still hadn't told Myra what was going on with him. I knew that I probably should, but wasn't ready to include what Shawne had known about me, and there wasn't much point in telling the story if I left that part out. I decided that I'd tell her when and if Shawne actually made his play, but that for now there wasn't any point, as there was nothing that we could do. "I just had a kid, a dealer, where the DA didn't go forward because they didn't have a case on him. But there was no missing the fact that he ran the corner they were trying to clear up."

"And it's bothering you?"

"It's not that I think they should have prosecuted him without any evidence," I said. "It's just . . . he was going to go right back out to that corner, keep dragging the neighborhood down."

"I've never gotten from you why you left your fancy-pants career to become a PD," Myra said. "You still just don't quite seem the type."

"I had my reasons," I said, wondering again if she knew more than she was letting on.

"What were they?"

"I'll tell you sometime."

"What's wrong with now?"

"Maybe after the trial's over."

"Whatever," Myra said. "If you think I find this intriguing you couldn't be more wrong."

The waitress arrived with our food—a turkey burger with mashed potatoes for me, a regular burger with blue cheese and bacon and fries for Myra. "You drink like you're on *Sex and the City* and eat like you're in a fraternity," I said.

"No one asked you."

"I find it intriguing," I said. "It's like you've got these dueling adolescents battling it out inside you."

"You know what I noticed?" Myra said. "Before, when I asked you what else was going on, you started telling me about work things."

"I assumed that was what you were asking about."

"It was a pretty broad question."

"It's not like you've ever shown any interest in my life outside of work."

"I wasn't aware that you had one."

"Why?" I said. "Do you?"

"Not so much," Myra said. "I used to, but it just sort of fell away over the years. I didn't really notice the steps; then all of a sudden it was basically gone."

"That sounds depressing."

"I don't mean for it to be. I love what I do. I don't really mind that it defines me. Something has to. I'd rather it be this than, you know, changing some squalling baby's diapers."

"Sometimes I think that drinking cosmos is the closest thing you have to a feminine characteristic."

"Maybe," Myra said. "That's what scared away my last serious boyfriend. Not the cosmos, the fact that I didn't see myself moving to the burbs and popping out little screamers. We'd been together for over a year before I realized that he viewed my job as some sort of phase I was going through."

"Doesn't sound like he knew you very well."

"I think he just didn't have the imagination to see those parts of me that he couldn't relate to," Myra said. "Like spending my time defending criminals and barely getting paid for it."

"Somebody who didn't understand *that* about you probably didn't understand very much."

"He was like most guys I've dated, I suppose," Myra said. "If I judged him, he seemed pretty lame, but if I compared him, he seemed like a good deal."

"And that's enough for you?"

"Well, not really, but what choice do I have?"

"You don't think any man can possibly be your equal, is that it?" I said with a laugh.

"It's not that so much as that men aren't looking for an equal," Myra said. "There's too much dirty work that has to get done in a relationship, and men are scared that if they settle down with an equal they might actually have to do their fair share of it."

"Some men want a woman who's their equal."

"What, like you, for instance? I'm sure you want a woman who's smart, but I bet you still want her to be the one who cleans up after you make the mess."

"Well sure," I said. "But that's just based on what I'm good at."

· P A R T ·
THREE

·28·

GOOD MORNING, ladies and gentlemen," ADA O'Bannon said, beginning the opening arguments in *People v. Lorenzo Tate*. He was standing at the podium in front of the prosecution's table. The ADAs had the table closest to the jury; Myra and I sat flanking Lorenzo at our table. Behind us were a half dozen rows of public seating, which was about half-full. The courtroom was new and antiseptic, lacking the imposing formality of the federal courts I'd generally practiced in while at Walker Bentley, but a good deal

nicer than the criminal court on Schermerhorn where I handled arraignments and misdemeanors. "This is a murder case. The murder
in question arose from a debt. The intended victim, Devin Wallace,
owed money to the defendant, Lorenzo Tate. You will hear evidence
that the defendant came looking for the intended victim at his home
in the Glenwood Gardens housing project on the night of the shooting. You will hear that the defendant made threatening remarks while
he was looking for Mr. Wallace that night. And you will hear that an
eyewitness saw the defendant actually do the shooting.

"Devin Wallace did not die, even though he was shot twice in the
back. But the defendant fired a full six shots, and one of those four
bullets that missed Mr. Wallace went into the head of a college student named Seth Lipton, killing him instantly. That is the murder in
this case.

"The People do not believe that the defendant set out to kill Seth
Lipton that night. There is no evidence that the defendant had ever
seen Seth Lipton before. We believe that Seth Lipton was simply in
the wrong place at the wrong time. The reason that Seth Lipton was
there, as strange as this might seem, was for his studies. Now, perhaps the defense will try to put a more sinister spin on it, but the fact
is that Seth Lipton was studying sociology in school, and he was doing his senior honors thesis on life at the Glenwood Gardens housing projects.

"Devin Wallace, on the other hand, was the intended victim,
hunted down and shot because of a debt. You will hear testimony
from Devin's sister, Latrice Wallace. Latrice Wallace lives with her
brother. She will tell you that a few hours before the shooting, the
defendant came knocking on their door. She will tell you that the defendant was looking for her brother, that he was looking for his

money, and that when she said her brother wasn't home and hadn't left any money, the defendant made a threat.

"Now, as I said, Mr. Wallace was shot in the back, so he did not see who shot him and Mr. Lipton. But there was a witness, a woman named Yolanda Miller.

"Ms. Miller, who also lives in Glenwood Gardens, was on her way to a deli to get some milk for her child. She had just stepped out of her building and had spotted Mr. Wallace, who she was dating. Ms. Miller will testify she was starting to approach Mr. Wallace and the deceased, Mr. Lipton, when the shooting started. She will testify that she saw the defendant run right by her with a gun in his hand, and that she was able to identify him by his street name, which is Strawberry, because she had seen him on several occasions prior to the shooting.

"The evidence will show, beyond a reasonable doubt, that the defendant shot and killed Seth Lipton, and shot and attempted to kill Devin Wallace. We will ask you to find him guilty on all counts. Thank you."

O'Bannon had given his entire opening while standing in front of the small podium placed a few feet in front of the jury box, occasionally glancing at notes. Myra had written out her entire opening, which she had then gone over with me before boiling it down into a page's worth of bulleted trigger phrases. Myra stood at the podium for a moment, looking from face to face, making sure she had fully gathered the jury's collective attention to her.

"I'd just like to clear a few things up," she began. "To begin with, nobody knows who the intended victim of this crime was. Two people were shot. One was killed, but the police and the prosecutor assumed that the actual murder victim just happened to be in the wrong place at the wrong time. We're going to present some evidence suggesting that Mr. Lipton's death might not have just been a matter of bad luck. That perhaps it wasn't just bad timing, but that something else was going on.

"It's true that Lorenzo Tate came looking for Devin Wallace that night, but that in no way makes Lorenzo Tate a murderer. Lorenzo Tate was friends with Devin Wallace. Lorenzo Tate often spent time at Mr. Wallace's apartment. That Mr. Tate had stopped by looking for Mr. Wallace earlier that night is simply not evidence that he had anything to do with the shooting.

"The prosecution talked about a motive in this, that motive being that Devin Wallace owed Lorenzo Tate money. But dead men don't pay debts. And as you will learn, Mr. Wallace was almost certainly in the midst of getting a significant amount of money at the very time he was shot.

"The assistant district attorney also told you they had an eyewitness, Yolanda Miller, who claims that she saw Lorenzo Tate do the shooting in this case. He told you that Ms. Miller was dating Devin Wallace at the time of the shooting. But there're a few things the DA didn't mention about that eyewitness. He didn't mention that she'd had a child with another man, Malik Taylor, not long before starting her relationship with Mr. Wallace. He didn't mention that this other man, Malik Taylor, had fought—physically fought—with Mr. Wallace just a couple of weeks before the shooting took place. He didn't mention that, despite the fact that Ms. Miller claimed to recognize my client, Lorenzo Tate, because she knew him from around the neighborhood, Ms. Miller failed to identify Mr. Tate when shown a photo array the day after the shooting. He didn't mention that Ms. Miller has herself been arrested for drugs since the night of the murder.

"The prosecution also told you that the victim who was killed,

Seth Lipton, was just an innocent bystander, a college student. But like just about everything he said, the truth is a little more complicated than what he told you. Seth Lipton was a college student, and he was studying drug dealing at the Gardens as his senior thesis in sociology, but that wasn't all he did down there. The truth is that Seth Lipton was in business with Devin Wallace. You will hear testimony regarding the fact that Seth Lipton himself dealt drugs on campus, drugs that Devin Wallace furnished him with."

There was a stir in the courtroom as Myra spoke. I resisted the urge to turn and look at Lipton's parents, who were seated directly behind the prosecutor's table.

"As will become clear to you over the coming days, perhaps any one of these facts would suffice to create a reasonable doubt of Lorenzo Tate's guilt in this case," Myra said in conclusion. "Taken together, they go much further than that. Thank you."

"SO, JOEL," Adam Berman said, sliding up to me as we filed out of the court for our lunch break. "You happy with my story?"

The sight of Berman made me feel awkward, even a little guilty. I forced myself to be civil, recognizing that he might continue to be useful, if not in this case then in future ones. I assumed the story had caused some shift in the public perception of Seth Lipton, transforming him from college student to drug dealer. But I hadn't been prepared for how grubby it'd made me feel. I saw ADA Williams watching us from down the hall. I stared back at her until she looked away. "Sure," I said to Berman. "You got pretty deep into it, I thought."

"That's what I do," Berman said. "I'm a dog with a bone when you give me a lead."

"I believe it," I said. "Anyway, I've got a lot of work to do."

"Listen," Berman said, leaning forward conspiratorially. "A lot of the reporters you're going to meet in this building, they just take what the prosecutors give them. The tabloids mostly just want to demonize a defendant. I try to get the full story across, which is why defense lawyers generally talk to me when they're going to talk to someone. I hope that's how you'll feel."

"I hear you," I said.

"Great," Berman said. "Anything I should know?"

"Not just now," I said.

"But if you're going to take something to the press, you'll bring it to me?"

"Who else?" I said with a smile.

·29·

THE PROSECUTION began their case slowly. Any criminal prosecution had to establish the elements of the crime in question, even when they weren't in dispute. So here they had to establish that Seth Lipton and Devin Wallace had in fact been shot, and that Lipton had been killed, even though such evidence shed no light on who had done the shooting. So the prosecution put on the off-duty emergency services worker who'd been on his way home when he'd heard the shots and had been the first person with any medical knowledge to arrive at the scene, as well as the medical examiner who had conducted the autopsy on Lipton, and a doctor who had treated Devin Wallace at the hospital. Myra and I took turns conducting cursory cross-examinations, but there wasn't anything here that we really took issue with.

It was late afternoon when the prosecution called their first important witness, Latrice Wallace. Latrice was dressed well, and looked as composed and attractive as she had when we'd interviewed her at her apartment.

ADA Williams took Latrice's direct testimony, establishing that she was Devin's sister and that she'd been home alone the evening of the shooting.

"Turning your attention to around seven p.m. that evening," Williams continued. "What, if anything, happened?"

"Somebody knock on our door," Latrice said, glancing over at Lorenzo as she said it. We'd talked to Lorenzo about the importance of his not showing emotion when hearing the evidence against him, and I was pleased to see how calmly he met Latrice's gaze.

"Did you recognize the person who was knocking?"

"It was Lorenzo Tate."

Williams took her time asking the next question. "And how were you able to recognize Mr. Tate?"

"He been over at our house, time to time."

"Do you see Lorenzo Tate in this courtroom today?"

Latrice dutifully pointed him out. These in-court IDs were an empty, offensive ritual. Identifications based on a lineup or photo array were one thing, but I hated that the prosecution could ask a witness to pick out the defendant in open court. Lorenzo sat at the defense table between two white lawyers in suits—how was anybody going to fail to identify him as the accused? We had dressed him up, putting him in a dark blazer and striped tie from the office's ragtag wardrobe of dress clothes that we kept for our clients' court appearances, but the clothes didn't look convincing on him: they looked more like a costume than an outfit.

"And what did you do after you recognized Lorenzo Tate as the person who was knocking on the door?"

"The door was on the chain. I opened it a little bit, but I didn't take the chain off."

"If you knew Lorenzo Tate, why didn't you just open the door all the way?"

"I know he gonna be looking for my brother, not me."

"What, if anything, did the defendant say to you once you'd opened the door a little?"

"He asked if Devin be home," Latrice said. "I told him I ain't seen him."

"And then what did the defendant say?"

"He ask if Devin left some money for him."

"And what did you say to that?"

"I said I didn't know nothin' about no money."

"And what, if anything, did the defendant say to that?"

Myra was quickly back on her feet. "Objection. Hearsay."

"Statement against penal interest, Your Honor," Williams replied.

"Overruled," Ferano said.

"He say that Devin don't know who he's fucking with, but he's going to get his," Latrice said, again glancing quickly over at Lorenzo.

"And then what happened?"

"Then he was out."

"Thank you, Ms. Wallace," Williams said, returning to her seat.

By the time the direct was finished it was just a few minutes before five. We didn't bother to protest when Ferano declared that we were finished for the day, as we knew it was no use. Myra was doing the cross on Latrice, and at least this way we'd have the night to look for any weaknesses in her direct testimony.

"SO WHERE are we so far?" I asked Myra. We'd walked over to Dumbo to review the day and preview tomorrow over a quick dinner. We were at Superfine, a couple of blocks from the East River, just steps out from under the Manhattan Bridge. The bar fit the neighborhood: stylish but quiet, underpopulated and well designed. It was just a block or two from Paul's apartment, but I did my best to push that last visit to Dumbo out of my mind.

"They haven't hit us too hard yet," Myra said. "But they haven't brought out their big guns yet, either."

"How about Latrice's testimony?" I said. "Think we survived that okay?"

"I do," Myra said.

"Lorenzo was talking to me about how he wants to testify, explain away his visit to the apartment that night, what he said to Latrice."

Myra's laugh carried little trace of amusement. "That's not going to happen," she said. "Not if we're earning our fees, anyway."

"Earning our fees?"

"It's an expression I understand real lawyers use," Myra said. "Lorenzo's one of those people thinks he can charm a jury all the way to an acquittal. It never happens. A defendant gets up on the witness stand, no jury ever sees the nice guy. They see a guy who's been called a killer."

"But it's Lorenzo's right to testify, isn't it?" I said. "I mean, if he wants to, don't we have to let him?"

"Technically," Myra said. "Which just means it's our job to make sure he doesn't want to. One of the victims owed our guy money for drugs? Please. Lorenzo wanders off the trail in his direct, he opens the door for this to come in. No way can we let him get crossed on that. It'd be game-over."

"So how do we explain that to Lorenzo?" I said.

"Pretty much like that," Myra said. "Sugarcoating things isn't going to help us with him."

I smiled.

"What?" Myra said, tilting her head quizzically.

"Nothing."

"What?" she repeated.

"I just . . . I was just thinking that I like watching you work."

"Oh, no," Myra said in mock horror. "No compliments."

"Hey," I said. "That was an entirely professional compliment."

"As compared to what?"

"I mean, it's not like I said something about how I like your perfume."

"Did you actually notice my perfume?" she said.

"Sure," I said. "I mean, I was sitting near you in court all day."

"That's what you were doing in court all day?" Myra said. "Smelling me? No wonder you're still on the market."

· 30 ·

Did your brother have a cell phone or pager?" Myra asked Latrice Wallace to begin her cross-examination the next morning, the question having its intended effect of catching the witness off guard. Myra was standing behind our table, barely having moved out of her chair before asking the question.

"He got a cell," Latrice said.

"So after Mr. Tate allegedly said this supposed threat about Mr.

Wallace to you, you must have called your brother right away to warn him, right?"

"No," Latrice said. "I didn't call him."

"You didn't?" Myra said, feigning surprise as she walked slowly over to the podium. "That was because you weren't actually worried that Lorenzo Tate posed a threat to your brother, were you?"

"Not just then I wasn't, no. Now—"

"Thank you," Myra interrupted. "Did you call the police after Mr. Tate's visit that night?"

"No."

"I see. Ms. Wallace, do you recall testifying before a grand jury regarding the same events you've just testified about here?"

"I got up at that thing before this."

"And at the grand jury, you testified about when Mr. Tate came to your door looking for your brother that night, didn't you?" Myra asked.

"That's right."

"And what you then claimed Mr. Tate said that night was: 'Oh, shit, he think I'm fucking with him'?"

"If that's what it say."

"That's what it says because that's what *you* said, right?"

"I went to that other jury and told the truth, same as I'm telling it now."

"But that statement is pretty different from what you just told this jury, isn't it?"

"No."

"No?" Myra said, appearing genuinely surprised by the answer. I doubted the jury could tell the difference between when she was pretending to be surprised and when she actually was, but I was pretty sure I could. Even I wasn't entirely sure: Myra was a pretty good actress. "You don't think 'Oh, shit, he think I'm fucking with him' is pretty different from 'He don't know who he's fucking with, but he's going to get his'?"

"No."

"Isn't it true that the second one sounds like a threat but the first one doesn't?"

"Don't know about that."

"To you, those two comments, they mean the exact same thing?" Myra pressed, wanting to make sure this got through to the jury.

"Asked and answered," O'Bannon said by way of objection.

"Sustained," Judge Ferano said. "You've made your point, Counsel," he said to Myra.

"I suppose I have, Your Honor," Myra said. "Now, you gave a physical description of Lorenzo Tate to the police, correct?"

"Yes."

"And in the description you described what Mr. Tate was wearing that night, right?"

"I can't remember everything I say."

"According to the police report, you said that Mr. Tate was wearing a bright-colored T-shirt, blue jeans, and a Yankees baseball cap; do you remember that?"

"If that's what it say."

"Ms. Wallace, do you know Yolanda Miller?"

"We know each other some."

"How do you know her?"

"We both come up in the Gardens. And she used to come 'round to see my brother."

"Ms. Miller used to come to your apartment to see Devin Wallace?"

"Sure."

"Are you aware of the fact that Ms. Miller used illegal drugs?"

"Objection," O'Bannon said.

"I'll allow it," Judge Ferano said. "The witness can answer if she has actual knowledge."

"I know she get high," Latrice said.

"You've seen her get high?"

"I see her when she be high."

"How many times have you seen Ms. Miller under the influence of drugs?"

"Objection," O'Bannon said. "The witness is not an expert in recognizing drug impairment."

"The witness grew up in our city's projects," Myra shot back. In addition to being comfortable as a performer, Myra also had the most important tool for any trial lawyer: she was quick on her feet.

"Objection overruled," Ferano said.

Latrice shrugged. "Few times maybe. Ain't like she high every time I seen her."

"When was the first time you ever saw Ms. Miller under the influence of drugs?"

"Didn't write down no date."

"Was it before the night your brother was shot?"

"Before then, uh-huh. I remember her coming over to our place all messed up."

"Thank you, Ms. Wallace," Myra said, turning quickly and taking her seat.

ADA O'Bannon did a brief redirect, focusing on the fact that Latrice was absolutely certain that it was Lorenzo Tate who'd come looking for her brother that night, and that he'd said words she now took to be threatening to her brother. After that the prosecution was ready to bring out its next witness.

"The People call Lester Bailey," ADA O'Bannon said.

This was our first look at the jailhouse snitch who claimed that Lorenzo had confessed to him. Unsurprisingly, Lester Bailey had refused to speak with me when I'd tried to visit him at Rikers. He was a wiry black man, with cornrows and a dead-eyed glare. You could take the gangster out of jail, I thought as I watched him approach the stand, but you couldn't take jail out of the gangster. Although they'd dressed him in a jacket and tie, to my eyes a prison jumpsuit hung over Lester's spindly frame like an aura. I hoped a jury would take one look at Lester Bailey and decide there was no reason to believe a word he said.

"Mr. Bailey, where do you currently reside?" O'Bannon asked.

"You mean, like, where I live at?"

"Yes."

"I don't know that I'd say I live there, truth to tell, but at the moment I'm at Rikers Island."

"Why are you at Rikers?" O'Bannon asked.

"They got me up on a B and E," Lester said. "They be sayin' I was someplace I got no right to be."

"You got arrested for breaking and entering?" O'Bannon acting as much translator as questioner.

"That's right."

"And those charges are still pending?"

"I got that over me," Lester agreed.

"Mr. Bailey, do you know Lorenzo Tate, the defendant in this case?"

"Sure I do," Lester said.

"Do you see Lorenzo Tate in this courtroom?"

"Can't help but see him," Bailey said. "He's sittin' right over there in the hot seat."

"Where do you know Lorenzo Tate from?"

"I know him from Rikers," Lester said. "We was in the same cell back in the day."

"Did you have occasion to talk to Lorenzo Tate?" O'Bannon asked.

"We used to talk all the time," Lester said. "We was friendly."

"Mr. Bailey, did there come a time when the defendant talked to you about the crimes he was accused of committing?" O'Bannon asked.

"What happened was this," Lester said, leaning forward slightly, appearing eager to tell his story. "I could always tell something was weighing on him. He was always talkin' about how he wasn't a bad person. And one time I was like, 'All right, then, you so good, how come you're stuck up in here?'"

"Did the defendant answer when you asked him that?"

"He got real quiet. And he wouldn't look at me or nothing. I was checking him, just to see what was up, and I see he be crying. Wasn't like he sobbing or nothing, wasn't making no noise, just that he got these tears on his face, you know. And he said that he was there 'cause he shot a man dead."

"Did he say who he shot?"

"He told me how he was trying to cap this dude he be beefing with, but that he ended up hitting this other dude too. He say the guy who got hisself killed wasn't nobody he even knew, how he just hit him by mistake. That's what he was bugging out about."

"How is it you came to testify here today?"

"Well, see, I started thinking about how I knew about a killing now. I didn't want to end up no accessory after the event or nothing like that. So what I did was, I thought I should say something to my lawyer, see what he thought I should do. I mean, that's what you all are there for, right?"

"And what happened after you consulted with your attorney?"

Lester shrugged. "He made *arrangements*, you know, whatever it is you lawyers do when you do what you do, and that's how come I'm here today."

"Why are you willing to testify against the defendant?"

"It's nothing I got any joy for, you know?" Lester said, looking over at Lorenzo, doing his best to look apologetic. "But it ain't like I'm up here speaking on this 'cause of some little thing he done. I'm not no saint, but you can't just be killing people—"

"Objection," Myra said loudly, not having to stage her anger. I knew how she felt: I felt ready to hit Lester Bailey over the head with a two-by-four. "Approach, Your Honor?"

"There's no need for that," Judge Ferano said. "I'll sustain your objection."

"There is too a need," Myra barked back as I rose beside her, placing a cautionary hand on Myra's arm.

"I'll instruct the jury to disregard."

"That doesn't unring the bell, Your Honor," Myra said. "Only a mistrial would."

Now it was Ferano's turn to be angry. He waved the lawyers up to a sidebar, glaring daggers at Myra as we approached.

"What kind of asinine stunt are you trying to pull, asking for a mistrial in open court?" Judge Ferano fairly hissed at Myra.

"The record will reflect that I sought a sidebar and was denied. I need to make my record, whether you plan on giving me the opportunity or not."

"You're one irritation away from contempt, Counsel," Ferano said. "I don't like stunts in my courtroom."

"And I don't like it when the prosecution puts on a witness who's trying to do the jury's job for them. I move that all of his testimony be stricken."

O'Bannon started to speak, but Judge Ferano waved him silent. "I've had enough of this. I'll strike the inappropriate testimony, but we're not even close to a legitimate grounds for a mistrial. You can continue your examination, Mr. O'Bannon."

We retreated from the bench, O'Bannon positioning himself again behind the podium.

"So was it the nature of the defendant's crime that prompted you to be willing to testify against him here today?"

"You mean I'm here on account of he capped somebody?" Lester said. "True that."

"You're also hoping your cooperation here will help you in your own case, aren't you?"

"My lawyer say it ain't gonna hurt," Lester said.

"You realize any favorable treatment you might receive would be conditioned on your telling the truth in this courtroom?"

"Nobody's ever told me to say nothing except the truth up in this chair," Lester said. "That's what I've done."

"Thank you, Mr. Bailey," O'Bannon said, and then the floor belonged to Myra.

Myra stayed in her seat even after O'Bannon had returned to his. After a long moment she began clapping. She managed to get four claps in (certainly enough, I thought, to make her point) before O'Bannon stood to object. "Your Honor—" O'Bannon began, before Ferano interrupted.

"That's quite enough with the theatrics, Counsel," Judge Ferano admonished Myra. "Or should I take that to mean you have no questions for this witness?"

"On the contrary, Your Honor," Myra replied, standing quickly and striding to the podium. She had the added energy and focus that anger gave her. "I'm now very confused, and am hoping this witness can straighten me out."

"Your Honor—" O'Bannon interjected, but the judge waved him off.

"I don't want to hear anything from you but questions," Judge Ferano said to Myra. "Starting now."

"Mr. Bailey, why don't we start with the first thing that confuses me. You said before that you became friends with my client out at Rikers, is that correct?"

"It was like that, yeah."

"And yet here you are, ratting him out."

"Objection," O'Bannon said, getting quickly back to his feet.

"I'll be happy to rephrase," Myra said quickly. "And yet here you are, offering testimony that may put him in jail for the rest of his life. Tell me, Mr. Bailey, how do you treat your *enemies*?"

"Objection."

"Sustained."

"Would it be fair to say that you are no longer acting as Mr. Tate's friend?"

"I ain't doing nothing but telling the truth."

"We'll get to that," Myra said, her arms crossed in front of her, everything in her trying to convey her skepticism. "This isn't your first visit to Rikers, is it?"

"I ain't never denied that."

"You've been there, what, two previous times?"

"Something like that."

"Actually, you've been there three different times, haven't you?"

"You say so, I won't say you're wrong."

"So when you said 'Something like that' when I asked you if it was two times, what you meant was 'No, more'?" Myra said, her sarcasm so strong I worried that for once she wasn't fully in control of it. I realized I was clenching my fists under the table; while I usually enjoyed watching Myra perform, now I was too invested in the case and, perhaps, in her, to have the necessary distance to enjoy it.

"I ain't sitting up here counting."

"You've got two pleas and one guilty verdict on your jacket, isn't that right?"

"Only one of those was for anything approaching serious."

"In the world according to Lester Bailey, breaking and entering and robbery are trivial, and armed robbery is only approaching serious?"

"Wasn't even a real biscuit on that," Lester protested.

"You've done six months at Rikers one time, a year another, then four years at Green Haven, isn't that right?"

"What you need me for if you know everything?"

"Is that right, Mr. Bailey?"

"That's the time I've done, yeah," Lester said.

"So you're what we could call a repeat customer at this, right?"

"Ain't like I'm no customer," Lester said. "But I been there."

"You know how the game is played, don't you?"

"Ain't none of this a game to me," Lester said. "You go sit out on Rikers, see if you still be talking about a game."

"You're aware that people at Rikers often claim that another inmate has confessed to them, come testify at trial like you're doing here, and get a better deal for themselves as a result, right?"

"Objection," O'Bannon said.

"I'll allow it."

"I know it helps you to help them," Lester said. "Everybody know that."

"And that's why you pretended to befriend Lorenzo Tate, isn't it?"

"I didn't pretend nothing."

"You were planning all along to snitch him out, weren't you? Regardless of whether or not he ever told you anything incriminating."

"That's all coming up out of your own head."

"Mr. Bailey, you are a three-time loser, a career criminal facing time on yet another crime. Why should anyone in this courtroom believe anything you say?"

"I ain't going to deny I been in trouble," Lester said. "But that ain't got nothing to do with this. I'm just here to tell the truth."

"You and the truth have never even *met*, Mr. Bailey," Myra said, and as she said it I relaxed: while I was sure her anger was genuine, I was also sure she had it under her control, that she'd been using it to set up this moment. "Allow me to introduce you. The truth is, everything you've said here has been a lie, a self-serving lie, and worse than that, a betrayal of a man who's never done you any harm."

"Objection," O'Bannon said.

"Withdrawn," Myra said. "I think I've heard enough from Mr. Bailey."

· 31 ·

"THE PEOPLE call Yolanda Miller," ADA O'Bannon said, bringing on the prosecution's star witness.

Even dressed for court Yolanda looked a good deal worse for wear than the first time I'd seen her in the spring. She'd gone from thin to skinny, sharp-angled, and jumpy. As Yolanda took the stand I noticed Devin Wallace in the spectator seats of the courtroom, but Yolanda did not even glance at him as she stepped through the well of the court. I leaned over to Myra and pointed Devin out. He was not on the prosecution's witness list, presumably because he was still not cooperating with them.

"Before we get to the events of April 6, Ms. Miller," O'Bannon began, "we have to talk about some more recent things. Have you ever been arrested?"

"That's right."

"How many times have you been arrested?"

"Three," Yolanda said flatly, no trace of embarrassment at having to talk about this in public. Her third and most recent arrest had been only a couple of weeks earlier; the DA's office had sent us the police report shortly before jury selection.

"All in the past year?"

"Yes."

"What have you been arrested for?"

"Two times for copping, one time for fighting."

"And what were you fighting about?"

"We was fighting over drugs."

"Ms. Miller, have you become addicted to drugs?"

"I got a need now, yeah," Yolanda said quietly, looking down at her hands, which were clasped together in her lap.

"And was that the case on April 6?"

"No. This all happen after that."

"You started doing drugs after April?"

"I started with the rock after that."

"And was that a coincidence?"

"How you mean?"

"What I mean is, did you start doing drugs because of what happened on April 6?"

"Objection," Myra said. "Speculation."

"Sustained," Judge Ferano said.

"Have you been offered anything in exchange for your testimony today in relation to the charges that are pending against you?" O'Bannon asked.

"I was offered what?"

"I'm sorry for being unclear. Put more simply, have you made a deal with my office concerning your testifying here today? Are you getting anything as far as your own criminal charges go?"

"Nothin' like that, no," Yolanda said.

O'Bannon then shifted gears, asking Yolanda about the night of the shooting. He led her through her going out to the deli, spotting Devin across the courtyard, and then seeing Wallace and Lipton getting shot as she started to approach them.

"What happened after you saw and heard Mr. Wallace and Mr. Lipton get shot?"

"I was looking around, you know, trying to find out what was going on," Yolanda said. "That's when I see Strawberry running toward me."

"When you say you saw Strawberry, do you know that person's actual name?"

"Lorenzo Tate."

"What, if anything, was the defendant carrying when he ran past you?"

"He got a gun."

"How did you recognize Lorenzo Tate?" O'Bannon asked.

"I seen him around the Gardens," Yolanda said. "I seen him with Devin too."

Myra tensed beside me, pushing her chair back from the table, preparing to jump to her feet at the first indication that Yolanda was going to make a connection between Lorenzo and Devin's drug dealing. The judge caught her movement, then looked sternly over at

O'Bannon. Because of the judge's *Molineux* ruling, any mention by Yolanda of Lorenzo being a drug dealer and we would potentially have a mistrial on our hands.

"You'd seen the defendant with Mr. Wallace?" O'Bannon said neutrally, obviously realizing the line he was approaching.

"Sure, I'd seen them," Yolanda said.

"How many times had you seen the defendant before the night of the shooting?"

Yolanda shrugged. "Maybe five."

"Did there come a time when the police had you look at a photo array in this case?"

"The lady detective brought me some pictures to look at."

"What happened when the detective showed you these pictures?"

"I told them I didn't want to pick Strawberry out by no pictures," Yolanda said. "I told them I know him better in person."

"Did they then arrange an in-person lineup for you?"

"Once they got him, yeah," Yolanda said. "Then they set that up."

"What happened at that lineup?"

"I pointed out Strawberry."

"How long did it take you to point him out?"

"Didn't take me no time," Yolanda said.

"When you say it didn't take you any time, was it a few seconds, a few minutes . . . ?"

"Five seconds, maybe. Wasn't no longer than that."

"There's no doubt that Lorenzo Tate is who you saw run past you with a gun in his hand after Mr. Lipton and Mr. Wallace were shot?" O'Bannon continued.

"I seen him," Yolanda replied.

"Thank you, Ms. Miller," O'Bannon said. "Nothing further."

"Good afternoon, Ms. Miller," Myra said to begin her cross, Yolanda just nodding in reply, her arms folded across her chest, her whole demeanor going hostile.

"I just need to clarify some of your earlier answers," Myra said. "You said you have three pending criminal charges against you, is that correct?"

"I already say that."

"And those are all for drug-related crimes, right?"

"One was 'cause I was beatin' on this girl," Yolanda said. "But that was on account of drugs too."

"And all of these charges are from after the night of April 6, is that right?"

"That's right."

"And did I understand you correctly earlier; was it your testimony that you didn't use drugs before that night?"

"This is all after Devin got capped."

"It's your testimony that you didn't use illegal drugs prior to April 6?" Myra tried again.

"Ain't that what I said?"

"You tell me," Myra replied evenly. Unlike with a witness like Lester Bailey, where she'd been extremely aggressive from the start, with Yolanda on the stand Myra was keeping her voice even, her tone polite, even when she asked a tough question. It was Yolanda's own hostility that we wanted to let take center stage.

"Like I already say, this all start after that."

"So would it surprise you to learn that Latrice Wallace has already testified that she saw you under the influence of illegal drugs prior to April 6?"

"I ain't got no idea why she'd say that," Yolanda said.

"Is it your testimony that Ms. Wallace was lying when she said that?"

"You got to ask her why she say what she say."

"I'm asking you," Myra replied. "If she said she saw you high on drugs before that, would she be lying?"

"I ain't going to call her a liar," Yolanda said. "But what she say ain't true neither."

"Fair enough," Myra said, smiling slightly. She'd gotten us what we wanted, established an area of disagreement between Latrice's and Yolanda's testimonies. "So you're awaiting trial on all three of these charges, right?"

"That's right."

"And the same office that has called you as a witness today will be prosecuting you on those charges, correct?"

"I guess so."

"You guess so?" Myra shot back. "Isn't that true?"

"They got different lawyers handling my cases."

"Do you just mean that there are different assistant district attorneys prosecuting your cases than the prosecutors who are having you testify in this case?"

"True that."

"But they all work in the same office, right?"

"How I supposed to know where they all work at?"

"Would it surprise you to learn that they all worked in the same office?" Myra asked, making a show of patience.

"Wouldn't surprise me, no."

"You've got a lawyer in those cases, right?"

"I don't got me a real lawyer," Yolanda said. "Just somebody like you that ain't getting paid."

"You hope that testifying today will help you with your own legal troubles, don't you?"

"I'm just saying what I know."

"That isn't what I asked you, Ms. Miller. Do you need me to repeat my question?"

"If you asking me do I want to go to jail, the answer is I don't."

"And you're hoping that testifying here today might help you stay out of jail, right?"

"They ask me to come and say what I saw, so that's what I be doing."

"Thank you," Myra said, trying to indicate to the jury just how hard it was to get Yolanda to admit the obvious. "Tell me, Ms. Miller, about how long had you been outside when the shooting started?"

"Just a few seconds is all."

"And you were looking over at Devin Wallace once you got out there, right?"

"I seen him, yeah."

"You didn't see the shooter until the shooting started, right?"

"I wasn't looking that way."

"So the first time you saw the shooter was when he ran past you with his gun out after he'd just shot your boyfriend in the back, right?"

"I seen him when he run by, yeah."

"Now, when the police questioned you on the night of the shooting you described the clothes the shooter was wearing as black pants, black shirt, and a white doo-rag, with a birthmark above his left eye; do you recall that?"

"If that what it say."

"It was pretty late when this happened, isn't that right?"

"It was nighttime."

"It was dark, right?"

"Sure, it was dark."

"And in the dark, late at night, after just seeing your boyfriend get shot, a man dressed all in black, with a doo-rag on his head as well, ran past you while holding a gun. Those were the circumstances under which you saw the shooter in this case, right?"

"He go running right past me."

"I understand that. You're not disagreeing with what I just said, are you?"

"I seen him."

"And you're sure that's what the shooter was wearing? Black pants, black shirt, and a white doo-rag?"

"He run right past me," Yolanda said. "I seen him right there."

"And that's how he was dressed?"

"That's right."

"Now, Ms. Miller, you're aware that Latrice Wallace had a conversation with Mr. Tate a few hours before the shooting, right?"

"Uh-huh."

"Would it surprise you to learn that Ms. Wallace described the clothes Mr. Tate wore that night as a bright-colored T-shirt, blue jeans, and a baseball cap?"

"Don't know why I'm supposed to be surprised."

"It doesn't surprise you that Ms. Wallace described Mr. Tate as wearing a completely different outfit that night?"

"I don't know nothin' about that."

"But you're sure that the man you saw was not wearing a bright shirt, blue jeans, and a baseball cap, right?"

"I already say what he be wearing."

"And you can't explain this discrepancy?"

"I can't do what?"

"Never mind," Myra said, not needing an answer to make her

point. She took a couple of steps so that she was standing directly between Yolanda and Lorenzo. "When this man ran past you, did you see his left side or his right side?"

"He ran past like this," Yolanda said, sliding her right arm leftward.

"So his left side would've been facing you, right?"

"His left, yeah."

"Did you see the birthmark on Mr. Tate's face when he ran past you?" Myra said.

"I can't remember that now."

"Because in your description, you said that Mr. Tate's birthmark was on his left side, the side you saw. You told the police that to indicate that you'd seen his birthmark, right? Because that was part of how you recognized him that night?"

"I saw him," Yolanda said.

Myra stepped away, gesturing back to Lorenzo. "Please look at my client, Ms. Miller, and tell me, on which side of his face does his birthmark appear?"

"It be on the other side."

"By the other side you mean the right side?"

"That's right."

"Thank you," Myra said. This was little more than razzle-dazzle, not substantive evidence, but razzle-dazzle was an important weapon in the defense lawyer's arsenal. Yolanda's lip was now curled as she glared at Myra; she looked defensive and angry, and was clearly getting flustered.

"Now, Ms. Miller, you were in an intimate relationship with Mr. Wallace, is that correct?"

"We were together," Yolanda agreed. "But it wasn't nothing too serious."

"How long had you been involved with Mr. Wallace?"

"Couple of months before the shootin'."

"You are the mother of a child, correct, Ms. Miller?"

"I got a little boy," Yolanda said.

"How old is your son?"

"Jamal's about to be two."

"Who is Jamal's father, Ms. Miller?"

"His name's Malik."

"Malik Taylor?"

"That's right."

"Were you and Malik Taylor ever married?"

"No," Yolanda said, giving Myra a little glare, some challenge in it too.

"Did you continue to see each other after you had your baby?"

"Even though Malik and me weren't together no more, he said it was important that he still see his boy," Yolanda said. "Malik would take Jamal some weekends. He buys him things—clothes, toys."

"Has Malik ever been in any trouble with the law?"

"Malik? The man work one job all week and then another one on the weekend. He ain't never been in trouble a day in his life."

"How about Devin Wallace? What does he do for a living?"

"You already know," Yolanda said, looking right at Myra, lifting her chin a little.

"Please answer the question."

"Devin be in the life."

"I think we all like to think of ourselves as in life," Myra countered. "Can you perhaps be a little more clear?"

Yolanda was staring at Myra skeptically, no doubt wondering if she was being toyed with. "The life mean the trade," she said. "Devin's a dealer."

"So he was a criminal, wasn't he?"

"I don't begin to know who's a criminal and who ain't," Yolanda said. "That's for you people to figure out."

"But you do know dealing drugs is illegal, don't you?"

"Course I do."

"So you do, in fact, know that Devin was a criminal, don't you?"

"I know what he do."

"How did Malik Taylor feel about his little boy being around a dealer like Devin?"

"Approach, Your Honor?" ADA O'Bannon asked, standing. Judge Ferano gestured us up for a sidebar. We all walked over to the far end of the bench from the jury. "This has gone completely outside the scope of the direct, Your Honor," O'Bannon said. "I fail to see any possible relevance to these questions."

"What I'm trying to explore, Your Honor, is the possibility that these shootings had nothing to do with my client, but arose instead out of an escalating dispute between two men who'd both been involved with Yolanda Miller," Myra responded. "If true, this would strongly suggest that Ms. Miller's identification of Mr. Tate is not a mistake, but rather a deliberate lie. Because the state's whole case essentially rests on Ms. Miller's identification, we're entitled to challenge her veracity, and to make it clear that she might have a reason to be making up her story."

Judge Ferano held up his hand to indicate that he didn't want to hear any more. When he spoke it was directed to O'Bannon. "I'm not going to create an appealable issue by limiting the defense's cross of your main witness," the judge said, before turning his attention to Myra. "I'll allow you some latitude. But don't get carried away."

The lawyers retreated to our respective corners, Myra returning to her cross. "The question, Ms. Miller, was how did Mr. Taylor feel about his little boy being raised around a drug dealer like Mr. Wallace?" Myra said.

"He didn't like it," Yolanda said softly. "We both wanted Jamal to be raised up right."

"And how do you know that Malik didn't like it?" Myra asked.

"Because Malik told me so. He told me we had to make sure Jamal came up okay."

"And Mr. Taylor was worried that Jamal wasn't going to be raised right if you were involved with Mr. Wallace?"

"He didn't like that Devin did what he do."

"Mr. Taylor and Mr. Wallace had an actual fight, didn't they?"

"One time they started shoving at each other some is all."

"They had a fight in your apartment, right?" Myra asked.

"They got into it a little there."

"And did you tell the police about this fight?"

"They ain't never asked me about nothing like that."

"You didn't want them to know about it, did you?" Myra pressed.

"It don't got nothing to do with nothing else that was going on."

"Sounds pretty clear that Mr. Wallace and Mr. Taylor didn't like each other very much, did they?" Myra said.

"Devin didn't like Malik coming 'round to see Jamal. He didn't want nobody I used to be with at my crib, 'specially when he wasn't there."

"Is that what they fought about?"

"That's right."

"Devin was jealous of Malik?"

"I don't know about being jealous," Yolanda said. "He just thought it was a lack of respect. He thought people would be talkin'."

"So Devin didn't want Malik coming to see his own son?"

"That's what he say."

"And yet it was important to Mr. Taylor to see his son, wasn't it?" Myra said.

"Far as I know."

"Sounds like they had a problem."

Yolanda didn't respond, but it didn't matter: Myra had gotten her point across. "You're still close to Mr. Taylor, aren't you?" Myra continued.

"We're all right."

"He's the father of your child. You're more than just all right, aren't you?"

"We ain't together no more."

"But you've been with Mr. Taylor since the night of the shooting, haven't you?"

"I see him from time to time 'cause of our boy," Yolanda said, either missing Myra's suggestion or deliberately ignoring it. Judging by her lack of reaction, I guessed she'd missed it.

"That's not what I was asking, Ms. Miller," Myra said. "Isn't it true that you've been with Malik Taylor sexually since Devin Wallace was shot?"

I could feel a stir in the courtroom behind me, the murmur of indistinct voices. The question had caught everybody's attention. From her perch in the witness stand Yolanda was glaring daggers at Myra.

"Objection," O'Bannon said, coming quickly to his feet.

"Sustained," Judge Ferano said.

I could see Myra making an effort to move past her disappointment. We'd known there was a fair chance that we wouldn't be able to get this in, even while we viewed it as compelling evidence to create a shroud of doubt in the minds of the jury by focusing them on Malik Taylor's motive for shooting Devin Wallace. But the objection might have helped us: we had no idea what answer Yolanda would've given, and a forceful denial from her would've neutralized the question. The lack of any answer left it hanging there, something that could bother the jury.

"You wouldn't want to see Malik Taylor go to jail for the rest of his life, would you?"

"What're you saying?" Yolanda asked. She was still visibly seething.

"The question is simple: you wouldn't want Malik to go to jail for the rest of his life, right?"

"Why would Malik be going to jail?" Yolanda asked.

"You want him to be there for your son, don't you?"

"Course I want that."

"Indeed," Myra said. "Why wouldn't you lie to protect him if he was in trouble? Especially if he was in trouble just because he was trying to stay close to your son."

"Was there a question there?" O'Bannon objected.

"Withdrawn," Myra said. "Nothing further."

Myra sat down, and as she did so O'Bannon stood. "The People rest, Your Honor," he said.

"We'll call it a day, then," Judge Ferano said. "The defense can start its case tomorrow morning."

AFTER LEAVING the courtroom for the day, Myra and I met with Lorenzo in a holding cell in the basement of the courthouse. Lorenzo was pacing, agitated. "How you gonna let that bitch get up there and lie like that?" he said. "She didn't see me do a goddamn thing that night; no way she saw me try and cap Devin."

"I understand that," Myra said.

"But you didn't get her to say that she was just goofin' when she say she saw me."

"I'm a lawyer," Myra said, "not a hypnotist. There's only so much I can get accomplished through crossing Yolanda. We're going to be calling Malik Taylor, and we can use him to explain why Yolanda would lie."

"What if the jury goes with what she say about seeing me?"

"Then we have a problem, Lorenzo," Myra said. "I thought we knew that. The state is prosecuting this case because they think they are going to win it."

"How about you?" Lorenzo asked. "You think you're going to win?"

"I never make promises about winning," Myra said. "But this is the moment where their momentum is at its strongest and ours is at its weakest. We always knew that Yolanda was going to be their star witness. This is their time to run the show, so that's how it generally works. Our turn will come soon enough."

"I can get up there my own self, tell them people that Yo-Yo's a straight-up liar."

"We can talk about whether or not to put you on when the time comes," Myra said. "Usually the cross of a defendant proves far more devastating than their direct proves helpful."

"How's it gonna play like that when I ain't done nothin' wrong?" Lorenzo said.

"I don't know," Myra said. "But it does."

· 32 ·

WE CALLED Amin Saberi as our first witness for the defense. Amin, dressed in a white shirt and blue tie, stumbled as he made his way through the well of the court. While virtually all witnesses were nervous, it was obvious that Amin was terrified.

I'd been in the office past eleven o'clock the night before getting ready, then gone home and drunk beer in front of the television for an hour, too worked up to sleep. To my surprise, though, I'd slept quickly and easily once I finally went to bed. The fear I'd expected never fully materialized. I took this as a good sign.

"Did you know Seth Lipton?" I began.

"Yes."

"How did you know him?"

"He was my roommate," Amin said.

"Did you go to school with him?"

"Yes."

"Where?"

"Brooklyn College."

"Were you friends?" I asked.

"Yes."

"Have you ever met Devin Wallace?"

"No," Amin said.

"Tell me, Mr. Saberi, were you surprised when you heard that your friend had been killed outside of a housing project that's well known for its drug activity?"

I asked the question bluntly, doing nothing to sugarcoat it. We'd subpoenaed Amin to come here today and were not expecting him to be cooperative; we'd received permission from Judge Ferano to treat Amin as a hostile witness, meaning we were allowed to ask him leading questions.

"Of course I was surprised," Amin said. "Seth was, like, twenty-one years old. I still can't believe that he's dead."

"But were you surprised that Mr. Lipton would be in an area like that, late at night?"

"I guess not."

"Why is that?" I asked.

"Seth would go down there sometimes."

"Down where?"

"To the projects."

"Why?"

"He was writing his senior thesis on the business of drug deal-ing," Amin said. "In sociology," he added.

"Was that the only reason?"

Amin looked around the room like he was searching for someone to come to his rescue.

"No," Amin said.

I had no choice but to drag it out of him. I told myself that this was necessary, however ugly it felt. "What was the other reason?"

Amin shifted in his seat, looking out into the well of the court-room; I guessed Amin was looking at Lipton's parents, who'd been present every day of the trial. "To get drugs," he finally answered, his voice hoarse.

"What kinds of drugs?"

"Coke and pot mostly. Sometimes heroin."

"And was this for his own use?"

"No."

"For whose use was it, then?"

"Other people," Amin said, giving off his first show of hostility.

"Was this something Mr. Lipton was doing as a favor?"

"No," Amin said, looking down and speaking so softly that Judge Ferano reminded him to keep his voice up.

"Was he selling them?"

The silence that followed was as complete as I could imagine in a room holding more than twenty people. As it lingered I began to wonder if Amin was simply not going to answer. "Yes," he finally said.

"Who was he selling drugs to?"

"To people from school. Seth would go buy a bunch of stuff from this guy; then he'd sell it to students for a lot more than he paid, because, you know, most kids at the college don't want to go get stuff on the street."

"Did you ever hear Mr. Lipton mention Devin Wallace?" I asked.

"I'd heard the name Devin, yeah."

"Was it your understanding that Mr. Lipton and Devin Wallace were in business together?"

Amin nodded.

"You have to answer verbally," I said.

Amin glowered up at me briefly, then looked back down at his lap. "Yeah," he said.

"So if Mr. Lipton was talking to Mr. Wallace on the street, it would be safe to assume that they were undertaking, or about to undertake, or had just undertaken a drug transaction?"

"Objection," said ADA O'Bannon. "Speculation."

"Sustained," Judge Ferano said. I didn't really care—the point was clear.

"To your knowledge," I continued, "did Mr. Lipton and Mr. Wallace socialize?"

"Not that I know of."

"Devin never stopped by your apartment for a beer or anything?"

"No."

"How much money would Mr. Lipton take with him when he went down to the Gardens to score?"

Amin winced slightly, as if answering these questions was causing him physical pain. "I don't know exactly," he said. "But from the amount of stuff he was moving, I'd guess it was kind of a lot."

"So assuming that Mr. Lipton and Mr. Wallace were about to complete a drug transaction at the time they were shot, Seth Lipton would've been about to hand Devin Wallace a substantial amount of money?"

"Objection," O'Bannon said. "Assumes facts not in evidence, calls for speculation."

"I'll withdraw it," I said. "So if someone was owed money by Devin Wallace, he would have been well advised to allow these two to complete their transaction, wouldn't he?"

"Your Honor—" O'Bannon began, still standing. But he was interrupted by Judge Ferano.

"That's quite enough, Counselor," Judge Ferano said sternly to me. No surprise there; Amin had no direct knowledge of what had taken place at the Gardens that night, and the purpose of my questions was not to get him to answer them but to get the jury to think about them. "Is there another line of questioning you wish to pursue with this witness?"

"No, Your Honor," I said, turning quickly on my heel and heading for my seat.

"Mr. Saberi, have you ever met the defendant in this case?" O'Bannon asked to begin his cross.

"I don't think so."

"And you've never met Devin Wallace?"

"I'd just heard Seth mention the name Devin, is all," Amin said. "I don't even know for sure if it's the same guy."

"So you don't have any idea what the relationship between Mr. Wallace and the defendant was, do you?"

"I don't have the first clue."

"Did you volunteer to come here today and testify for the defense?"

"They subpoenaed me."

"Do you have any knowledge as to why Mr. Lipton was killed, or who killed him?"

"No."

"Thank you, Mr. Saberi," O'Bannon said, returning to his seat.

■   ■   ■

MYRA AND I left the courtroom together when we broke for lunch after Amin's testimony. We were walking down the hallway leading to the elevator, debating between the diner on Clark and an Italian place on Montague, when Seth's mother came charging at us, her husband a few paces behind. They were dressed formally, the father in a dark suit and yarmulke, the mother in an ankle-length skirt.

"You must be so proud of yourself," Mrs. Lipton said once she was directly in my face. "Dragging my son's name through the mud like that, and him being dead. How dare you!"

In court I'd made a point of avoiding looking over at Lipton's family, although it was impossible not to be aware of their presence. "I can't talk to you, Mrs. Lipton," I said. "It's not appropriate."

"You son of a bitch," Seth Lipton's mother said, looking like she was ready to strike me.

"He didn't say anything that wasn't true," Myra said to Mrs. Lipton. "Now, please, we can't talk to you."

"So he deserved to be killed by that man?" Mrs. Lipton said, including Myra in her fury. "Is that what you're saying? What kind of Jew are you? I don't know how you can stand to look at yourselves in the morning. You don't care about the truth at all, do you? You're only doing this for the money."

Seth Lipton's father was standing behind his wife now, hands on her shoulders, trying gently to drag her away. Myra and I quickly resumed walking, leaving the Liptons behind.

We were both silent until we were out on the street. Once we were outside I turned to Myra. "For the money?" I said.

· 33 ·

M R. TAYLOR, we've heard testimony that you are the father
of Yolanda Miller's son," I said to begin my examination of
Malik Taylor when court resumed after lunch. I had glanced into the
spectator section of the court before getting started, making eye contact first with Adam Berman, then with Devin Wallace, who stared
back at me. Looking away from Wallace, I caught the eye of somebody slouched in the very back row of the courtroom, all the way in

the corner, nobody else within ten feet. I flinched as I recognized Shawne Flynt, who nodded at me, a mirthless smile on his face. The mere sight of Shawne caused my heart to start pounding. I'd been hoping that I'd seen the last of him, that whatever game he'd been playing with me was over. I couldn't imagine what had made him decide to show up in court.

Whatever he was doing here, I wasn't going to figure it out now. Instead I willed myself to focus on Malik Taylor to the exclusion of everyone else in the room.

"That's right," Malik said. "Jamal's my son."

I knew I had to be careful in questioning him. Although we were calling Malik as our witness, he, like Amin Saberi, was testifying under subpoena and would presumably be hostile. If he wasn't to begin with, Malik certainly would become so once he realized we were putting him forward as an alternative suspect.

"And even though you and Ms. Miller are no longer a couple, you've made an effort to stay in your son's life?"

"I try to be a father to my boy, best as I can."

"And what is your relationship with Ms. Miller like now?"

"We're not together no more, but we still awright. We both get how it's important to raise Jamal up right, and we try to be together on that."

"So how did you feel, then, when Ms. Miller began seeing Devin Wallace?"

"I ain't gonna say I liked it."

"And how did you feel about your son being around someone like Mr. Wallace?" I asked, keeping my voice neutral, not wanting to get confrontational with Malik until I absolutely had to.

"I didn't like that neither."

"In fact, you had a fight with Mr. Wallace about it, didn't you?"

"We had words, yeah. I pushed at him, he pushed me back, it went on like that some. It wasn't no real fight—nobody swung."

"These words you had, where did they take place?"

"At Yolanda's crib."

"And how did this exchange of words begin?"

"I was dropping Jamal off. Devin came by while I was still there. He started talkin' about how he didn't want me coming 'round like that. I tell him I'm just dropping off my boy. But Devin didn't want to hear that. He keep talking at me. I tell him I'm not gonna stop seeing my own son."

"What happened then?"

"We cursed at each other some. Ain't like neither of us was gonna back down. Then it was like I say, we shoved each other."

"So how did the situation end?"

"Yolanda started saying for me to go. She didn't want us fighting in there, especially in front of Jamal. I respected that, us being in her crib and all, so I was out."

"So Devin Wallace essentially told you that he didn't want you spending time with your own son anymore?"

"At least not so that I'd see Yolanda."

"How'd that make you feel?"

"What you want me to say?" Malik said.

"I want you to tell the truth," I replied with a smile. "Did Mr. Wallace make you angry?"

"Course he did," Malik said, letting his frustration show despite himself. "Who's gonna like having to put up with that kind of nonsense?"

"Did you know that Mr. Wallace was a drug dealer?"

"Everybody knew. Wasn't like he was trying to hide it."

"You wanted to be able to see your son without some drug dealer interfering?"

"That's right," Malik said.

"And how long before Mr. Wallace got shot did he and you have this confrontation?"

"Couple of weeks, maybe."

"Was it two weeks?"

"Something like that."

"Did you approve of Ms. Miller raising your child around someone like Mr. Wallace?" I asked.

"Course not. Would you?"

I ignored the question. "Did you worry about what effect it would have on your boy?"

"Sure I did."

"And did you still care about Ms. Miller too?"

"She's my boy's mama."

"Did it bother you that she would be with someone like Mr. Wallace?"

"It bothered me, sure," Malik said. "I didn't like Yolanda falling into that."

"And were you aware that Ms. Miller had started doing drugs herself?"

"I heard about when she got picked up," Malik said. "I tried to get her some help. I even went with her to some meetings, just to be sure she went."

"So you spent some time alone with Ms. Miller after she was with Mr. Wallace?"

"True that."

"In fact, you had sexual relations with Ms. Miller shortly after this crime, didn't you?" I asked, throwing it out there once again in the spirit of having nothing to lose, doing my best to seem casual, although I could hear a slight tremor in my voice as I spoke. I wanted to hammer home the point, not really expecting to get an answer but not really caring if I didn't.

"Objection," O'Bannon said loudly.

"I've already ruled before that this line of inquiry isn't relevant to this case," Judge Ferano said. "That's the last I expect to hear of it, Mr. Deveraux."

I nodded brusquely, not wanting to appear distracted by the judge's ruling. Malik was glaring at me; then his gaze shifted out into the spectator section of the courtroom. "Tell me, Mr. Taylor," I asked. "Did the police ever question you about Mr. Wallace's shooting?"

"No real police did," Malik said. "Just you and that lady lawyer, pretending to be five-oh."

I'd been prepared for Malik to bring up our questioning of him, but I wasn't prepared for his claiming that we'd actually pretended to be police. I tried not to look thrown off, but decided I needed to do some damage control. "You're referring to when my colleague and I spoke to you at your workplace?"

"You took me out of there and talked to me on the street."

"You thought we were the police?"

"Who else going to be rousting me out of where I work at?"

"Did we ever say we were police?"

"That's how you carried it."

"If we had been the police that day, then the police would've learned what we've all learned today: that you had a motive to shoot Devin Wallace, didn't you?" I said, abandoning any remaining pretense that I wasn't going after Malik. The best defense, after all.

"I didn't shoot him. I didn't shoot nobody."

"That wasn't what I asked you," I said. "Or should I take that to mean you're admitting that you did have a motive to shoot him?"

"Objection," O'Bannon said.

"I'll withdraw it," I said. I decided that I'd gotten what I could get, and turned and sat down.

Once again ADA O'Bannon was in the position of crossing a witness who presumably had no desire to hurt the state's case. "Mr. Taylor," O'Bannon began, his voice neutral, nothing to indicate that this was a cross-examination, "where were you the night Seth Lipton and Devin Wallace were shot?"

"I don't even remember what night that was."

"Mr. Taylor, did you shoot Seth Lipton and Devin Wallace?"

"I never shot nobody."

"Thank you."

O'Bannon strode back to his seat. Judge Ferano thanked Malik for his testimony and dismissed him. The judge then turned to us. "Does the defense have any more witnesses?"

Myra stood. "Approach, Your Honor?" she said.

Judge Ferano gestured us all up for a sidebar.

"Your Honor," Myra began once we were all assembled at the side of the bench. "We've yet to make a final determination as to whether Mr. Tate will testify. I would ask the court to adjourn for the day, and when we come back in the morning we will either put on Mr. Tate or we can go straight to closing arguments."

Judge Ferano turned to O'Bannon. "Any objections?"

"I suppose that's fine," O'Bannon said after a moment. "I'd assumed we'd do closings tomorrow."

"We'll leave it at that then," Judge Ferano said.

■　■　■

"IT'S SIMPLE," Myra said to Lorenzo once we were all down in the holding cell. I'd dawdled leaving the courtroom; by the time I did the room was empty, no sign of Shawne Flynt. "Right now that jury is thinking about Malik Taylor. They're wondering why the hell the police never talked to him, and thinking that this love triangle gone bad seems like a plausible explanation for what's happened here. We put you on, they get to ask about your relationship with Devin, and despite the judge's ruling they will still turn everybody's attention to drugs. It won't be hard for them to get the jury to connect the dots even without something explicit coming up. We want to end the case with everyone thinking about Malik."

"I feel you," Lorenzo said, smiling at Myra without looking remotely amused. "But you been playin' me on this. You waited to say it till after Malik got up there. I could have testified before, but now you saying it's too late."

"It was never a good idea for you to testify, Lorenzo," Myra said. "The cross would've been brutal, and the jury wouldn't have found your alibi convincing. Trust us."

Lorenzo furrowed his brow, staring hard at the wall as he thought it through.

"I liked what your boy did to Malik, yo," he finally said to Myra with a smile. "You all say for me not to talk, guess I'm not talkin'."

AS SOON as we stepped out of the building into one of the first brisk days of early fall I saw him, leaning against a lamppost across the street, the same vaguely amused look on his face that I'd seen in court. There didn't seem to be any point in avoiding him; obviously he could find me whenever he wanted to. Whatever it was that

Shawne Flynt wanted, I might as well find out. "Go ahead without me," I said to Myra, who looked puzzled, glancing over at Shawne.

"Who's that?" she asked.

"Former client," I said. "I'd better see if he's in a jam."

Myra nodded, apparently satisfied by my answer, and headed off back to the office while I crossed the street and walked over to Shawne Flynt. I hadn't actually spoken to Shawne since his case had been dismissed; I'd simply called the cell phone number he'd given me and left a message telling him the DA had dropped the charges.

"You looking for me, Shawne?" I asked once I was standing in front of him. We were maybe twenty feet from the entrance to the courthouse, a steady stream of people walking past us, a couple of cops doing guard duty just outside the court. It seemed like as safe a place as any to let Shawne make his play, whatever it was going to turn out to be.

"You had it going on in there, yo," Shawne said. "You were taking that boy down and shit. I could see how you used to be some kind of real lawyer. Almost made me wish they'd been able to make some charge stick on me, could've watched you go to war."

"I think you're better off the way things stand," I replied, looking up at Shawne. Somehow we'd ended up closer to each other than I wanted to be, which emphasized Shawne's height as he loomed over me.

"True that, true that. Never good to be jammed up on a charge, even if it's just some bullshit."

"Everything okay now? You in any kind of trouble?"

"Naw, man, everything's cool."

"Then why are you here, Shawne?" I said, trying to keep my voice neutral, not wanting to provoke him, but also not wanting to let him have even more control over the situation than he already did.

"I just never got no chance to pay you back for what you've done for me," Shawne said.

I didn't know how to interpret this. "You know you don't have to pay me," I said. "That's the point of having a public defender."

"Sure, but you used to be a real lawyer and all, you probably got paid mad cheddar to help people out back in the day. Me, I can get you what you need, know what I'm saying?"

"No, Shawne, I don't know what you're saying."

"Awright, yo," Shawne said. "You got my digits, you ever want to reach out." Shawne held out his hand, his thumb tucked oddly against the flesh of his palm. I reached out to shake it, and as I did he moved his thumb and something fell into my hand, as Shawne reached out with his other hand and gently closed mine into a soft fist. Then he turned and walked quickly away.

I knew what he'd done. It took me a moment before I opened my hand slightly, keeping it cupped to shield its contents from the view of passersby. But even before I saw the two small packets I already knew what was there.

Shawne Flynt had just paid me in heroin.

My first thought was that I was being set up. I flashed back to Shawne's behavior from the start of his case, his lack of concern, his knowledge of my past. Could the whole thing be a sting, Shawne working off a collar by taking me down? If so, the fact that I hadn't asked for it wouldn't necessarily matter; it'd be my word against Shawne's, with me having to explain why I was standing on a city street holding dope.

I thought about just throwing it away, walking over to the trash can on the corner and tossing it. Of course, if the police were watching even that wouldn't necessarily get me out of trouble; they'd just claim that I saw them coming.

Besides, dropping some smack into a trash can a few feet away from the courthouse in broad daylight seemed like a pretty bad idea. In addition to the two cops stationed in front of the courthouse, there was also a steady stream of cops and prosecutors going in and out of the building; I might have already drawn some attention for standing frozen on the middle of the sidewalk with my hands now jammed in my pockets.

There was something else, too. There was the buzzing in my veins, an electrical charge dancing in my blood. The back of my throat had gone dry; my stomach had clenched into a fist. It had taken only a few seconds of having the stuff nestled in my hand for me to be deep in the clutches of a jones.

It wasn't just the drug itself that I missed. I'd ended up doing most of the copping back when I was doing it with Beth; I'd come to enjoy that part of it too. I'd done it up on Amsterdam Avenue and 106th Street, sometimes buying from the dealers who worked out of a Chinese take-out joint, other times from the crew across the street that operated out of the vestibule of an apartment building. I'd enjoyed the charge of going up there, often the only white face around, trying not to get busted or burned. I hadn't expected to like it but I had. I liked scoring it and I liked having it, the illicit feeling of having heroin tucked in my pocket as I walked down the street. I had no illusions that any of this was a good thing.

I couldn't just stand here in front of the criminal courthouse indefinitely. Not knowing what else to do, I decided to just go back to my office. When I turned around to head back I found myself staring into the eyes of Devin Wallace, who stood by himself five feet away. I stopped instinctively, then forced myself to keep walking past him, Devin just standing there, a smile on his face, his eyes locked on mine.

I MADE it back to my office without being arrested. Whatever Shawne Flynt was up to, it apparently didn't involve the police.

Back in the office and at loose ends, I went to check in on Myra to see if she wanted any help with tomorrow's closing argument, the heroin still tucked into my pocket. Myra's door was closed. I knocked, but got no response. I decided to leave her a note, telling her that I was going home but that she should feel free to call me if she needed anything. I opened her office door and started to step inside when I saw that Myra was sitting with her back to the door, her head cradled in her folded arms on the desk. She looked up quickly, allowing me a glance of her pain-etched face before looking quickly away.

"Sorry," I said. "I didn't think you were here. I was just . . ."

"What?" Myra said after I'd trailed off. "You just what?"

"What's wrong?"

Still without looking at me, Myra picked up a short document and held it out. "I got this in the mail," she said. "I found it when I came back from court."

I walked over behind Myra's desk and took the court's order, glancing quickly through it. It was the decision of the Appellate Division in *The People v. Terrell Gibbons*. The entire opinion was no more than a half dozen paragraphs, just a quick and dirty disposal of all claims. They'd affirmed the conviction, and Terrell Gibbons had lost his one clear chance at reversing his guilty verdict.

"Shit," I said. "Myra—"

"No platitudes," Myra interrupted. "I swear to God, Joel, you say some kind of platitude right now and I won't be held responsible."

"I don't know what to say. Obviously there're still other av-
enues—"

"The chances of getting the Court of Appeals to even hear this
are maybe one in twenty," Myra snapped. "And even that's probably
optimistic. And winning a federal habeas these days is like winning
the lottery—there's maybe a couple a year in this whole circuit. The
only real shot we had was this appeal."

"You never know," I protested.

"You don't ever know," Myra agreed. "But sometimes you're
pretty damn confident."

I put my hand on Myra's shoulder, wanting to offer whatever
comfort I could. She was still wearing her suit jacket, so I all I felt under my hand was its shoulder pad. To my surprise, Myra reached up
and put her hand on top of mine. After a moment I turned my hand
slightly, taking hers between my thumb and fingers. I looked down at
Myra, who was looking at me in a way I hadn't seen before. I felt my
throat constrict suddenly in a rush of nerves.

"It's not your fault," I said, my voice coming out hoarse.

"Whose is it if not mine, Joel?" Myra said. "The guy didn't do it,
and now he's gone away for life. Who's that on, if not me?"

"You're a great lawyer, Myra," I said. "You can do things that nobody at my fancy firm could even dream of doing. I'm sure you did
everything that could've been done for Terrell."

Myra smiled at me, taking her hand away from mine and swiping
at her eyes. "I'm pretty sure that was a platitude," she said. "But I'll
let it go."

IT WAS a little after nine when I got home. I'd stayed around in the
office even though I didn't really need to, returning some phone

calls, scheduling appointments, closing out the paperwork on cases I'd pled out. It was the sort of work I always had a backlog of, the stuff that I usually put off.

I'd thought about trying to find someone to keep me company, calling Paul or asking Zach to get a drink. But I hadn't actually tried to make it happen, and it was clear that at least on some level I didn't want to. I told myself it was for the best to just face it head-on, do whatever I was going to do when I got home.

So here I was, alone with the dope. I pulled it out of my pocket, dropped the packets down on my glass living room table.

I didn't want this, I told myself. I hadn't gone looking for it, not once since Beth had died. I'd learned my lesson from what had happened to her. The only way the story of doing smack ended well was if you stopped on your own, and did so before it got the best of you.

But what harm would one more little snort do? What was the danger, really, of one last toot for the road? It was all famous last words, I knew that, but any attempt at logic was swimming upstream against an ocean of brutal need.

But there was also the fact that I still didn't understand what Shawne Flynt was up to, and what role Devin Wallace might have in his plan, or if the two were even connected. I didn't need to do it, I told myself. It was as simple as that. I'd gotten clear of the stuff, stayed clear for well over a year now. There was no reason to put myself back down in that hole. I was strong enough not to.

But I wasn't strong enough to just throw it away. Instead I tucked it inside a thick law school textbook on the bottom of my bookshelf. Out of sight, for now, but hardly out of mind.

· 34 ·

I'**D ARRIVED** at the courthouse a half hour before we were scheduled to resume for closing arguments, wanting to be available to help Myra out if she needed anything. I'd asked her if she wanted my help preparing the night before, but she'd insisted that she'd be fine. I was worried she wouldn't be able to focus on putting together her closing after losing the Gibbons appeal, but there wasn't much I could do about it.

The courtroom was empty, and I sat at our table, feeling both exhausted and charged up with adrenaline, that feeling your body gets when it's running on nothing but caffeine and nerves. It'd been a long night; I'd managed to fall asleep readily enough, but I found myself suddenly wide awake a scant three hours later, jolted into consciousness as if I'd been thrown there. I'd awoken with a need like hunger, a craving as deep and primitive as any the human animal can feel. My hands were clenched together so tightly it felt as though I'd developed arthritis overnight. The hours had dragged by with the slow grief of a funeral as I lay curled up, blinking in the gradually lightening dark. I hadn't managed to doze off again until dawn was creeping into the room.

I told myself the night was over now, that it was time to turn my attention back to this courtroom and the task at hand. My perspective was long gone: I had absolutely no idea whether we were winning or losing, no clue whether the prosecution had proven Lorenzo's guilt beyond a reasonable doubt in the eyes of the jury. I'd long ago stopped wondering about what had actually happened that night in the Gardens, long ago left the truth for the jury to figure out.

Seth Lipton's parents were the first people to arrive. They took their customary seats in the front row directly behind the prosecutor's table. Trials were like weddings in that the audience seated themselves according to their sides, only instead of bride and groom it was prosecution and defense. Lipton's mother glared over at me, and I quickly turned away.

The courtroom gradually got more crowded, with additional family members, Adam Berman and some other reporters, and, in the very back row, Devin Wallace. There was no sign of Shawne Flynt. Myra, who was usually early to court, didn't arrive until a couple of minutes before nine thirty, when we were scheduled to begin closing arguments. "You ready?" I asked.

"Why wouldn't I be?" Myra said, not looking at me.

"THE PROSECUTION'S case hinges on exactly two people," Myra said to begin her closing argument. She stood before the jury without notes, pacing slightly away from the podium. "One of these people, the sister of one of the victims, claims that Lorenzo Tate came looking for Mr. Wallace that night. Another supposed witness, who just so happens to be the then girlfriend of that same victim, claims she saw the crime. These two people represent the only real evidence against Lorenzo Tate. And both of them are, very obviously, interested parties. And that's not just my opinion."

Myra proceeded to go through everything we considered to be weaknesses in Latrice's and Yolanda's testimonies. She talked about how Latrice had changed what Lorenzo had supposedly said to her when she'd told him that Devin hadn't left the money to make it sound more threatening. She talked about Yolanda's spate of arrests, the suddenness of the crime that had happened outside late at night, how Yolanda's description of what the shooter was wearing was completely different from the clothes Latrice had described Lorenzo as wearing a few hours earlier.

"It's possible that Yolanda Miller was simply mistaken about what she saw that night," Myra said. "But something else is possible, too. It's possible that Ms. Miller is deliberately not telling us the truth.

"Her reasons to lie include protecting her son, Jamal, and protecting Jamal's father, Malik Taylor. And let's bear in mind, these weren't reasons that the prosecution supplied you with. They didn't even *mention* them. You never even heard Malik Taylor's name from the prosecution. You never heard from them about the fight Malik Taylor had with Devin Wallace a couple of weeks before this crime. You never heard about how Devin Wallace told Malik Taylor that he wouldn't let Malik stay in touch with his own son.

"I think we all have a pretty good idea of what kind of guy Devin Wallace is. We know that what he was doing on the street that night related to selling drugs on a college campus. A guy like that tells you to stay away from somebody, you're going to take it seriously. You're going to take it as a threat.

"But let's think about what exactly Devin Wallace was demanding. He was telling Malik Taylor that he couldn't see his own son anymore. Now, that's bad enough, of course, but let's stop and think for a minute about what exactly it would mean in this case. Let's think about what it would mean for that little boy, Jamal. Instead of being raised by his own natural father, a young man who was working two jobs, a young man who was trying to educate himself, a young man who was trying to make a better life for himself and his community, instead of being exposed to all that, what would Jamal be exposed to? A drug dealer whose innovative business practices included selling drugs right on a college campus. Think what this would mean for Jamal's future.

"Then ask yourself this: what would you do if you were Jamal's father? To defy Devin Wallace would be to risk your life; I think we all know that. We know that disrespecting the neighborhood drug dealer is not a ticket to longevity, not in the projects. So this is the Catch-22 facing Malik Taylor. He either agrees to never see his son again, or he risks getting killed.

"Maybe Mr. Taylor found a third way. Maybe that third way was to get rid of Devin Wallace. That way he could see his son without risking his own life: a perfectly understandable thing to want.

"You may have noticed I only said maybe. The reason I only said maybe is because the police never investigated Malik Taylor. They never even *talked* to him. The police can't get to the right answer if they don't ask the right questions. I don't know whether Malik Taylor shot Devin Wallace and killed Seth Lipton. But I do know that the case against him would be every bit as strong as, if not stronger than, the case against Lorenzo Tate.

"Because let's remember, there's no evidence against Lorenzo Tate other than the word of two people who had abundant reasons to lie, or at least to exaggerate. The police didn't recover the murder weapon. There's no physical evidence linking my client to the crime.

"I said the prosecution's case hinged on two people, the two purported witnesses from the night of the shooting. Of course, the DA would have you believe that they have another witness, Lester Bailey. But Lester Bailey isn't actually a witness to anything. He's a hardened criminal working an angle. Lester Bailey wants to play let's make a deal with the DA's office, he wants to do anything he can to help himself out, and he doesn't mind who he has to hurt to do so. He has no credibility, he's a repeat felon, he's testifying here in hopes of getting himself a better deal in his own criminal case. His testimony isn't worth the air it took to speak it.

"As I'm sure you all know from watching TV, to convict my client you have to find him guilty beyond a reasonable doubt. The judge will instruct you as to what exactly that means. I think your doubts here will at least be reasonable. I think you will be far from sure that the police got the right man here. In fact, I think you will wonder whether they even spoke to him. Thank you."

"**THIS IS** a straightforward case," O'Bannon began his closing remarks. In contrast to Myra, he was standing at the podium with a few pages of notes. As always, his delivery was dry and methodical, devoid of emotion. "Devin Wallace owed the defendant a sum of money. On the night of April 6, the defendant decided he'd waited long enough to get that money back."

O'Bannon proceeded to summarize the testimonies of Latrice Wallace, Yolanda Miller, and Lester Bailey. He acknowledged Yolanda's recent arrests, but argued that they had nothing to do with her ability to make an identification of Lorenzo Tate.

"The defense has tried to distract you," O'Bannon said once he'd finished summing up the state's evidence, turning and pointing his finger directly at Myra as he spoke. "They've tried to create an alternate suspect, a reason for one of our eyewitnesses to lie. They are trying to create confusion where clarity exists. Don't fall into that trap, ladies and gentlemen. Keep focused on what you actually know.

"For example, did anything in the defense's supposed theory actually contradict Latrice Wallace's testimony? Did they explain how it just so happened that the defendant was out looking for Devin Wallace that night, uttering threats against him? Was it just a coincidence that he said these threats on the same night that Mr. Wallace got shot? Did they present some harmless explanation for the defendant's exchange with Ms. Wallace that night? No. In fact, ladies and gentlemen, the defense didn't really refute any part of our case. Instead, they simply tried to distract you from it.

"The defense also tried to distract you by claiming that Seth Lipton was a drug dealer. Ladies and gentlemen, I don't honestly know whether Seth Lipton was involved in some way with illegal drugs or not. But I do know this: no matter what put him on that street, he didn't deserve to be shot and killed. So why did the defense drag the victim's name through the mud? To distract you. And I ask you not to let yourself be distracted.

"Don't be fooled by smoke and mirrors. Pay attention, instead, to the simple facts of this case. Those facts will lead you to find the defendant guilty, beyond a reasonable doubt, for the murder of Seth Lipton and the attempted murder of Devin Wallace. Thank you."

· 35 ·

I **'VE NEVER** been so exhausted in my entire life," Myra said, draining the last of her cosmo. Her voice was hoarse with fatigue, her body slumped.

I nodded and took a long drink of Maker's Mark. We were at the Henry Street Alehouse, the only PDs still there. Zach, Julia, Max, Michael, and Shelly had all come out after work, but none of them had stayed long. There wasn't much to say to lawyers who were waiting on a verdict; little you could do but keep them company. Neither

Myra nor I was fit for conversation, both staring off into space, withdrawn and distracted, lost in our waiting. Our colleagues had drunk with us for as long as they felt obligated to, then went off to do something more entertaining than watch two worn-out lawyers marking time.

Judge Ferano hadn't finished charging the jury until late afternoon, so the jury had only deliberated for a little over an hour before calling it a day. There was, of course, no telling how long a jury would be out—it could be a few minutes; it could be a couple of weeks. Myra and I would try to get other work done tomorrow, although I suspected that I wouldn't be able to concentrate until we had a verdict, my mind constantly tugged back into speculating on what the jury was up to.

Even though Myra had done much of the heavy lifting at the trial, I felt completely exhausted myself. The pressure had been there even when I was just sitting at counsel's table. It had been like being onstage for eight hours a day, still performing even when you didn't have any lines. The jury was always watching, or at least it felt like they were. The slow grind of a trial had worn me to the bone.

"We did what we could do," I said.

Myra fixed me with a look, evaluating me. "So," she said. "Was it what you expected? Was this what you threw away your big-money corporate job to do with your life?"

"I didn't actually throw away my law-firm job to come work here," I heard myself reply. It was something that had been there for me to say to her for some time, and it felt both scary and good to have said it.

"What do you mean?"

"I mean I didn't actually quit my job to come work here," I said. "In fact, I didn't quit my job at all."

"I don't understand what you're telling me," Myra said.

"I was fired from my law firm," I said, my hand shaking slightly as I took a sip of my bourbon. "They were old-school about it—officially I was asked to resign. Then I was suspended from the practice of law for six months. Then I came here."

"You punking me?" Myra asked, tilting her head quizzically.

"This isn't really when or how I would do that."

"This is what, then? Your confession?"

"Isaac's known all along," I said. "I'd actually just sort of assumed it would leak out."

"Not to me it hadn't. Why was your license suspended?"

"Long story short, it was drug related."

"Drugs, huh?" Myra said. "Yeah, I guess I can see that with you." I laughed sourly. "Thanks."

"You're okay now?"

"I don't get high, if that's what you're asking."

"I guess that's part of what I was asking," Myra applied. "You in NA?"

"Not since I was required to be," I replied. I'd been obligated to go to meetings the whole time my law license was suspended, but they'd just been a waste of my time. I'd never spoken more than the bare minimum that was required of me, never even been tempted to open up. I had nothing in common with the true down-and-outers whose bottomed-out lives were the focus of our nightly discussions. I was not really an addict. At least, that's what I'd told myself to get through.

"It was like that, huh?"

"It was, yes," I said. "Losing my law license was a real possibility."

"What're we actually talking about in terms of drugs?"

"Heroin," I said. "And that wasn't all of it. I had someone, a young woman, a person from my firm, whom I did it with. She OD'd."

"OD'd as . . . ?"

"She died, yes. In the firm's library bathroom. It was a bit of a scandal."

"Shit, Joel," Myra said. "You're a badass motherfucker."

We laughed, cautiously, then descended into silence. Myra had again picked out songs on the jukebox, and the music abruptly shifted from The Clash's "Guns of Brixton" to an acoustic song by Aimee Mann.

I propped my window up and then
I turned my back to lure you in
To rifle through what I might have been

"So what actually happened?" Myra asked.

"I don't like talking about this stuff with people."

"I'm not a roomful of strangers drinking bad coffee in a church basement," Myra said. "Tell *me* what happened."

And so I did.

I'D CALLED Beth at home a week or so after the night when she'd first told me about her using. I wasn't calling out of curiosity about heroin, though I supposed that was there, but rather out of lust. I'd called her from my office on a night when I was working late. It didn't make a lot of sense on one level—we spoke at work a couple of times a day—but I wasn't about to ask her out within the transparent confines of the firm.

Beth sounded amused but not surprised by my call. I'd made the briefest possible small talk, then asked her if she was free that Friday.

"Why?" Beth had said. "What did you have in mind?"

"I figured we could play it by ear," I said.

"Are you calling from work?" Beth asked.

"Yes," I said.

"Okay then," Beth said. "I guess we'll leave it at that."

WE HADN'T talked about it during the rest of the week at work, interacting as we always had. I suspected there was a lilt of self-consciousness, or perhaps self-parody, to our banter now.

On Friday the forecast was for a severe winter storm, perhaps even a blizzard. By the time I left Walker's Midtown office to take the subway uptown to Beth's apartment in Morningside Heights, the sky was thick with drifting snowflakes.

It was snowing even worse by the time I got there, ankle-deep and growing, dancing through the air in angry gusts. I trudged the two blocks to her apartment through piles and drifts.

When I rang Beth's buzzer there was no response. I pulled out my cell phone and was dialing her number when Beth walked up behind me and tapped me on the shoulder. She was wearing a peacoat without a hat or scarf, her hair covered with snow.

"What're you doing out here?" I said.

"I was doing some last-minute shopping before the blizzard," Beth said, walking past me and opening her building's front door.

Beth's studio apartment was both cluttered and dirty, old newspapers and magazines on the floor, dishes stacked in the sink. It reminded me of how I'd lived in my very first apartment, as a sophomore in college.

"The maid's week off?" I said as I shook snow from my coat.

"I was going to tidy up," Beth said, plopping down on her futon. "But then I didn't."

"So what kind of shopping were you doing this time of night?" I asked, sitting on the swivel chair by her desk.

"You're the kind of person who always has to know, aren't you, Joel? I bet you think your curiosity knows no bounds."

"It hasn't come up against them yet."

With a small sigh and a lift of her hips Beth reached into the front pocket of her jeans, drew something out, and handed it over to me. Upon inspection it proved to be several things: identical white packets that looked like miniature envelopes. The same words were stamped in bleeding ink upon each: *Lethal Injection.*

"Is this what I think it is?" I asked.

"Do I know what you're thinking? But my guess would be yes."

"This is H?"

"It's not called H anymore," Beth said. "It's called D now."

"Do you mind if we just take a time-out for a moment?" I said. "Like if we put the movie on pause or something?"

We tried for a few minutes to speak of other things, but with little success. I felt as though I'd been set up, although I realized this feeling was not particularly supported by the facts. We'd talked about it before, after all. I had made my curiosity known. Beth was, perhaps, only doing what I'd asked her to do. This was, apparently, something I wanted.

"Okay," I said. "I'll admit to being curious. There's a grim sort of appeal. But there are practical considerations as well."

"Such as?"

"Such as the fact that people die from it."

"You're scared?"

"Goddamn right I'm scared," I said. "If there was a loaded gun sitting there on the table between us I'd be scared of that too."

"It's not a loaded gun."

"If that's the best thing you can say in its defense, I have to say your case is pretty weak."

"It doesn't in any way resemble a loaded gun," Beth said. "It's not at all what you're thinking it is. After you do it, you won't even believe we had this conversation."

"I already can't believe we've had this conversation," I said.

BUT LATER I realized Beth was right. By then I was lying down on her futon, unable to remember the last time I'd moved. Beth was on the floor, slack-limbed, propped up against a wall. There was a complicated geometry of knots in my stomach: it was like I could feel every one of my internal organs, the whole intricate mechanism of sustaining my body. Yet the feeling was not an unpleasant one; no feeling was an unpleasant one. The pleasure was almost sexual, yet lacking sex's strain, its battle with self-consciousness, its animal need.

"It's like sex without the sex," I said.

The heroin had come in tiny doses of blocky gray powder. Beth had cut it with a steak knife on the surface of a CD case. The lines were small and dirty-looking, uneven and vaguely woebegone. They'd gone down with a slight burn, a chalky taste at the back of the throat, like a new manner of thirst.

"What?" Beth said.

At first I had felt nothing. Before the high came a spell of nausea, as brief as it was unsettling. When the dope hit it wasn't with the rush I'd expected, but rather a loosening, a final triumph of detachment.

"Never mind," I said.

It was a glorious physical glow, a slow burn. The room acquired a stillness. Movement had become unnecessary, extraneous. We were both still, our eyes closing as if in sleep, some deeper species of rest.

"No," Beth said. "You're right. That's exactly what it's like."

"It's not what I expected," I said. "Not at all. It's much, much easier."

We'd turned off all the lights. The only illumination came from the street below, leaking through the curtains and into the room. Everything was shadowy, inert, the shadows slow dancing in the pattern the wind made with the tossing tree branches just outside the window.

"It's the easiest thing in the world," Beth agreed.

I sat up and instantly regretted doing so. Nausea rippled through my body in a swelling wave. "So you do this a lot," I said, swallowing hard, waiting for the tremors to subside.

"I wouldn't say a lot," Beth said. "I'd say enough. Want some orange juice?"

I nodded weakly, my eyes open now. Beth slowly leaned forward and slid the carton along the floor toward the couch. I looked down at it helplessly. After a long moment Beth noticed that I'd made no effort to pick it up.

"You feeling sick?" she asked.

"I'm great so long as I don't move," I said.

After another minute or so Beth stood up and handed me the carton.

I drank deeply and rashly, the juice tasting as good as anything ever had. A moment later I was in the bathroom, throwing up. I was pleasantly surprised that my vomiting had been sufficiently foreshadowed to allow me to make it to the toilet.

It was the best puking experience of my life, the orange juice still cold coming back up. I walked back into the living room feeling terrific, better than ever. Beth was now sprawled on the futon, blinking fast as I flicked on the overhead light. "Another round?" I said.

THE SNOWSTORM had turned into a blizzard, and I had ended up spending the entire weekend with Beth in her cramped apartment. We hadn't even kissed on that first night, but then somehow the next morning, both of us coming up out of nodding off in Beth's bed, we'd ended making tentative, fragile love.

I hadn't been expecting it—I thought heroin had already taken the place of sex between us. We'd gotten high again that night. By the time I left on Sunday evening, emerging onto wet city streets with slush and gray chunks of icy snow, I felt sick and exhausted and more than a little afraid.

Back home, I went straight to bed, slept for nearly twelve straight hours, woke up Monday morning feeling almost back to normal. I wasn't looking forward to seeing Beth at the office, could not decide how to play it when I did. I knew the obvious: I should never see her again outside of work, should stop things now, should probably even try to get her transferred off of the case, avoid working with her.

But I also knew that things between us weren't over, knew it through my resignation, as though I myself had no choice in the matter.

When I'd seen her Monday morning the sight was a jolt. My body reacted to her mere presence: a thudding heart, awkward shyness, all the tired symptoms of a pounding high school crush. My resolution drained away at once: I was officially in trouble.

Later in the week I confided in Paul. We'd been working late, were taking a dinner break in a conference room, each of us with nearly fifty dollars' worth of food, an easy indulgence since it was billed directly to our clients. It took me only a minute to convey the relevant facts, after which we'd sat in a long silence.

"I'm trying to come up with something to say that you won't already know," Paul said at last.

"I do already know."

"But I can tell that knowing isn't really doing it for you."

"I suppose that's right," I said.

"If you just need confirmation of what a bad idea this is," Paul said, "I'm happy to give it to you. You're risking everything—your job, your health, your bar license, your fucking life."

"Yes."

"But you're not going to stop." Paul did not say it as a question.

"Not just yet."

Paul shook his head. To my surprise, he looked genuinely sad. It occurred to me that my confession had altered our friendship, perhaps permanently.

And so it began. Soon I was spending every weekend with Beth. Our getting high always outnumbered our lovemaking. I did stick to my rule that I would do heroin only on the weekend. I was well aware that Beth had no such rule; her job performance continued to suffer. I found myself in the uncomfortable position of increasingly having to cover for her, right up to that day when her death had burst everything out into the open.

Did I love her? Even to this day I wasn't sure. I knew, I always knew, that she didn't love me, and I liked to think I was pragmatic enough to restrain my own feelings when certain they would not be reciprocated. I suspected Beth was permanently incapable of love; what I knew for sure was that she was incapable of it in her current condition. What there was of our sex life quickly devolved from mediocre to lousy: Beth seemed fundamentally uninterested, her libido shut down by her addiction.

The situation had become increasingly untenable, as I had known it would. I wondered how long I could maintain myself as a heroin dilettante, a weekend snorter, before things got out of control. I would have to do something.

I was spared having to take action, but not in any way I ever would've wanted. The situation had taken on its own momentum, which led to its own resolution. Perhaps Beth's death had saved my life; who knows where I would've ended up if I'd continued down that path awhile longer?

But I'd hardly gotten off scot-free: I'd lost my job, been suspended from practicing law for half a year, had to start all over again at the bottom. Of course, that was nothing compared to what Beth had lost.

WHEN I was finished telling it I couldn't look at Myra. It was the first time I'd told the story to anyone. I hadn't looked at her while I was talking, my gaze fixed at some vague spot on the table. It'd been a long time since I'd been naked before another person—truly naked, not merely unclothed—and the feeling of total exposure felt terrifying. But it was necessary too: I needed to open myself to Myra. If anybody was going to be able to accept my wrecked little self it was her. I wanted to offer her that chance.

"Do you miss heroin?" Myra asked after a long moment had passed.

"What?" I replied, although it was clear to both of us that I'd heard her.

"I would think you must still miss it," she said.

"I don't, actually," I said. "Honestly. Heroin's like the best love-less sex you've ever had. But that's all it is."

"Well, that can still be pretty amazing," Myra said.

I looked at her, started to say something, didn't. "Anyway," I said, "as to the drug thing, I don't feel anything about it but shame and guilt."

"Guilt?"

"Sure," I said. "I hate that I was a part of the damage drugs do. I hate that I helped create the world that people like Lorenzo and Devin Wallace live in. I recognize my responsibility for it."

"I think you're giving yourself too much credit," Myra said. "That's the world our client would be living in regardless of whether someone like you decided to experiment with dope."

"Yes and no," I said. "I mean, one person more or less doesn't make any difference, sure, but if there wasn't any demand there wouldn't be any supply."

"There'll always be demand," Myra said. "But let's not change the subject to the big picture. What about you?"

"What about me?"

"You sure you got it beat?"

"Sure becomes a little relative when talking about such things," I said, thinking about the heroin from Shawne Flynt that was still wait-ing for me in my apartment.

"Come on, Joel," Myra said. Her cell phone started ringing, audi-ble from her purse, but she ignored it. "You don't even go to meet-ings? You're that sure of your own uniqueness? Of your own strength?"

"I didn't claim there was anything unique about me," I said, fin-ishing off the last of my Maker's Mark. "Just because everybody else announces their problems on *Jerry Springer*, that doesn't mean I can't choose to deal with my problems myself."

"I think you're just another guy like me," Myra said.

"And what're guys like you?"

"People who just can't deal with the idea of having other people be in their lives."

"Is that really how you think of yourself?"

"I think that's why I like being a lawyer so much," Myra said. "It's a way of engaging with the world by way of other people's problems."

"You let Terrell Gibbons into your life," I countered.

"Sure," Myra said. "In a sense I did. But I mean, how safe is that? The guy's borderline retarded and accused of murder. I took on his problems as my own the best that I could, but at the end of the day they're still his problems, not mine. I had a couple of bad nights because I lost the appeal. But he's the one doing twenty-five to life in Sing Sing."

"Well," I said, "there wouldn't be very many criminal defense lawyers if we had to serve our clients' sentences."

"And I'm not saying I would trade places with Terrell even if I could. That's the point, though, isn't it? We get to go to war, but it's always someone else's battle. Win or lose for us, we live to fight another day. We're in the fight but not of the fight."

"I know what you mean," I said. "But I don't agree that I'm somebody who can't let other people into my life."

"Have you been with anyone since that girl died?" Myra asked softly. It wasn't a question I'd expected.

"Not in a way that meant anything," I said. I looked up at Myra, but she kept her gaze down.

"Do you want another drink?" I asked.

"I don't think I can stay here any longer," Myra said. "The sound of other people having a good time is bugging the fuck out of me."

The force of my disappointment surprised me. "Okay."

"It's not that I want to be alone right now," Myra said quickly. "I don't, actually. We can still hang out."

"Sure," I said. "I'm not going to be falling asleep anytime soon."

"You want to come over?"

"Yes," I said. "I do."

Myra nodded, at last meeting my eyes. "Let's go, then," she said.

WE WENT out onto Henry Street to hail a cab, walking down to the intersection. As we waited for the light to change, I stepped forward and kissed her. Myra leaned into me, her hand coming up to my shoulder, then my neck. After a few seconds she broke it off, resting her head against my chest as I held her. Her skin felt cold in the evening's chill. Only her mouth felt warm. "We know about one hundred people who work within six blocks of where we're standing right now," Myra said, a softness in her voice I hadn't heard before.

"I think they all went home for the night some time ago," I replied.

"When did you first know that you were going to kiss me?"

"When did I first actually *know*? About thirty seconds ago. I've known that I wanted to for a while before that."

"Let's find that cab," Myra said.

MYRA AND I didn't speak on the short cab ride to her apartment on South Portland Avenue in Fort Greene. "There's beer in the fridge and vodka in the freezer," Myra said once we were inside. I could tell she was nervous, which only compounded my own nerves. Her apartment was muted and tasteful, considerably more adult than I'd been expecting: Myra had clearly nested here, built a home.

"Which do you want?" I asked.

"Would drinking vodka be too obvious an admission that I was getting myself drunk so that you could take advantage of me?" Myra asked.

"Vodka it is," I said. "You got anything to mix with it?"

"Does ice count?"

I poured us a couple of drinks and brought them over to the couch. Myra had left the overheard light off, turning on a couple of lamps. She'd put on some music, something ambient and vague.

"Your apartment's nice," I said.

"What'd you think, there'd be pizza boxes on the floor?"

"Something like that, yeah," I admitted.

"You're still not convinced I'm a girl, are you?"

"I'm getting there."

"Is that so?" Myra said, peering at me as she sipped at her drink. I was still settling in, getting used to the fact that I was here, and wasn't sure I was quite ready to actually go to bed with her.

"The thing about this kind of music," I said, "I like it, but then there's this moment where I'm about to suggest somebody put some music on."

"You want thrash, Joel?" Myra said. "Because I can give you thrash."

"Is that a fact?" I said, reaching out for her.

This kiss was different from the one on the street, less tentative, with a bit of an edge to it. Myra softly bit my lower lip. I responded by sliding my hand under her shirt. I was moving it up toward Myra's breasts when her phone rang.

"Do you need to get that?" I said, wondering who the hell was calling her this time of night.

"I don't answer the phone this late," Myra said. "Anybody ever call you with good news after midnight?"

After four rings the machine picked up, Myra's recorded voice saying her number but not her name. After the beep a man's voice came over the speaker. "Myra, this is Adam Berman at the *Journal*. Give me a call when you get this. We've got some breaking news over here relating to your case, and would love to get your comment. It seems Malik Taylor was just murdered."

I UNDERSTOOD when Myra kicked me out shortly after returning Berman's call: suddenly we both had a lot of work to do before the morning. Myra had assigned me the task of researching whether Taylor's death gave us grounds for reopening the trial to present evidence regarding his murder.

Back in my apartment I went straight for my bookshelf, shaking my contracts textbook so that the packets of heroin fell to the floor. I snatched them up, moving quickly now, not allowing for any pause to let myself think or try to rationalize away what I was about to do. I didn't even know when I'd made the decision to do it, hadn't even realized that I had.

I didn't turn on the bathroom light, just stood over the toilet and opened my hand, letting the packets fall. I looked down at them a moment as they floated there, then watched as they disappeared in the soft roar of the flushing toilet.

I was clear. For now, I was clear.

·36·

"You WANT me to do what?" Judge Ferano asked. It was a little after nine a.m., and Myra and I were gathered in the judge's
chambers along with O'Bannon and Williams.

I'd stayed up most of the night reading cases on my laptop, trying to establish a legal basis for our getting news of Malik Taylor's
death in front of the jury, while Myra tried to find out whatever facts
she could. We'd met up at the courthouse at eight thirty in the morn-

ing, Myra brisk and entirely businesslike, no acknowledgment of what had happened between us the night before. I wondered if it had all been a temporary aberration, a frisson born of anxiety, stress, and a primitive need for comfort.

"You should declare a mistrial," Myra said firmly to the judge. "In the alternative, we move that you instruct the jury to cease deliberations, and then allow us to reopen our case to present evidence relating to Malik Taylor's murder."

"Your Honor—" O'Bannon began, but Judge Ferano held up his hand to stop him.

"I don't see how this is possible grounds for a mistrial," Judge Ferano said. "As for telling the jury to stop deliberating, I've been a judge for seven years, and I've never had a party ask to reopen the case after the jury had begun deliberations. You have any authority for this proposition?"

"The Court of Appeals has established that a trial court can reopen a criminal case when new evidence of a defendant's guilt or innocence has come to light during the jury's deliberation. *People v. Olsen*," I said, handing first the judge, then O'Bannon, copies of that opinion. "It's obviously not a commonplace thing, but our situation here provides a perfect example of when it needs to be done."

"Let me read this," Judge Ferano said. We were all silent for a minute while the judge quickly scanned the opinion, O'Bannon doing the same with Williams looking over his shoulder.

After a minute Judge Ferano turned to O'Bannon. "It appears from this decision that I do have the authority to reopen the trial if new evidence has come to light," he said. "So it seems the real question is whether or not this constitutes new evidence. What do you know about Malik Taylor's murder?"

"I don't have any independent knowledge that he's even dead, Your Honor," O'Bannon said. "All I know is what defense counsel has said."

Judge Ferano turned back to Myra and me.

"Explain to me precisely why you believe that Taylor's death is evidence of Lorenzo Tate's innocence in the shooting of Seth Lipton and Devin Wallace."

"It has been the contention of the defense throughout this case that the police should have investigated Malik Taylor as a suspect in that shooting," Myra said, "given that he was an equally plausible, if not more plausible, suspect as our client. The fact that he's now been murdered strongly supports our theory. Devin Wallace has not cooperated with the police in this case, and it is obviously possible that Taylor's murder is a case of street justice."

"Do you have any actual evidence that Taylor's murder was in any way related to this case?" Judge Ferano asked.

"Taylor's murder happened less than twelve hours ago," Myra said. "I've left messages with the investigating detectives but have yet to speak to them. Which in all fairness, I might not always return an after midnight call by nine the next morning either."

"So what you're telling me is that you don't have any knowledge of the circumstances of this murder," Judge Ferano said. "For all you know Taylor was mugged on the street, or the police have already arrested somebody for the crime and established that it was unrelated."

"Barring someone else already having confessed or a batch of eyewitnesses, I can't imagine the police wouldn't consider Mr. Wallace a potential suspect," Myra replied.

"On the basis of what?" O'Bannon said. "Ms. Goldstein's speculation, coupled with her innuendo in your courtroom?"

"Now, Counsel," Judge Ferano said to O'Bannon. "However

tenuous the defense's claims might have been in regards to establishing that Malik Taylor shot Wallace and Lipton, they did legitimately show bad blood between Taylor and Wallace. I would think the police will likely have some interest in talking to Wallace about Taylor's death if they don't have a clear suspect. But really, everybody in this room is just whistling in the dark here, because none of us knows what actually happened last night."

"Your Honor," I began quickly, ready to hand out additional case law to try to keep Judge Ferano from denying our motion.

"Relax, Mr. Deveraux," Judge Ferano said. "Here's how I see it. If Wallace is legitimately a suspect in Taylor's death, then it looks to me like jury deliberations should be suspended and you should be allowed to present evidence in that regard. But if it looks like Taylor's murder was just a coincidence, then there's no reason it should go before the jury. The interests of justice suggest that I shouldn't let the jury continue their deliberations until we sort this mess out."

"But, Your Honor—" O'Bannon began.

"What else would you have me do?" Judge Ferano interrupted, glaring over at O'Bannon. "Think it through, Mr. O'Bannon. Let's say the jury reaches a guilty verdict today, and then tomorrow the police arrest Wallace for killing Taylor, who promptly confesses that he did it because he believed it was Taylor who tried to kill him. We'd have to try this whole case over again, assuming your office could even reprosecute. Meanwhile the *New York Journal* is running front-page articles asking how an innocent man had been convicted of a crime he didn't commit, and that doesn't help any of us."

O'Bannon and the judge looked at each other for a moment; then O'Bannon shrugged. "I understand that it would be relevant evidence if the police believe Wallace actually killed Taylor," O'Bannon said. "I would just stress that if there is no evidence of such a link, the defense should not be able to just present evidence that Taylor was murdered. I mean, the guy lived in a bad neighborhood; who knows what happened?"

Judge Ferano proceeded to work out the details of how we'd go forward. The jury would be told to stop their deliberations, while the judge attempted to get the details of Taylor's murder from the police.

Lorenzo was brought to court from Rikers every morning; the first time we would usually see him was when the COs brought him to the courtroom. We hadn't had a chance to even tell him what had happened, so we went down to the holding cell where Lorenzo was being kept in case the jury reached a verdict.

Myra ran through everything, moving so quickly from Malik's death last night to the suspension of the jury's deliberations a few minutes ago that I felt vertigo, even though I'd just lived through it. I watched Lorenzo carefully to make sure he was following; his shocked expression told me he was.

"So you think Devin might have gone after Malik?" Lorenzo asked.

Myra cocked her head slightly; she hadn't actually suggested that yet, although that was where she was going. "We don't actually know one way or another," she said after a moment. "But we think the police have to at least be considering that possibility."

"Devin gone after Malik because he heard about how Malik be hooking back up with Yo-Yo," Lorenzo mused. "I can see how he'd come to do that."

"You never know," Myra said. "The point is, we don't have to prove that Devin did it. If the DA can't disprove that, then it could be enough for reasonable doubt."

"So what happens now?"

"I'm kind of curious about that myself," Myra said.

■　　■　　■

IT WAS a little after eleven by the time Detectives Dwayne Franklin and James Scott arrived at the judge's chambers. Franklin was black, late thirties, dressed more like a businessman than a cop. Scott was white, fleshy, on the far side of fifty. They did not look like partners with too much in common, though they were united in how unhappy they looked about being there.

Now that we were all gathered in chambers nobody seemed quite sure what to do, everyone looking to Judge Ferano, who for the first time in the case appeared distinctly uncomfortable with the attention. He offered Franklin and Scott an elaborately courteous greeting, which neither detective acknowledged with more than the slightest of nods.

The judge then proceeded to summarize the relevant parts of our trial, emphasizing our attempts to put Malik Taylor forward as an alternative suspect, the detectives keeping their expressions neutral while the judge spoke.

"So," Judge Ferano concluded, "the question I have for you, Detectives, is this: are you investigating, or are you aware of, any possible links between the shooting of Devin Wallace and the murder of Mr. Taylor?"

"We spoke to Yolanda Miller last night, after we learned that she was the mother of Malik Taylor's child. She told us about this case, and about the previous disagreement between Mr. Taylor and Mr. Wallace," Franklin said. Franklin must have spent a lot of time on the witness stand, because what he was doing now was so clearly cop in a courtroom. "She also indicated her own suspicion that Mr. Wallace might have been looking to go after Mr. Taylor based on this situation, and what had come out in court."

"When you say 'what had come out in court,' is there something specific you are referring to?" Judge Ferano asked.

"Yes," Franklin answered. "Ms. Miller told us that the defense attempted to question her about a recent sexual encounter she'd supposedly had with Mr. Taylor."

"I remember that," Judge Ferano said. "I sustained the objection. I didn't allow her to answer and told the jury to disregard it."

"Apparently she thought maybe Devin Wallace didn't disregard it."

"And have you questioned Mr. Wallace?" the judge asked.

"We haven't been able to locate him yet," Franklin replied.

Judge Ferano tilted his head skeptically, giving a long look at the detectives, who looked back at him, Franklin deadpan polite, Scott through hooded lids. "When you say you haven't been able to locate Wallace," he said, "does that mean you have police actively looking for him?"

"Yes."

"And you've tried his apartment, I take it?"

"Of course," Franklin replied.

"Do you have people watching his apartment?" Judge Ferano asked.

"We're keeping an eye on it, yes."

"So he's hiding out from the cops," Myra couldn't resist saying.

"I don't want to hear from you, Counsel," Judge Ferano said sternly, glaring at Myra briefly before turning back to Franklin. "Do you have any reason to believe he's hiding from you?"

"All we know is, he doesn't appear to have come home last night." This was Scott, finally interjecting. "Lots of men don't sometimes—it doesn't necessarily mean they're hiding from the police."

"Are there any witnesses to the crime, or any other evidence suggesting either that Wallace is a viable suspect or that he isn't?" the judge asked.

"All we got from witnesses was two black men in a car, a darker-skinned man at the wheel, a lighter guy who did the shoot," Scott said.

"With all due respect, Your Honor," Franklin began, showing more animation than he had so far, "you're putting us in an impossible position. We understand that the reason we're here is to see if our investigation is tanking another murder case. And the simple fact is, we just don't know enough yet to answer that. We talked to Detective Spanner, who handled the Lipton murder, this morning. She told us she's sure that Tate was the right guy. Now maybe there was some underlying beef between this Wallace and Taylor, but even so, that doesn't mean it has anything to do with the shootings—"

"With all due respect to you, Detective," Judge Ferano interrupted, "don't try to tell me how to do my job. I don't like this either—the jury has started deliberations—but I can't ignore it when the person proffered by the defense as an alternative suspect is murdered. I'm sure you're not ignoring the problems between Wallace and Taylor in your investigation, and I can't ignore them either.

"However," Judge Ferano continued. "I do also, and I want to make this clear, understand that you are in the midst of a murder investigation that began just a little over twelve hours ago. We've got a lot of cross-purposes at work here, and my job is to try to balance them as best I can. So, Detectives, let me ask you this: it is my understanding that the first forty-eight to seventy-two hours of a homicide investigation are the most important; would you agree with that?"

"Absolutely, Judge," Scott said immediately, clearly thinking he saw a way out of this room. I caught Franklin giving his partner a look.

"Am I correct, then, in taking that to mean you will be investigating this case all weekend?" the judge continued.

Now even Scott sensed a trap. The two detectives looked over at each other, neither immediately responding. "Unless we make an arrest today, we will, yes," Franklin said at last.

"So here's what I propose," Judge Ferano said. "We have enough of an issue here that I'm going to send the jury home for now. I'm going to require at least one of you to appear before the court at nine a.m. sharp on Monday to inform me as to where your investigation stands. Based on what I hear, I will either let the jury resume deliberations, or I will reopen the case to allow the defense to call one of you to testify about Taylor's murder. Detectives, I wish you luck in your investigation, and I very much hope you can shed some light on it come Monday."

·37·

A LL RIGHT," Myra said. "Let's try it where you're just a total asshole."

It was late Sunday afternoon, and Myra and I were in the neutral
territory of a conference room in our office. We were role-playing,
with me pretending to be the detective and Myra crossing me. With
the other witnesses we'd at least had some idea of what their testimony was going to be and how we were going to attack it, but with
the detective—based on their appearance before Judge Ferano we

were guessing it was going to be Franklin, but we didn't even know that—we were going to be totally winging it. So Myra and I had brainstormed for every possibility we could come up with of what the detective's testimony would be and how he would present it, and had spent the afternoon running through the possibilities.

It was also entirely possible that the police would've found a way to clear Devin Wallace in Malik Taylor's murder by the time Monday morning rolled around. If so, the detective wouldn't testify, and the jury would just be allowed to resume its deliberations. On the other end of the spectrum, it wasn't out of the realm of possibility that the police would've come up with direct evidence connecting Wallace to Taylor's murder. It wasn't impossible that they would've arrested him.

We'd run through that scenario at the start, but hadn't spent much time on it: if Wallace had been arrested Myra wouldn't need much practice to get the important concessions out of the detective. It was the middle ground that mostly concerned us, situations where there was enough that the judge let us go forward and bring in the detective's testimony but not enough to make it a slam dunk that Wallace was involved. If that was the case, we'd be hard-pressed to get much out of the detective, homicide cops being old hands at rebuffing defense attorneys.

We'd been at this for a few hours now, and I was running out of ways to pretend to be a recalcitrant cop. We spent about twenty minutes with me in asshole mode—hostile, sarcastic, refusing to admit the obvious.

"Okay," Myra finally said. "I think I'm as prepared as I can be, under the circumstances. Let's call it."

Myra and I hadn't talked about the other night, hadn't even acknowledged it. Now that we were suddenly back in the throes of the trial, I didn't feel comfortable bringing it up. If it was bothering Myra at all she was doing a good job of hiding it; she seemed entirely focused and businesslike, lacking any trace of the openness and vulnerability that occasionally leaked out of her.

"You think it's a game changer if we get this sort of testimony before the jury?" I asked.

"If we get the judge to reopen the case at all, I think it's at least a bit of a game changer. The jury will understand that something strange is happening."

"Where are we if the judge just throws it back to the jury without letting us call the detective?" I asked.

Myra shrugged. "No worse off than we were a few days ago," she said. "Latrice's evidence is collateral, Yolanda's shaky in three different ways, and Lester Bailey's a lying snitch. I guess the question is whether we've given the jury enough for them to think Yolanda's lying. She was an eyewitness, after all, and she made the ID right off the bat. The problem is, we never came up with a reason why she'd pin it on Lorenzo."

"Why would she?"

"I don't have the faintest idea," Myra answered. "Nobody ever gave us anything between them suggesting why she would."

"Well, if she was just looking for a fall guy, she knew Lorenzo did business with Devin," I said. "One way or another, that would've led the police to a motive. Or maybe Yolanda heard something about Lorenzo coming to look for Devin earlier. She could've known Devin owed Lorenzo money, known a charge on him was likely to stick."

"You never know," Myra said. She'd finished packing up her bag and was putting on her coat. I realized that I didn't want her to leave, not yet. My earlier resolve not to broach the subject of the other night crumbled. I lacked her apparent ability to wall off doing the job from everything else. I didn't know whether I should admire her for it or take it as a sign of just how fucked-up she was.

"So," I said, trying to keep my voice playful, "anything else we should talk about?"

"We've got to go back to court tomorrow, Joel," Myra said. "Isn't that enough drama for now?"

"Why does anything else have to be drama?"

"You think you and me wouldn't be drama? I'm not the easiest person in the world, and I'm guessing you still can't put one foot in front of the other without looking down."

"I'm doing fine," I protested. "I even fall asleep most nights."

"I was raised by someone in recovery, Joel," Myra said. "And you don't look to me like someone who's there yet."

"It doesn't have to be drama," I said. "At least, not anytime soon."

That at least got a smile from Myra. "I don't need an office fuck buddy," she said.

"I wasn't offering to be your office fuck buddy. All I was going to say was, after the trial—"

"Let's deal with after the trial after the trial," Myra said.

·38·

IT WAS a little after ten on Monday morning, and nobody knew what was about to happen.

Detective Franklin had arrived alone at Judge Ferano's chambers at nine o'clock. The detective had done his best not to tell us anything, but he'd said enough that Judge Ferano had decided to reopen the case so that we could call him.

Judge Ferano had addressed the jury briefly, merely informing them that he was suspending their deliberations to allow the defense to call a new witness. The jurors looked to be visibly unhappy with this turn of events; no doubt they'd been hoping their service had been nearing its end.

Myra began by asking Franklin some innocuous background questions, trying to give the jury time to settle back down and focus on what was happening, while also giving herself a chance to get a sense of the detective's courtroom demeanor.

"Detective Franklin," Myra said, "are you testifying here today because you want to be?"

Franklin appeared slightly surprised by the question. "I don't know many people who come to court for fun," he answered. "Except lawyers, of course." This got a small laugh from the jury.

"You're here at the instruction of the judge, correct?" Myra said.

"That's right."

"And do you know why Judge Ferano asked you to be here today?"

"Malik Taylor was killed last Thursday night," Franklin said. "I'm investigating his murder."

Myra paused, letting the detective's words sink in. She had positioned herself near the corner of the courtroom behind the jury box, so that the detective was looking in the jury's direction. I was watching the jury as Franklin spoke, and the effect was electric: we finally had their full attention.

"Thank you, Detective," Myra finally said. "And are you aware that Malik Taylor testified in this case?"

"Yes, I am," Franklin said.

"Are you aware whether or not Devin Wallace was present in this courtroom when Malik Taylor testified?"

"Objection," O'Bannon said.

"I'll allow it," Judge Ferano said.

"It was my understanding that he was," Franklin said.

"Is it your understanding that Devin Wallace watched much of this trial here?"

"Your Honor, the witness has no direct knowledge of this," O'Bannon protested.

"The witness has been conducting an investigation," Judge Ferano said. "He can answer as to what his understanding is."

"I've been told that he was present, yes," Detective Franklin said.

"Tell me, Detective," Myra said, "have you questioned Devin Wallace regarding Mr. Taylor's murder?"

"No," Franklin said. "I haven't."

"You never tried to talk to Mr. Wallace?"

"We haven't been able to locate him," Franklin said quietly.

"Have you tried his apartment?"

"Yes."

"More than once?"

"Yes."

"Are you keeping an eye on his apartment?"

O'Bannon stood and started to object, but Judge Ferano cut him off. "We don't need to get into the nitty-gritty of an ongoing police investigation, Counselor," Ferano said to Myra. "Let's move on."

Myra nodded. "How about Yolanda Miller, Detective?" she asked. "Did you talk to her?"

"Yes."

"Did you talk to her before you tried to talk to Mr. Wallace?"

"Yes."

"Did Ms. Miller tell you things that made you want to talk to Mr. Wallace as part of your investigation of Mr. Taylor's murder?"

Franklin took his time with that one, clearly wanting to think it through, or perhaps hoping for an objection. "Yes, she did," he finally said.

"After your conversation with Ms. Miller you considered Mr. Wallace a suspect, didn't you?"

"We were interested in talking to him."

Myra held the moment, looking at Franklin. He looked back at her impassively. "Nothing further," she finally said.

O'Bannon did only a cursory cross of Franklin, confining himself to establishing the obvious. He had Franklin say that the police did not know that Wallace had killed Taylor, and had no direct evidence linking Wallace to the murder. His strategy appeared to be to try to minimize the importance of Franklin's testimony by having his cross be as brief as possible.

The judge had agreed to allow the parties limited additional closing arguments solely to address the new evidence presented. "If you're thinking this all seems very strange," Myra began as she walked toward the podium, "you're right. This hasn't happened on any other case I've ever had. New evidence isn't just supposed to arise at the very end of a trial. But that's what happened here, and it's now going to be your duty to put aside any conceptions you had before and reevaluate this entire case in light of this new information.

"That isn't an easy task. But if you don't think you can do it, you need to take yourself off this jury, because it's what's required of you. There can't really be any doubt, can there, that this new evidence changes the outlook of this case?

"It is now clear that the police are investigating Devin Wallace as a suspect in the murder of Malik Taylor. Ladies and gentlemen, Devin Wallace sat in this very courtroom and listened to the evidence we put on that it was Malik Taylor who shot him," Myra said, pointing toward the spectator section of the courtroom as she spoke. "He was right there, taking it in. I have no way of knowing whether that evidence convinced you, ladies and gentlemen, but I have reason to suspect that it convinced Mr. Wallace.

"I'm sure you noticed that Detective Franklin wasn't exactly enthusiastic to be called here to testify. I don't blame him. He's in the middle of his own investigation, plus he's not in the business of coming to testify on behalf of criminal defendants. I'm not saying anything bad about the detective; I'm just saying I don't think he was happy to be here, which I understand. As he said, nobody likes coming to court but us lawyers, and to tell you the truth, even we aren't thrilled most of the time.

"But despite the fact that he didn't enjoy his time in the witness chair, Detective Franklin still made it entirely clear that Devin Wallace was his only real suspect in the killing of Malik Taylor. He also made it clear that Devin Wallace hasn't been seen since that killing.

"I've already talked to you about reasonable doubt, and what that means," Myra said. "The judge has also instructed you on what it means as a matter of law. I won't say all that again; I'll just tell you how important it is that you evaluate this new evidence when you consider whether the state has met its burden of proving its case beyond a reasonable doubt.

"I submit to you that, regardless of whether that was possible before, it is no longer possible here today. Frankly, ladies and gentlemen, I suspect your doubts about this case are not just reasonable; I suspect they are severe. For that reason, this new evidence makes it clear that the only just verdict in this case is not guilty."

Myra took a moment, looking from juror to juror, before turning and heading back to her seat.

"**THERE'S NO** doubt that Malik Taylor was just recently murdered," O'Bannon began his rebuttal. "There's no doubt that his death is a tragedy and a shame.

"But that doesn't mean that there's any doubt in the case you are here to decide. Because, ladies and gentlemen, you are not here to decide what happened to Mr. Taylor, or who might have murdered him. And from the evidence you heard in this courtroom, you do not know much of anything about what might have befallen Mr. Taylor. You don't know who might have wanted him dead, or why, how likely it might be that this was a random killing, that Mr. Taylor was simply in the wrong place at the wrong time. You just don't know. And that's okay, because you are not here to decide who killed Mr. Taylor.

"The detective who testified here today told you that the police do not know who killed Mr. Taylor. He told you that he did not know if Mr. Taylor's murder had anything whatsoever to do with this case. And even if—just supposing, because there's no evidence that this is actually the case—even if Mr. Wallace did have some role to play in Mr. Taylor's murder, that wouldn't mean that the defendant didn't shoot Mr. Wallace and Mr. Lipton. We have no actual basis for thinking these crimes are related.

"It's important to remember that this new evidence does not have any special weight just because it was brought in at the eleventh hour. You need to look at the evidence in the case as a whole, not just what you were told today. When you do so, you will find that you have more than enough evidence to convict the defendant. Thank you."

·39·

AGAIN WE were waiting. It was late afternoon; the jury had
renewed their deliberations just over four hours ago. After the
closings Judge Ferano had briefly addressed the jury, instructing
them that they were not to give this new testimony any more or less
weight than if it had been presented earlier in the trial, but that they
were nevertheless to begin their deliberations anew, ignoring anything they had previously discussed.

I was spending the afternoon returning the many client phone messages that had piled up over the last couple of weeks. I was in midconversation with a chronic shoplifter when Myra appeared in the doorway of my office. When she caught my eye she drew a finger across her throat. I got off the phone quickly, grabbing my suit jacket. I didn't even need to ask: one look at Myra's face had told me that we had a verdict.

"Why'd you slit your throat?" I asked her on the walk over to the courthouse.

"I just meant for you to hang up," Myra said. "It wasn't anything other than that."

"I took it to mean bad news."

"Just for you to end the conversation," Myra said. "It's not like they tell us the verdict over the phone."

"It kind of freaked me out."

"I got it," Myra said. She was walking so fast it was an effort for me to keep up with her. I got the distinct impression she wished we weren't talking.

I had felt sure the jury would be out at least a couple days. That they'd reached a verdict in just a few hours had me worried.

"What does it mean that the jury came back so fast?" I couldn't resist asking.

"I'd say it's more good than bad," Myra said. "But you never know."

"THEY BACK with a verdict?" Lorenzo asked once he'd been brought up to the court from the holding cell in the basement.

"That's right," Myra said.

"Thought you said they gonna be talking for a couple of days," Lorenzo said to Myra, a hint of accusation in his voice.

"I said that's what I thought would happen," Myra said with a shrug. "Juries are unpredictable. Remember, if they convict, it's not the last word. We'll appeal. If they acquit, that's the end of it."

There were three loud knocks on the door behind the judge's bench, indicting that Judge Ferano was about to enter the courtroom. "All rise," the bailiff intoned. Looking over my shoulder as I stood, I realized there were at least half a dozen reporters present, Adam Berman among them, all bunched together in a row. The judge took his place slowly in the silent room, then peered out into the well of the court. The bailiff called the case, counsel stating our appearances for the record.

"I understand we have a verdict here," Judge Ferano said. "Let's bring the jury in."

I studied the jurors as they took their seats, though I didn't know what I was looking for. They appeared tired, slightly withdrawn, not looking at anyone. The jury didn't look to me like a group of people who had just agreed upon anything, and I quickly gave up trying to read the verdict from their expressions. As for Myra, I noticed that she didn't even glance in their direction.

As I sat there with my hands gone clammy, my heart skipping around in my chest, I had to remind myself that it wasn't me who was on trial. I thought about what Myra had said the other night, about how being a lawyer allowed her to live vicariously through other people's troubles. There was a part of me that wanted to be judged and found not guilty—to be absolved, I suppose. Or perhaps there was just something in me that felt the need to stand accused. Whatever it was, it flooded through me now; I felt as though my life was on the line as starkly as Lorenzo's.

"On the first count of the indictment, murder in the second degree of Seth Lipton, how does the jury find?" the bailiff asked.

"Not guilty," the foreman said.

The bailiff, without missing a beat, began asking them about the second count—the attempted murder of Devin Wallace—but everyone in the courtroom was already reacting. We all knew that the rest of the verdict was contained in that first not-guilty. Lorenzo Tate was a free man.

·40·

AFTER THE verdict, we waited around for Lorenzo to be processed, then left the courthouse with him. Lorenzo had never had any visible supporters in court, no sign of friends or family. He'd remained a stranger to us.

"That it then?" Lorenzo said once we were outside. "I'm done?"

Myra smiled. "You're done," she agreed. "It's over."

"Damn, y'all," Lorenzo said. "Ain't like I even know what to say. You did right by me."

"That's what we do," Myra said. She looked every bit as embarrassed as I felt. Lorenzo didn't seem like he was enjoying this either.

"So I just get on the subway and go back home," Lorenzo mused, looking baffled by the prospect, as if the idea of going back to his old, free life was unfathomable. "Ain't no more to it than that."

"That's right, Lorenzo," Myra said. "You've got your life back. Use it wisely."

"No doubt," Lorenzo said, not looking at us. "No doubt." After a moment he turned and headed for the subway entrance. I watched as he descended the stairs without looking back.

Myra and I headed over to the office in silence. Winter was threatening to emerge: the temperature was approaching freezing. As I braced myself against a stiff, chill wind, the feeling I'd had while waiting for the verdict vanished entirely. I'd felt a momentary elation when the verdict had been read, but it had quickly faded. Any illusion that I was being judged alongside Lorenzo, that we were connected in some fundamental way, had disappeared the second the case was over. The rush of it had been fierce, but it had also been fleeting. The endorphin flood, the quick elation, followed by the sudden empty crash—it was, I thought, much like a drug.

Myra was again walking quickly, cutting through the weave of pedestrian traffic, using the cigarette in her hand as a weapon to clear space in front of her. "You okay?" I asked as we approached our building.

Myra nodded without looking at me. "Just tired," she said.

I stopped walking, and after a moment Myra noticed, stopped, and turned back toward me. "We should celebrate," I said, trying to fight off the sudden gloom that had covered both of us. "An acquittal in a murder trial doesn't come around every day. Let's go out to a nice dinner."

"I don't know, Joel," Myra said.

"You don't know what?" I asked.

"We *work* together," Myra said.

"We just won a big case," I said. "A murder case. I'd like to take you out for a fancy meal to celebrate. What's the problem?"

"Sorry," Myra said. "I'm sorry, Joel. I'd love to have dinner tonight, okay?"

"Great," I said, though I wasn't sure if I still meant it.

I'D BEEN able to get us a last-minute reservation at the River Café, one of Brooklyn's fanciest restaurants, best known for its wall of windows that looked out on the East River, the Brooklyn Bridge, and Lower Manhattan. The food at the River Café was excellent, the atmosphere romantic and elegant, but Myra still didn't seem quite herself. She had changed out of her suit and into a black dress that clung to her angular body. It was the loveliest I'd ever seen her. I was still in my suit, this being the sort of restaurant where men dined in jacket and tie.

Despite the restaurant's best efforts, our conversation throughout dinner was strained and fitful. Even when we hadn't gotten along in the past, we'd never been at a loss for conversation. But Myra was quieter than I'd ever seen her, and nothing I said seemed to fully capture her attention. I ignored it for as long as I could, hoping that sooner or later she'd relax and things would go back to normal, but finally I gave up and asked her what was wrong.

"It doesn't have anything to do with you," Myra said, forcing a smile.

"I'm not sure that makes me feel better," I replied.

Neither of us said anything for a stretch. I finished the wine in my glass, refilled it. The bottle was nearly empty; Myra had been drinking methodically, although without any sign of pleasure.

"Shit," Myra said. "I'm just making it worse, aren't I? Okay. Here's the thing. If Devin knew all this time that Malik had shot him, no way would he wait this long to do anything about it. But he was sitting in that courtroom. I think it's what happened in court that got Malik Taylor killed."

"You mean that Devin was the first person we convinced," I said.

"We know that Devin didn't see his shooter," Myra said. "There's no reason to think he had any firsthand knowledge of what happened that night."

"And you think we convinced him?" I asked, tilting my head skeptically. "You're blaming yourself—you're blaming *us*—for Malik Taylor's getting killed?"

"I didn't say that—"

"That certainly seems to be where you're going."

"Well goddammit, he *is* dead, isn't he?" Myra snapped, finally meeting my eyes. Her own were brimming with tears. "He was alive when we started our trial and now he's been gunned down on the street. And I think we probably put the bullet out there. I think we're accessories."

"Please," I said instinctively. I'd never seen Myra like this and had assumed she was immune from it. "First of all, we don't even know that Devin shot Malik."

"Do you think Devin shot Malik?" Myra challenged.

"I think it's possible," I said. "But I don't have enough information to know. I guess I'm just surprised to hear this from you. I mean, I think of you as a true scorched-earth type. We did what we needed to do to represent the best interests of our client, and that's the only thing that can matter to us."

"I say that and mean it, sure, but I'm still human," Myra said. "I can't just blindly follow some absolute and ignore the consequences."

I smiled. "That's what I'm trying to do. I find things go down easier for me if I just try to mindlessly follow the rules. I've tried it the other way, and, believe me, the percentages just aren't there."

Myra looked at me, curiosity replacing sorrow in her eyes. "This really doesn't bother you, does it?"

I thought about it. "If I knew for a fact that we were really responsible I'm sure it would. But I don't know that, and we had a responsibility to our client."

"Our client was a drug dealer," Myra protested. "And Malik Taylor was a citizen, a dad, trying to do right by the world."

"Well, fuck, Myra," I said. "We don't get to represent the people trying to do right by the world."

Myra smiled at this, wiping at her eyes. "Pretty much never," she agreed.

In the silence that followed I thought about her theory of what had happened. I thought about how we'd more or less made up our version of events out of whole cloth, coming up with a story that we'd hoped would be vaguely plausible to those who heard it. Lorenzo Tate, the one person who unequivocally knew whether or not he'd shot two people on that April night, had offered us his own story, his own alibi witness, and we'd rejected it as insufficiently convincing, with no regard for whether or not it was actually true. Lester Bailey had come into court and offered his version of the truth, a version I was thoroughly convinced was a fabrication. Meanwhile our story, cobbled together out of stray facts, innuendo, and supposition, might well have been sufficiently convincing to cost Malik Taylor his life. Or it might have been enough that we'd insinuated the sexual encounter between Malik and Yolanda, that

Devin Wallace had committed murder simply to maintain his reputation on the street.

If uncovering the truth of what had happened in the Gardens that night had ever been the goal, it had receded far from view. But that was little different from what had happened to Terrell Gibbons, a victim of his own words and of the story told by Kawame Jones. If there was a thread connecting the truth to the law it was far too thin for me to see. It wasn't the truth; it was simply competing stories. It was storytelling as a form of combat. As this understanding came to me I realized it was the very understanding that Myra had long lived with, but which, just now, had overwhelmed her. I put aside my desire to speak honestly about what we knew in favor of trying to provide whatever form of acceptable consolation I could.

"There's nothing we can do to change any of it now," I said. "We did the job, that's all."

"You're right," Myra said, taking a sip of her wine. "I think I just needed to say it out loud."

The waiter came over, asked if we were finished, then took our plates. We'd ordered a prix fixe meal, so we were getting their famous Brooklyn Bridge dessert, even though I was pretty sure that neither one of us was particularly in the mood.

"So, anyway," Myra said, a false brightness in her voice, as the waiter brought out the desserts, an impressive rendition of the iconic bridge made out of chocolate cake. "I really didn't mean to talk about any of that. I was thinking about it before, when I went home after work, and I realized you were right. We should be celebrating tonight, no matter what. Winning an acquittal in a murder case— years can go by where that doesn't happen. So I bought us a bottle of good champagne."

"Really?" I said, surprised by the gesture. "Where is it?"

"Where is it?" Myra repeated. "Where do you think it is? It's at my apartment."

"I see," I said after a moment, unable to keep a smile off my face.

"Do you?" Myra asked, and now she was smiling too.

"I think so, yes."

"Because I don't think I'm being particularly subtle."

"No," I said. "I don't suppose you are."

"I can be harder to get, if that's what you're looking for."

"What about the whole 'we work together' thing?"

"I guess I'm just going to have to get you fired," Myra said.

·41·

AFTER DINNER we walked out to Myra's car. In the parking lot I took her hand, partially just to see if she'd let me. She did.

We took Front Street over to Gold Street, cutting down through Dumbo to Fort Greene, the neighborhood feeling so quiet as to almost be abandoned. Myra had just coasted to a stop at an intersection when somebody drove right into the back of her car.

The car behind us hadn't been going fast, but the collision was still jarring. I tasted blood from biting my tongue. "What the fuck,"

Myra said angrily. "How drunk does this asshole have to be to rear-end me at a fucking stop sign?" Before I could say anything she'd jumped out of the car.

I stretched my arms and shoulders, which felt like I'd just been tackled, though I didn't think anything was seriously hurt. I heard Myra's raised voice from outside the car, though I couldn't make out the words. Before getting out myself I turned back to see what was happening.

To my surprise Myra was moving quickly back toward her car. But she wasn't alone. Someone else was climbing into the backseat as Myra opened her door. I looked back instinctively, seeing little more than a black man in a hoodie before my attention was hijacked by the gun in his hand, which was pointed directly at my face. In a flash of panic I realized we were being carjacked. I was too disoriented to have any reaction but raw fear. "Just start driving," the man in the backseat said. "Drive like there ain't nothing happening. I'll be telling you where to go."

The voice sounded familiar, but I wasn't able to place it. I didn't want to turn around to look because I figured that was an invitation to getting shot. Myra did as ordered, driving slowly, following instructions. When I looked at her I could see the muscles of her jaw working even in the darkened car. She didn't look at me.

We got onto Flatbush, driving within twenty feet of my apartment, then drove deeper into Brooklyn for another several miles in complete silence. My panic had receded enough that I was starting to be able to think. If this was just a carjacking, why wouldn't the thief have taken the car back in Dumbo, which was far more deserted than where we were now? And Myra's beat-up Volvo was hardly the best car around in that expensive neighborhood. Plus, there was no mistaking the direction we were heading: out toward the Gardens.

Whatever this was, it had to do with the case we'd just tried; I was sure of that. And it didn't seem like it was somebody's way of saying thank you for a job well done.

I was wrong about our destination, though: we kept going past the Gardens, farther into the no-man's-land between Midwood and Flatlands. Finally the man in the backseat told Myra to turn. We were on a faded industrial street, warehouses and small factories instead of apartments, the only illumination coming from the streetlights. "Pull over here," the man in the back said. "Turn the car off but leave the keys in there. Now get out the car. If you try and book on me I'll cap you in the back."

The car lights came on as we opened the doors and got out. I caught a quick glimpse of the man behind me. It was Shawne Flynt.

"Shawne," I said instinctively.

Myra looked at me across the top of the car. "You know this guy?" she said.

"Both of you best just stop talking now," Shawne said, standing beside Myra, the gun steady in his hand and pointed in her direction. "Now, Mr. Lawyer, why don't you just come over here and stand next to your lady friend."

I was trying to figure out what I could possibly have done to Shawne Flynt that would make him want to do this. Of course, Shawne had always been operating from a playbook I hadn't understood. "He was a client," I said to Myra, keeping my voice even. "He knew things about me that I couldn't figure out how he knew."

"All right, you've said what you got to say," Shawne said, his own voice still calm. "Now come on over here."

I did as he told me, moving slowly, scanning for a weakness. Shawne had to be close to half a foot taller than I was, something I'd never been more aware of. When I was in front of him Shawne stepped up and, with a quick flick of his wrist, swiped the side of my head with the gun. It was only a halfhearted blow, but enough that I staggered, Myra catching me, the taste of metal in the back of my throat. "This is where it's at, Mr. Lawyer," Shawne said, nothing different in his voice. "I tell you not to do something, you best not do it. You feeling me?"

I nodded, wincing back the pain. I tried to take comfort from the fact that Shawne hadn't hit me to really hurt me; if he was planning on killing us he'd have no reason not to have given me a full swing. I didn't know if that was true, but it was something to believe. "You two just walk in front of me now. We going to go nice and slow toward that place right across the way."

The building Shawne directed us to was boarded up in front with graffiti-tagged plywood. As we approached I saw that there was a crude door carved out from the wood, a padlock on a loop of chain sliding through a hole in the door. The window frames were boarded up. No light showed anywhere.

As we got to the front of the building I realized the padlock was actually unlocked and dangling. "Right through there," Shawne said. "That's all you got to do. See how easy this is?"

I didn't want to go inside the building. Any hope we had of being seen, of someone coming to our aid, depended on our being out on the street. But there was no way to make a break for it without being in plain sight for Shawne to shoot me in the back, and anyway, I couldn't attempt it without abandoning Myra. I tried to think of something—anything—that I could do.

Shawne noticed my hesitation and jammed the gun into my back. I swung the plywood door open and stepped through, Myra beside me. The darkness engulfed us; I could only vaguely see the outline of the building. Shawne still had the gun nudged into the small of my back. "Just keep on walking. See them stairs going down?" Shawne said, prodding me. I could barely make them out, a handful of steps to the left of the building's entranceway. "That's where you want to be going."

The stairs were just wide enough that Myra and I could walk side by side. There were about a half dozen steps down, ending in a metal door. "It be open," Shawne said. "Just go right on through. We're all expected and shit."

I pushed the door open. It was surprisingly heavy, and it screeched sharply against the floor as it gave. As the door opened I was surprised to see that the room beyond it was glaringly bright with light. There was also a strong odor wafting out. I recognized the smell even before I actually stepped into the room and saw that it was filled with row after row of marijuana plants.

The plants were elevated a couple of feet above the ground, fluorescent lightbulbs arrayed just a few feet above them. The walls were covered with aluminum foil, which reflected back the light and made the room even brighter. The room was large and open, I guessed at least two thousand square feet of space, almost all of which was taken up with pot plants. Space heaters burned in the corners.

"You know where you are?" a voice boomed from the far end of the room.

I glanced over at Myra, who looked rigid with fear, her sharp features screaming in the glaring light. The man who'd spoken was walking toward us, he too with a gun in his hand.

"My guess is we're where Lorenzo Tate used to grow his pot," I replied to Devin Wallace. "My guess is you took it over while he was at Rikers."

"True that," Devin said, smiling as he approached. "You got to nurse these bitches, you know. They got all sorts of needs. This shit's mad complicated. With Strawberry in the pen, this fine chronic would've all just withered up and died if my people hadn't stepped in."

"I'm sure you're a hero to pot plants everywhere," I said. "But what do you want with us?"

Devin's smile was without a trace of amusement. "Guess you all think you can say what the fuck you want so long as you do it inside of court. You want to step up to me, looks like now's your chance."

"We weren't ever trying to step up to you," Myra said, her voice going soft, no trace of confrontation. I'd expected outrage and bluster from her; that she was playing it so low-key struck me as a bad sign. I took it to mean she didn't think Devin was bluffing. "We were just doing our jobs."

"Bitch, the fuck did your job have to do with me?" Devin barked, his face contorted with rage. "What reason you got for putting some bullshit about my business out there? Saying my bitch been stepping out on me with some no-account motherfucker she be with back in the day. You put that out there in front of my crew, ain't like I got no choice but to cap the motherfucker. Now I got the five-oh coming down to the Gardens, fucking with my shit. All that over something that ain't even true. But you all think you can skate because what? Because you fucking *lawyers*?"

"What makes you say it wasn't true?" Myra asked.

"You think I wouldn't know if Yo-Yo was stepping out on me in the Gardens? Shit, there ain't nothing that goes on in there that don't get back to me. That was just some shit you all made up, try and make it look like it was Malik who come at me."

Devin was wrong about that. We hadn't made it up. Lorenzo Tate had told us about it. Had Lorenzo been mistaken, or was Devin? It wasn't a question I could try to answer now; no matter what the truth was it wasn't going to placate Devin Wallace. However the story had started, our adopting it as Lorenzo's defense had led us directly to where we were now. The story we'd told had been folded into a larger story, one in which it looked like we were the victims rather than the heroes.

"Yo, Devin, you got this?" Shawne said. "I don't want to be seein' nothing I don't be needing to, you feel me?"

"You know what you do next?"

"Take their ride out to Malcolm's, get it chopped," Shawne said. "Busted-up old thing ain't even gonna be worth shit."

"You drive slow and steady, and don't be taking no detours."

"You ain't gotta tell me that," Shawne said.

For the first time Devin's attention shifted from us. He turned to Shawne, taking a slow step in his direction. "You telling me what's what now?" Devin said softly. They were looking at each other, distracted, but Shawne was still between us and the door.

"Ain't like that, D," Shawne said, taking a small step backward. "I just saying I know what to do."

"What you best be telling me is how I ain't gonna be hearing some shit on the street 'bout how you helped cap some white lawyers. You feel me? This ain't some corner shit where the five-oh not gonna give a fuck what anybody be broadcasting in the projects. I hear you been talking, I ain't even gonna start with you. First it'll be your grandma over at that house on Putnam. Your little girl Kinesha after that."

"Yo, D, why you got to be puttin' that out there? I ain't gonna burn you."

"You do, won't be for long," Devin said. "You feel me?"

Shawne had taken another step back, so that he was framed in the doorway. His face was taut, his mouth pulled back in a grimace. He clearly wasn't in the habit of taking this sort of threat from anyone, but was restraining himself from giving it back to Devin. "I feel you, D," he said.

"Then go," Devin said. Shawne turned and quickly went out the door he'd just led us through, leaving us alone with Devin.

Shawne had just abducted us and hit me in the head with a gun, but I instinctively felt sorry to see him go. His laconic, offhand threats were nothing compared to Devin's businesslike sadism.

"You see all this shit you stirred up with your nonsense?" Devin said, turning back toward us.

"We thought it was just as likely that Malik shot you as that it was Lorenzo," Myra said, still speaking quietly, but her voice was shaky, like she couldn't catch her breath.

"You going to try and sell me that shit, right in the here and now? Like you really don't know?"

"We don't know what?"

"Course it was Strawberry who tried to cap me," Devin said matter-of-factly. His anger had disappeared; he seemed calm, which made him even more frightening. "Even if he ain't never told you, you got to know that."

"We don't know that," I said.

Devin turned to me, a sneer on his face. "Didn't expect to see you even make it to the end of the trial," he said to me. "Guess you didn't like that present I sent you?"

It took me a moment to understand what he was referring to.

"You ain't never tasted that shit?" Devin asked.

"I flushed it down the toilet," I replied, glancing over at Myra, who was looking over at me, puzzled.

"That there's a shame," Devin said, shaking his head. "Best dope you ever would've had, too. Shit was so pure, one little toot would've sent you all the way up to heaven."

I wasn't sure at first that I understood what Devin was saying. But as I looked into his eyes a chill came over me. Any lingering possibility in my mind that Devin was just toying with us was completely erased. "Why did you want me to OD?"

"I couldn't find a way to reach your boy Strawberry at Rikers," Devin said. "You were going to be my little message to him."

"How'd you know about me?"

"Shit, you think I ain't got me my own lawyer? And I mean a real lawyer too. Didn't take him no time to check you out."

It wouldn't, I realized. The public record was there for anyone who knew how to look, had access to the right databases. Any competent lawyer doing basic due diligence on me could've put it together in half an hour. I just hadn't been looking in the right place, had let my assumptions get in the way of my understanding.

"What makes you so sure that it was Lorenzo who shot you?" Myra asked, going into her lawyer mode a little, like she was conducting an interview. "Did you see him?"

"Naw, I ain't see him, but Yo-Yo did. And I knew he might be coming at me; I just didn't think he'd have it in him to try and hit me right in the Gardens."

"Why was he coming after you?" Myra asked.

Devin shrugged. "So now's the time for you two to just come on back to this door here; we going to step outside."

I looked over at Myra, who was keeping her gaze trained on Devin. He was directing us to a back door in the room that I hadn't even noticed, kitty-corner from where we'd come in. This was probably our best chance to fight back. I scanned the room quickly, but other than the rows of pot plants and the lights and the foil along the walls it was empty.

A fleeting image of Beth's pale, desolate face ran across my mind.

As it did it suddenly occurred to me that maybe I'd been wrong about one crucial thing with her: I'd always thought Beth had picked me out as someone she could corrupt, but maybe instead she'd hoped that I would find a way to save her. I hadn't saved Beth, had barely saved myself, but I wasn't going to let the same thing happen to Myra. If there was a way out of here I wanted Myra to have it. I wanted her to survive. It was on me to find a way.

Myra and I walked slowly through the narrow aisle between the rows of the hydroponic pot, making our way toward the door. Devin stood about five feet away from it, his gun trained on us. I couldn't lunge at him without offering him plenty of time to shoot me. We were on his turf, playing by his rules, and there was nothing I could think of to do. Devin was clearly so confident that he could handle us that he didn't even have any backup with him; I guessed that doing us this way was part of his restoring his street cred.

"It's open," Devin said as I reached the door. "You just go on out."

I pushed the door open, stepping back out into the cold, wondering if this was finally my chance. I could slam the door shut behind us, give us at least a couple of seconds to run. But run where? As I peered into the darkness outside I realized the backyard—a grassless patch of dirt—was completely fenced off, nothing that would provide shelter, no signs of life nearby. There was nowhere to go.

"That's right," Devin said from behind me. "Just keep on walking."

Myra was a step or so behind me, but I kept my back to her as I desperately scanned the yard for a way out. I felt a tingling along my spine from the expectation that any second now Devin would shoot me. I heard a noise from behind me, a metallic screeching sound, and I turned back toward Devin.

He'd come through the doorway and was heading toward us. "This ain't even personal," Devin said evenly. "It's like what you said about how you called me out in that court—just doing my job here. You all should be able to respect that."

I'd continued to walk backward as Devin approached us, getting out to the middle of the yard. "All right, you can stop moving now," Devin said. "You've come to your final spot here in this world."

"The police are already looking for you on Taylor's murder. You don't think they'll connect the dots if we turn up dead?" Myra said, the last trace of calm drained out of her voice. "This isn't some drive-by that nobody will look at."

"Looks to me that you all are going to turn up missing, which ain't the same as dead," Devin said. "Look where you be at. Who going to find you buried back here?"

"Even if they don't, we disappear the same day Lorenzo Tate gets acquitted, you don't think the police are going to focus on you?" Myra said. "They already are because of Malik."

"You think the five-oh never knock on my door before? They don't got no bodies, they ain't got no crime."

"What about Shawne Flynt?" I said, trying the only thing I could think of. "You really think he won't flip on you the first time he's staring down real time on a possession with intent?"

"You just might be right on that," Devin said. The only illumination came from the open doorway, the light behind him making it impossible for me to see his expression, just the puff of his breath when he spoke into the cold air. "So maybe now I got to take him out too. Not gonna help you all, though, is it?"

Devin had been holding the gun at his side, but now he raised it up so that it was pointed at me. I decided to run at him, to go down fighting, at least give Myra a slim chance to get away. As I gathered myself to charge a shadow dampened the light behind him.

Devin must have noticed it too, because he turned to look back.

The bark of a gun was so loud I almost jumped out of my skin. Instinctively I dived to the ground, rolling away from Devin as shot after shot rang out.

A second later the only sound was the ringing in my ears. I was curled up into a fetal ball in the dirt. I looked over and saw Myra crouched a couple feet away. When I looked back to where Devin Wallace had been standing I didn't see anyone there.

Someone else was in the yard, framed in the illuminated doorway. He began walking toward us, then stopped about ten feet away, bending down. I was still on the ground, trying to see what was happening. After a moment I realized the man who'd just been approaching was standing over the crumpled body of Devin Wallace.

"Wasn't no way I was going to miss taking out that motherfucker twice," Lorenzo Tate said, walking toward us, the silhouette of a gun visible in his hand.

"What're you doing here?" I said.

"Looks like you needed me, son," Lorenzo said. He seemed different, but of course he did: it was the first time I'd seen him as a free man, and he was standing over a dead body with a gun in his hand while I was still sprawled down in the dirt. I sat up, but something kept me from standing. I looked over and noticed that Myra was still crouched as well, looking ready to dive or run.

Lorenzo noticed it too: he let out a low chuckle. "Well, c'mon, now," he said. "You two all right."

"What're you doing here, Lorenzo?" Myra said, her voice low.

"I didn't know the motherfucker would go after you," Lorenzo said. "And that there's the truth. I trailed him out here, but I ain't got clue one what was up. I was just biding my time till I get what the score be; next thing is I see you two brought in. You all did right by me, so I knew I wasn't having that."

"You shot him before," I said, realizing as I said it that I probably shouldn't. "Back in the Gardens."

"Ain't like you just thought of that now, homey," Lorenzo said with a smile. "Course it was me. Five-oh had a witness to that shit. What'd you think?"

"You shot him over the money?" I asked.

"Devin thought he could cut me out. His crew had found this place here. He wasn't never going to pay me, and he was going to move in on my product. He thought there wasn't nothing I could do, being as I don't got me a crew like he do. He'd made his move to put me out of the game, and there wasn't but two things I could do. Either I stand down or I step up. Wasn't no choice at all." Lorenzo stopped talking and cocked his head, looking down at us. "How come you all still ducked down like that?"

"You've still got a gun in your hand, Lorenzo," Myra said.

Lorenzo looked down at the gun as if he'd forgotten it was there. "That ain't nothing for you two to worry about."

I stood up slowly, swiping at my pants, which were ripped at one knee. I didn't think Lorenzo planned on hurting us, but on the other hand we were now witnesses to a murder he'd just committed. Myra still hadn't moved. "What about Malik Taylor?" she asked.

Lorenzo shook his head, something like a smile on his face. "I tried to give you my boy Marcus as an alibi, but you weren't going for it. Then you started in about Malik, and it just, like, came to me, you know. No way was that dumb proud-ass motherfucker Devin going to even wait till after the trial to take Malik out, not if you put it out there that the dude was tapping Yo-Yo."

"You lied to us about Malik and Yo-Yo getting back together," Myra said.

"I just gave you what you were looking for is all," Lorenzo said.

"I didn't have nothin' against the man. But I wasn't seeing no other way. Way it works out here, I got to go through you to stay alive, then that's what I gotta do. That ain't on me, though. I got no beef with Malik."

"But you caused him to be killed," Myra said.

I turned to her, raising a cautionary hand. "Myra—" I said.

"She can say what she gotta say," Lorenzo said evenly. "You all can't put that on me without putting it on your own self. All you got to tell me is that we're all right with what went down here."

"Devin was going to kill us," I said quickly, not wanting to give Myra a chance to speak. "You acted to save our lives. You didn't commit any crime."

"That's nice to know, but we ain't gonna find out," Lorenzo said. "The po-po don't come into what happened back here, you feel me? You all did right by me. I figure now we're something approaching even."

"We understand," Myra said before I could speak. I turned to her in surprise but she kept her focus on Lorenzo. "You saved our lives. We can walk away from here and never look back."

Lorenzo took a moment, studying her closely, the gun still in his hand. Finally he nodded. I realized that it was necessary that Myra had been the one to say it.

WE LEFT Lorenzo there and went back out to the street. I was still on guard, looking for any sign of either Devin Wallace's men or of anyone who'd heard the recent gunshots. But the street was empty and quiet. Myra's car was gone.

Suddenly all the fear of the last hour hit me and I felt myself shaking. I clenched my hands into fists and tried to ride it out.

I looked over at Myra, who looked back at me in the gauzy dark. "You really willing not to report what just happened?" I asked.

"What's it get anybody if we do?" Myra said. "Lorenzo really did kill Devin Wallace to save our lives. He would've done it even if we weren't there, but we were, and Devin was going to kill us. Lorenzo can't be charged again on the Lipton murder. He's not legally responsible for Taylor's death, even if he did cause it."

"So we just let it go?"

"What else do you want to do, Joel?"

"What if it comes out down the road?"

"You mean if Lorenzo is someday arrested for Devin's murder?" Myra said. "I don't see that happening. Nobody who could point the police to that building is going to do so."

I looked around again, amazed at how ordinary everything appeared. The city didn't know, or care, that we'd just witnessed a murder and almost died ourselves. The city just kept right on going, too vast and impersonal to stop for any one person's death.

I realized that a rough justice had played out here. The battle had always been between Lorenzo Tate and Devin Wallace. We'd merely been pawns in a larger chess game we hadn't even known was being played. Unlike Malik Taylor, we'd survived. If anyone here deserved justice, it was Malik. But Myra was right: that justice wasn't going to be forthcoming from the law. The person directly responsible for his death, Devin Wallace, was himself dead, and after that the guilt was diffuse, covering us nearly as much as it did Lorenzo.

We at least had the excuse that we'd just been doing our jobs. But Lorenzo felt the same way: he'd been jammed up on a murder charge, and he'd just been looking for whatever way out he could find. That the way he'd chosen had led to an innocent person's death was nothing more than collateral damage, as far as he was concerned.

Of course, none of this would've happened if it'd been the truth we'd been looking for. The truth had been staring us in the face from the beginning, so obvious that we'd essentially been forced to ignore it in order to mount a defense. We'd done our best to pick away at it—attacking Yolanda's ID, putting forward Lorenzo's manufactured suspect—but none of that had anything to do with the truth.

"You really flushed it down the toilet?" Myra asked.

I looked back at her, thrown off for a moment by the question, then nodded.

"Did you suspect it was meant to kill you?"

"Other than it being heroin, no. I flushed it because I didn't want it. Actually—" I cut myself off.

"What?"

I couldn't look at her as I said it. "I flushed it when I got home that night. After I went over to your place."

"Oh," Myra said. "Okay."

I forced myself to look at her. "Is that too much to put on you?"

Myra looked back at me; then she reached out and touched my face. In that touch came my first full understanding that we had actually survived what had just happened. I took her in my arms, both of our bodies trembling. The feeling of being alive flooded through me, more powerful than any drug, but clean and pure and good.

"We should get out of here," Myra said softly, her breath against my neck. "We're a long way from home."

ACKNOWLEDGMENTS

A tip of the hat to: Alice Peacock, for everything; Betsy Lerner, for vision and persistence; Gerry Howard, for wisdom; Anna Roberts, for details; Brett Dignam and Stephen Bright, for legal education; Holley Bishop, Stephen Koch, and Maureen Howard, for help along the way; and Bertolt Sobolik and Loren Noveck, for being there.